Step into Reading, Random House, and the Random House colophon are registered trademarks of Penguin Random House LLC.

Visit us on the Web!
StepIntoReading.com
rhcbooks.com

Educators and librarians, for a variety of teaching tools, visit us at RHTeachersLibrarians.com

ISBN 978-0-7364-4257-2 (trade)

MANUFACTURED IN CHINA

10 9 8 7 6 5 4 3 2 1

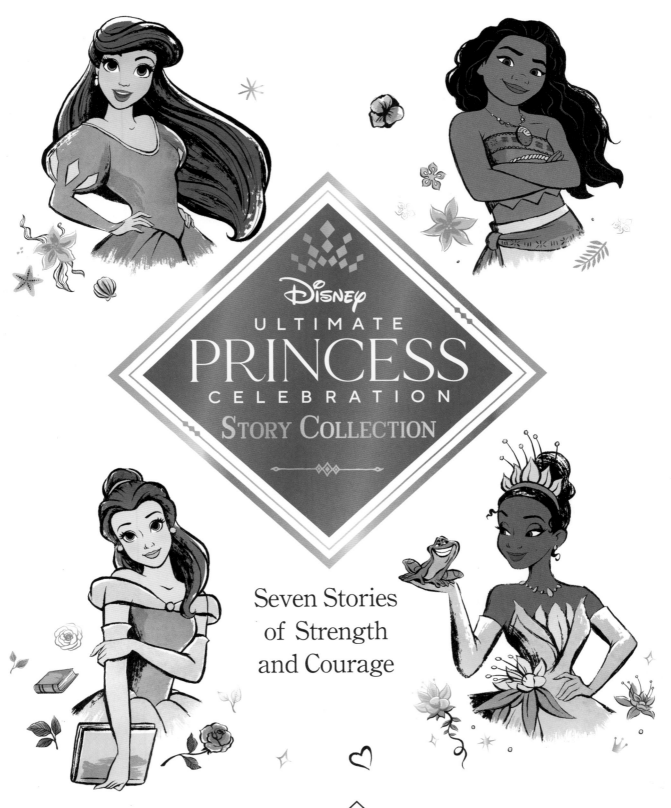

Disney

ULTIMATE
PRINCESS
CELEBRATION
STORY COLLECTION

Seven Stories
of Strength
and Courage

Random House 🏠 New York

Contents

STEP
2
READING WITH HELP

STEP INTO READING®

Disney

Aladdin

by Mary Tillworth
illustrated by the Disney
Storybook Art Team

Aladdin is poor.

He steals bread to eat.

But he is also kind
and brave.

At night,

Aladdin looks at a palace.

He dreams of being rich.

One day, Aladdin
sees a young woman.
Her name is Jasmine.
She gives an apple
to a hungry child.

Jasmine cannot
pay for the apple.
The apple seller is angry!

Aladdin protects Jasmine.
Together, they run away.

Guards capture Aladdin!
They take him
to the dungeons.

Jasmine tries to stop them.

She is really a princess!

In the dungeon,
an old man frees Aladdin.

He asks Aladdin
to find a lamp.
Aladdin goes into a cave.
He gets the lamp.
He is trapped!

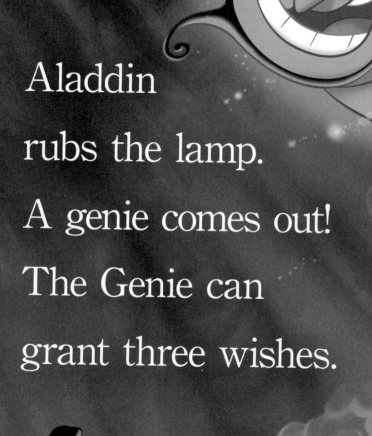

Aladdin
rubs the lamp.
A genie comes out!
The Genie can
grant three wishes.

Aladdin wishes
to be a prince!

Aladdin rides to the palace.
He finds Jasmine,
the Sultan, and
the evil Jafar.

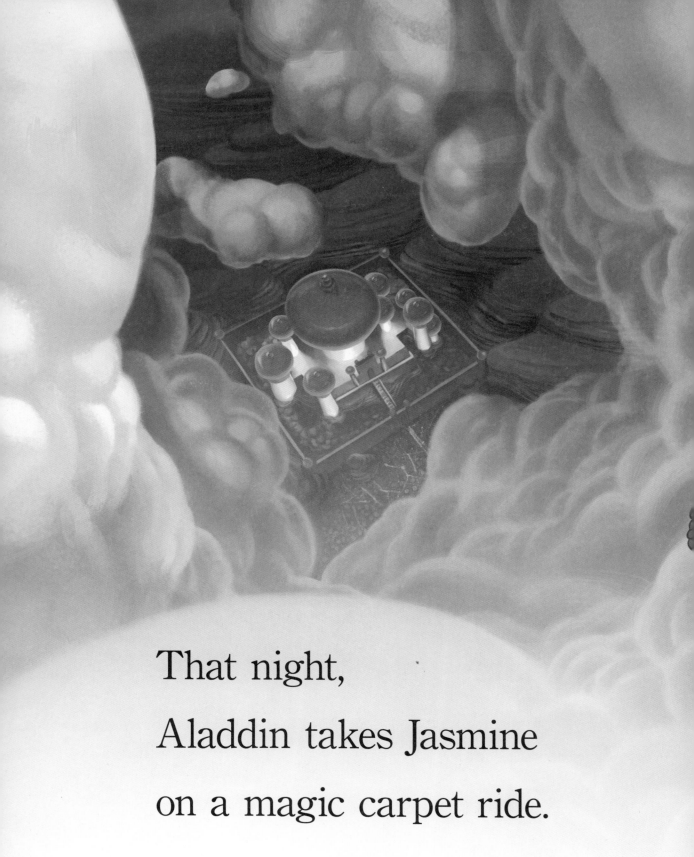

That night,
Aladdin takes Jasmine
on a magic carpet ride.

They have fun.

They fall in love!

They want to marry.

But Jafar wants
to marry Jasmine!
He throws Aladdin
into the sea.
Aladdin uses his
second wish.
The Genie saves him.

Jafar finds the magic lamp.

He wishes to be the sultan!

Jafar uses another wish.

He turns into a huge snake.

He squeezes Aladdin.

Aladdin tells Jafar
the Genie is more
powerful than he is.

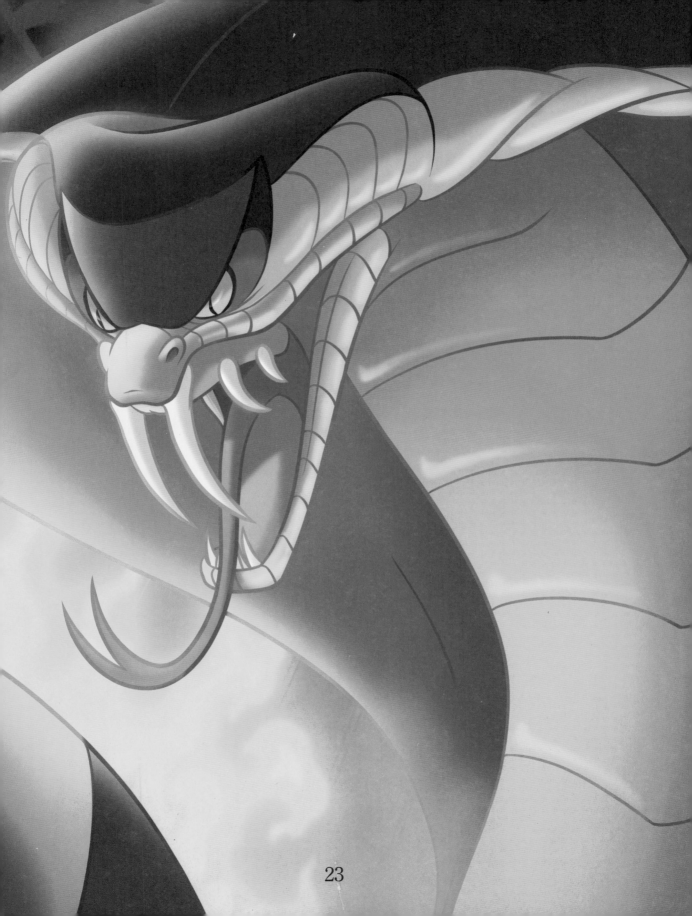

Jafar uses his
third wish.

He becomes a genie!

He traps Jasmine.

Aladdin saves her.

Jafar forgets that every genie lives in a lamp. He is trapped forever!

Aladdin uses his third wish.

He frees the Genie!

The Genie hugs everyone.

Kindness and bravery win!

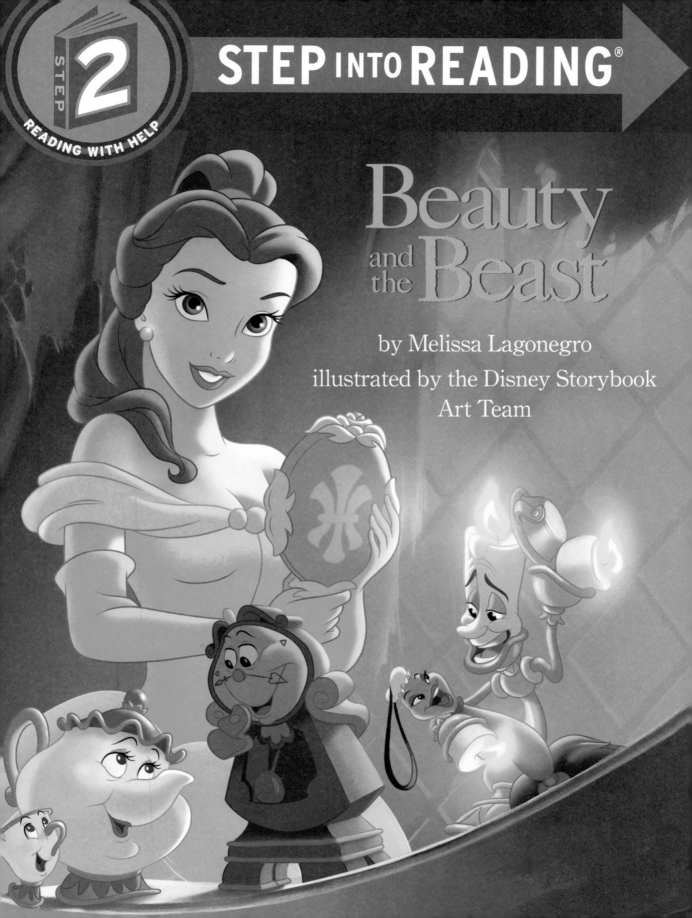

STEP INTO READING®

STEP 2 READING WITH HELP

Beauty and the Beast

by Melissa Lagonegro

illustrated by the Disney Storybook
Art Team

Belle is kind
and smart.
She loves
to read.

Gaston wants
to marry Belle.
She does not
like him.

Belle's father, Maurice,

is an inventor.

He goes on a trip.

Maurice gets lost
in the forest.
Wolves surround him!
He finds a castle.
He goes inside.

Maurice meets
magical objects.
Lumiere is a candlestick.
Cogsworth is a clock.

The castle belongs
to the Beast.
He locks Maurice
in a cell.

Belle finds Maurice.
She asks the Beast
to free her father.

She tells the Beast
to keep her instead.
The Beast agrees.

Belle meets
the magical objects
in the castle.

Lumiere sings.

Belle explores
the castle.
She finds a magic rose.

The Beast finds Belle.

He grabs the rose.

Belle is scared!

Belle leaves the castle.

Wolves surround her.

She is in danger!

The Beast arrives.

He fights the wolves.

He saves Belle!

Belle returns
to the castle.
She and the Beast
become good friends.
They spend time outdoors.

Belle teaches the Beast
to dance.

They are happy.

Belle sees her father
in a magic mirror.
He looks sick.

Belle leaves
to help him.
The Beast is sad
when Belle leaves.

Gaston wants
to find the Beast.

He goes to the castle.

He attacks the Beast!

The Beast is hurt.

Belle is very sad.

"I love you,"

says Belle.

The Beast
is really a prince!
Belle's love changes him
into a human.
They live happily
ever after.

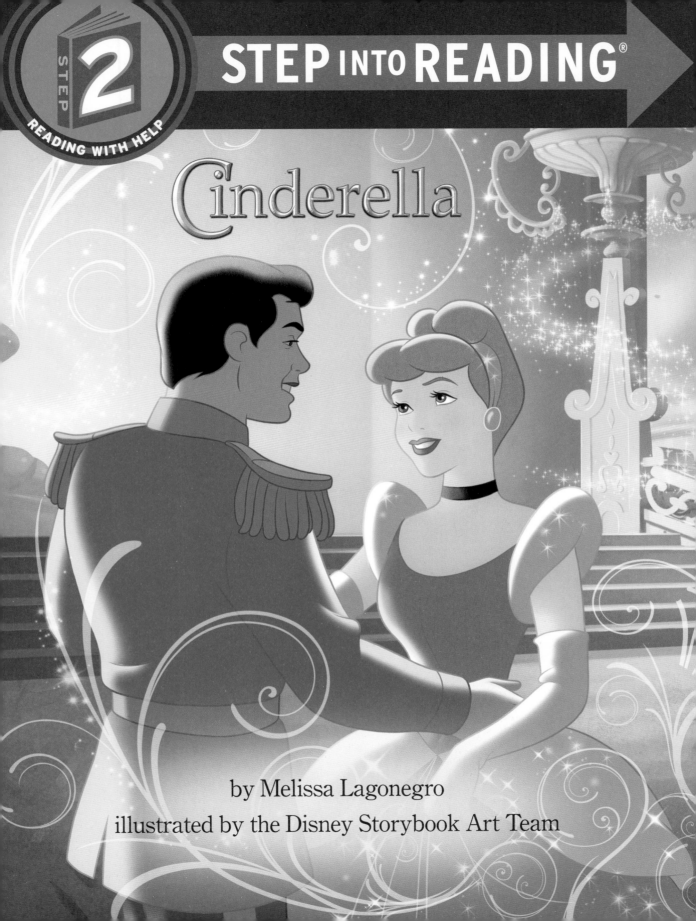

Cinderella

by Melissa Lagonegro

illustrated by the Disney Storybook Art Team

Cinderella is a kind
and pretty girl.
She has many
animal friends.

Cinderella lives
with her mean
stepfamily
and their nasty cat.
She does all the chores.
The stepsisters yell
at Cinderella.

Cinderella's stepmother
is Lady Tremaine.
She does not like
Cinderella.

She gives Cinderella
more chores to do.

The family gets a letter.
The Prince is having
a royal ball!

Everyone in the kingdom is invited.
Cinderella must finish her chores before she can go.

Cinderella finds
an old dress
in the attic.
She can fix it.

She can make it pretty!
Cinderella
and her friends
are excited.

Lady Tremaine gives
Cinderella a pile
of clothes to sew.

Cinderella's friends
fix her dress for her.
The birds add bows.
The mice add ribbons
and beads.

Surprise!
Cinderella loves
her new dress.
Her chores are done.
She can go
to the ball!

Cinderella looks pretty.
Her stepsisters are mad.

They do not want
Cinderella to go
to the ball.
They tear her dress
and pull her beads.

Cinderella is sad.
The Fairy Godmother
appears.

She turns a pumpkin
into a coach.
It will take Cinderella
to the ball!

The Fairy Godmother
gives Cinderella
a sparkling dress
and glass slippers.

Cinderella is ready
for the ball!
She must be home
before the magic stops.

Cinderella arrives
at the palace.
She meets the Prince.
He asks her to dance.

They take a walk.
They fall in love.

It is late!

Cinderella must go.

She runs down the stairs.

She loses a glass slipper.

The magic stops.
Cinderella's dress
and coach change back.
She has one glass slipper.

The Prince's true love
is gone.

He has her glass slipper.

The Prince's father
wants to find her.

Lady Tremaine locks
Cinderella in her room.
She does not want
the Prince to find her.

Cinderella's friends
get the key to her room.
They unlock the door.

Cinderella tries on
the glass slipper.
It fits!
She is the Prince's
true love!

Cinderella and the Prince get married. They live happily ever after!

THE PRINCESS AND THE FROG

Kiss the Frog

by Melissa Lagonegro

illustrated by Elizabeth Tate,
Caroline LaVelle Egan, Studio Iboix,
Michael Inman, and the Disney
Storybook Art Team

Tiana works hard.
She has no time
for fun.

She has a dream.

She wants to own

a restaurant.

Prince Naveen
likes to have fun.

He loves music.

He visits New Orleans.

Facilier is a bad man.
He plans to trick
Naveen.

Facilier uses bad magic.
He turns Prince Naveen
into a frog!

Tiana goes
to a costume party.
She wishes on a star.
She wishes
for her restaurant.
Naveen sees her.

Tiana meets Naveen.
She looks like a princess.
Naveen thinks her kiss
will make him human.
He wants to kiss Tiana.

Tiana kisses Naveen.
But she is not
a real princess.

The kiss does not work!

Naveen is still a frog.

Tiana turns

into a frog, too!

Tiana and Naveen
get lost.
They do not like
being frogs.
They do not like
each other.

They meet

Louis the alligator.

Naveen has fun!

Tiana does not.

The frogs try
to catch a bug.
They get stuck together.

Ray is a firefly.

He helps the frogs.

They all become friends.

Tiana shows Naveen

how to cook.

They like
each other now.

Tiana and Naveen find Mama Odie.

She makes good magic.
She can help them.

Mama Odie
shows Naveen
a princess.

He must kiss her.
Then he and Tiana will
become human again!

Tiana and Naveen
are happy!
They are in love.

Naveen kisses a princess.

But it is too late.

The spell does not break!

Naveen is still a frog.

Tiana is still a frog.

Tiana and Prince Naveen
go back to Mama Odie.
They get married.

Now Tiana is a <u>real</u> princess.

They kiss. <u>POOF!</u>

They become human again!

Tiana's dream comes true.

She gets her restaurant.

She has love.

She has everything
she needs!

THE LITTLE MERMAID

by Ruth Homberg

illustrated by the Disney
Storybook Art Team

Ariel is a mermaid.

She is also a princess.

Flounder is her friend.

Scuttle is her friend, too.
He teaches Ariel
about humans.

Ariel dreams of life
above the sea.

King Triton
is Ariel's father.
He is angry
with Ariel.

He does not
trust humans.
He wants Ariel
to stay home.

At night,
Ariel swims
above the water.
There is a storm.

She sees a human.

His name is Prince Eric.

He falls off a ship!

Ariel saves Eric.

Ariel sings
to Eric.
She falls in love
with him.

Ursula is an evil witch.

She takes Ariel's voice.

She gives Ariel legs.

Ariel must kiss Eric.

She has three days.

If they do not kiss,

she will lose her legs

and her voice forever.

Ariel is human!

She can live on land.

She loves her new legs.

Ariel's friends help her.
Scuttle makes
her a dress.

Eric is looking

for the girl

who sang to him.

He thinks it is Ariel.

But she has no voice.

Eric brings Ariel
to the palace.

She combs her hair
with a fork!
Eric laughs.
He likes Ariel.

Eric and Ariel
go on a boat ride.
They almost kiss.

Ursula's eels tip

the boat over!

Ursula does not want
Eric to kiss Ariel.
She changes herself.
She uses Ariel's voice.

Eric loves her voice.
He thinks he is in love
with Ursula!

Eric is going
to marry Ursula!
Scuttle finds out
about her trick.

Scuttle and his friends
stop Ursula.

Ariel's voice is back!

It is too late.

She turns

into a mermaid again.

Ursula laughs.

She turns

into a huge monster!

Eric stops her for good.

King Triton wants Ariel
to be happy.

He makes her
human again.

Eric loves Ariel.
Now they can be
together forever.

Eric and Ariel live
happily ever after!

STEP 2 READING WITH HELP

STEP INTO READING®

Disney MOANA

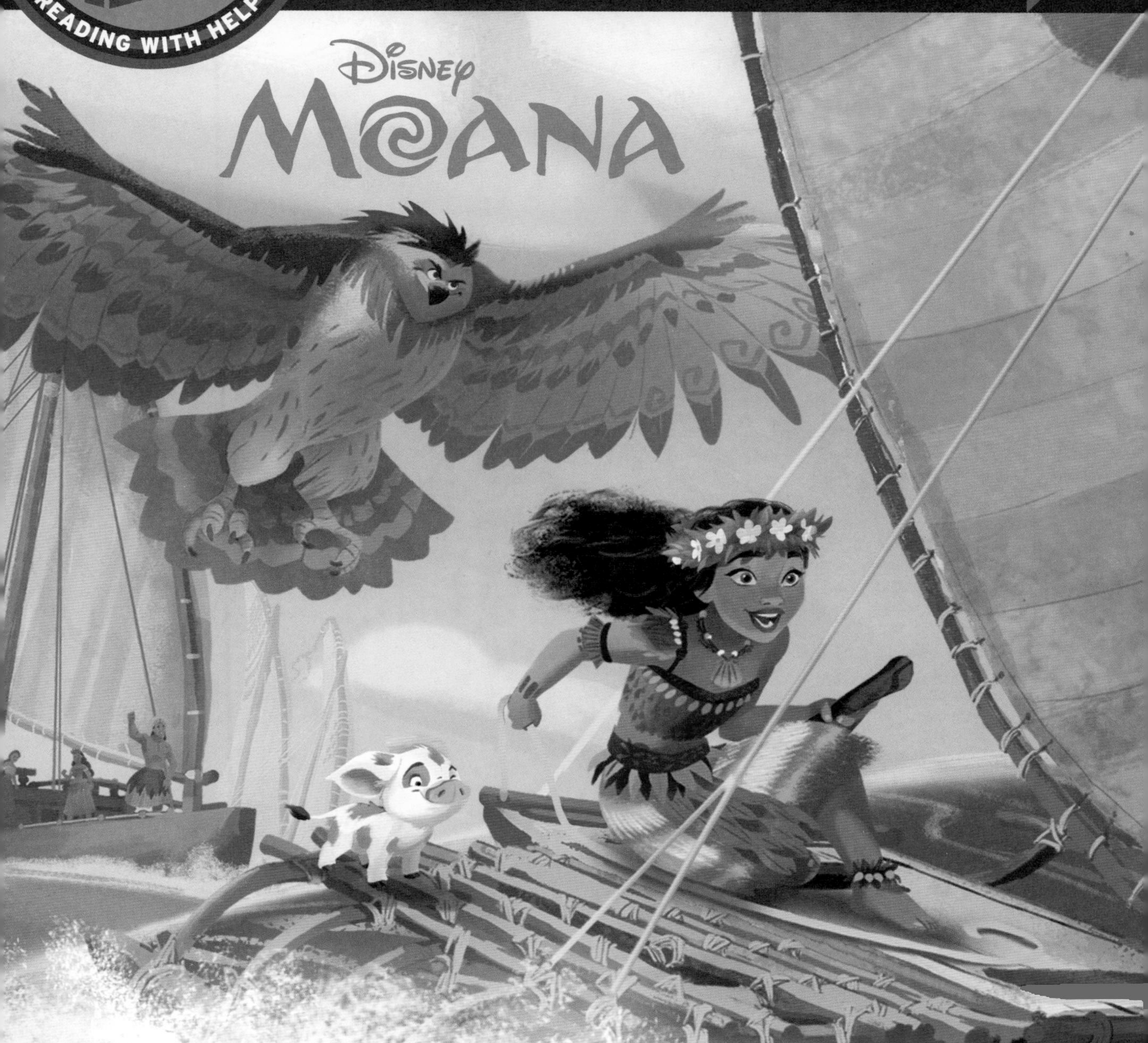

Moana Finds the Way

by Susan Amerikaner

illustrated by the Disney Storybook Art Team

Te Fiti is an island.
She once gave life to all.
The demigod Maui
stole Te Fiti's heart.

Maui lost the heart.
Darkness spread.
People stopped sailing
on the open ocean.

Moana lives
on an island.
She loves the ocean.

It gives her a shiny gift.

It is the heart of Te Fiti!

Moana grows up.
Gramma Tala shows her
a cave full of boats.
Moana's people once
loved to sail!

Moana thinks she would
love to sail, too.

Gramma Tala tells Moana
she must find Maui
and return Te Fiti's heart.

Moana agrees.

She will sail!

She will wayfind!

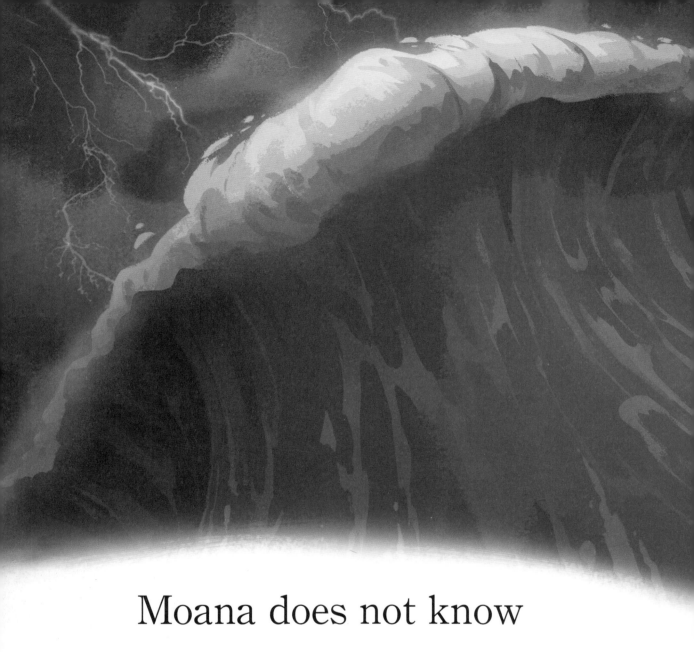

Moana does not know
how to sail.

But she loves the ocean.

She tries to sail.

A storm comes.

Moana is lost.

Moana finds Maui.
Maui does not think
Moana can learn
to wayfind.

He does not want
to help.
The ocean makes
him teach her.

Moana must learn
to use the sun.
She must learn
to feel the waves.

Moana works hard.

She uses the stars.

She feels the waves.

She finds the way!

Monster Te Kā comes.

Big waves rock the boat.

Moana sails fast.

She holds on.

Te Kā is strong.

Moana is smart.

She finds a way.

Moana returns
the heart of Te Fiti.

The darkness leaves.

Plants grow.

Te Fiti blooms.

Life returns

to the islands.

Moana finds her way
back home.
Her family is happy
to see her.

Moana leads her people
to new islands.
She is a great
wayfinder.

She is Moana.

STEP 2

READING WITH HELP

STEP INTO READING®

Disney

MULAN

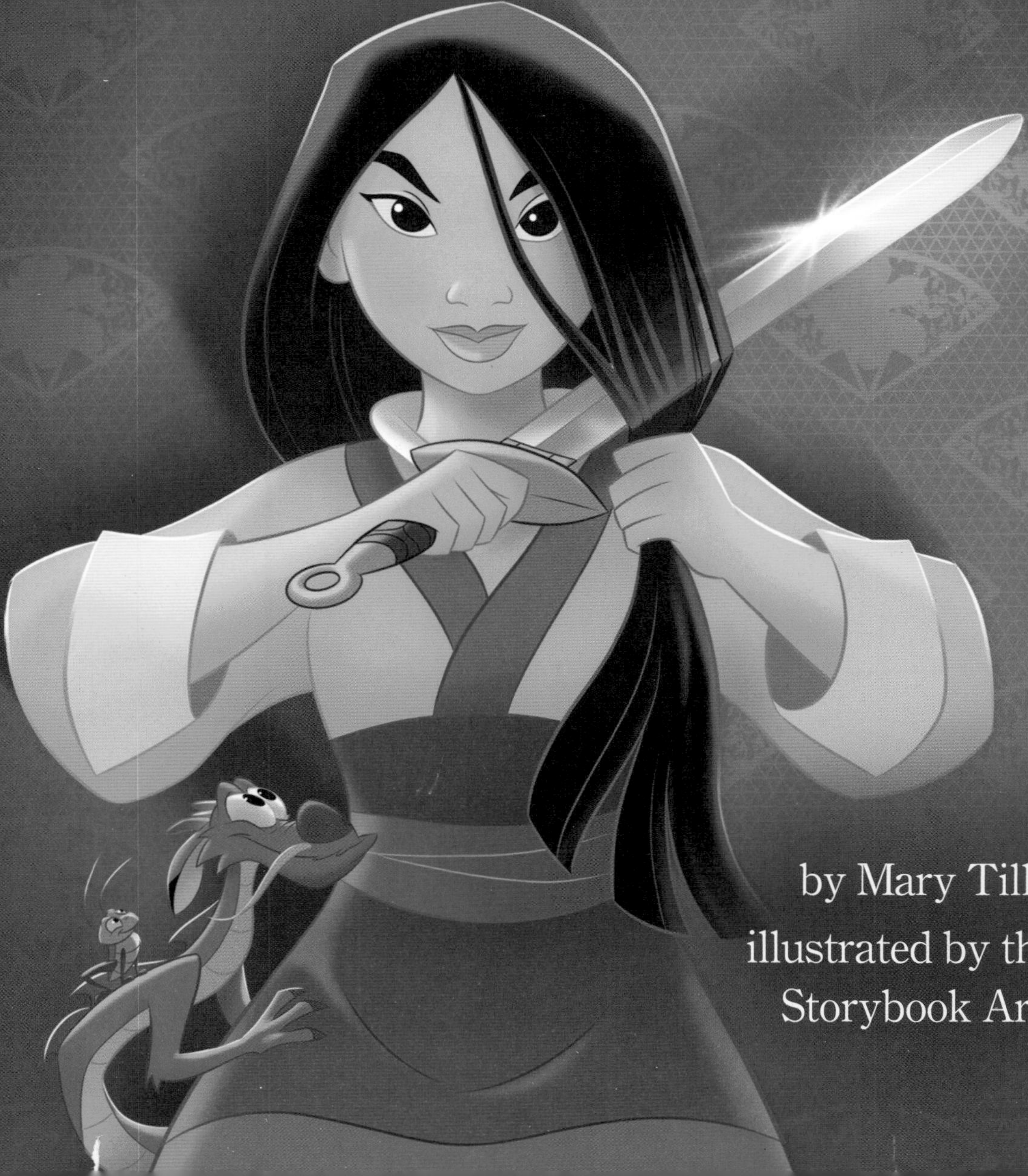

by Mary Tillworth

illustrated by the Disney Storybook Art Team

Mulan is a young woman.

She lives in

a small village.

She is smart and strong.

One day,

men on horses bring news.

There is a war!

One man from each family

must join the army.

Mulan's father is the only
man in Mulan's family.
He has orders
to join.

Mulan knows her father
is too old to go to war.
She will take his place.
She cuts off her hair.

She puts on armor.
Now she looks like a man.
She rides off to join
the army.

Shang is the army trainer.
Mulan gives him
her father's army orders.

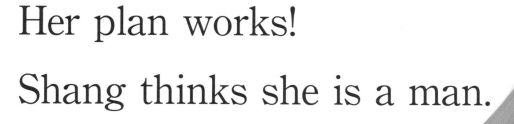

Her plan works!

Shang thinks she is a man.

Shang tells the men
to climb a tall pole.

They all fail.

Mulan does not give up.

She makes it to the top!

Shang leads Mulan
and the men into battle.
They fight Shan-Yu
and his army.

Shang's army is brave.
But Shan-Yu's army
is very big.

Mulan meets a spirit dragon
named Mushu.
She uses him
to light a cannon.
She stops Shan-Yu!

Mulan is hurt.

A doctor treats her.

Then he tells Shang

that Mulan is a woman.

Shang is angry.

Mulan learns Shan-Yu
is coming after them!
She tries to warn Shang.
He does not listen.

Shan-Yu captures Shang!

Mulan will save him.

She holds her hair back.

Now Shan-Yu sees the soldier

who defeated his army!

Mulan and Shan-Yu fight.
Mulan pins Shan-Yu
to the roof.
Mushu soars in with a rocket.

The rocket stops
Shan-Yu.

Mulan and Shang
watch fireworks from
the rocket light the sky.

The emperor thanks Mulan.
He bows to honor her.
Shang and the other soldiers
bow to her, too.

Mulan returns to her village.

She hugs her father.

He is very proud of his

brave Mulan.

Guide to Lighting

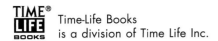

Time-Life Books
is a division of Time Life Inc.

TIME LIFE INC.

Jim Nelson
Chairman and CEO

Steven L. Janas
President and COO

TIME-LIFE TRADE PUBLISHING

Neil Levin
Vice President and Publisher

Jennifer Pearce
Vice President of Content Development

Carolyn Clark
Director of New Product Development

Inger Forland
Director of Marketing

Dana Hobson
Director of Trade Sales

John Lalor
Director of Custom Publishing

Robert Lombardi
Director of Special Markets

Kate L. McConnell
Director of Design

TIME-LIFE GUIDE TO LIGHTING

Anna Burgard, Jennie Halfant
Project Editors

Monika Lynde
Technical Specialist

Carolyn Bounds
Production Manager

Jim King, Stacy L. Eddy
Quality Assurance

HEARTWOOD BOOKS

Jeff Day
Editorial Director

Margaret Nolting Gallos
Editor

Kenneth S. Burton Jr.
Writer

Barbara Sabella
Writer

Mary Jane Favorite
Illustrator

Linda Watts
Designer

Beth Kalet
Copyeditor

Nan Badgett
Indexer

Library of Congress Cataloging-in-Publication Data
is available upon request:

Time-Life Books
2000 Duke St.
Alexandria, VA 22314

ISBN 0-7370-0318-9 Hardcover
ISBN 0-7370-0319-7 Softcover

Books produced by Time-Life Trade Publishing are available at a special bulk discount for promotional and premium use. Custom adaptations can also be created to meet your specific marketing goals. Call 1-800-323-5255.

Guide to Lighting

By the editors of

TIME
LIFE
BOOKS

Alexandria, Virginia

Contents

Layers of Light

LIGHTING FUNDAMENTALS

A home has to be more than practical. It has to be comfortable. It ought to be attractive. The lighting in your home is no different. It helps you see your dinner, read a book, get across the room without tripping. But it also creates an atmosphere or calls attention to certain parts of the room, like the fireplace or bookcase. Focused on a wall, light can be pure decoration.

When most people buy lighting, they focus not on what it does, but on what it looks like. Lighting may decorate the home, but no one light does everything, and the people who want good lighting need to think about light the same way they think about the rest of their home: It has to be practical, it has to be comfortable, and it ought to be beautiful.

Recognizing Layers

Unlike most things in your home, light is something you can't touch, lift, or move. Designers—who are used to thinking in physical terms—overcome this by thinking in terms of what they call "layers of light."

The first layer, ambient or general light, is the light you use to cross a room at night. The second layer, task light, gives you the light by which you read, apply makeup, or work in the kitchen. The third and final layer, accent light, adds interest. It splashes across a wall, highlights a piece of furniture, or draws your eye to a particular feature of the room.

These layers aren't necessarily stacked like those in a cake. A single lighting fixture can provide more than one layer of light, for example. The reading lamp beside your chair provides both ambient and task light. A lighting fixture above a kitchen counter can be both a task and an accent light. The layers blend together, surface in pairs, and sometimes stand alone. In most houses, the lighting is only two layers deep—ambient and task lighting. Top-notch lighting design uses all three layers.

Ambient Light

Ambient light fills the room like a cloud, establishing its basic atmosphere. Done well, it can be flattering. Good ambient lighting provides a smooth transition between areas of brightness and shadow and reduces the eyestrain caused as our eyes adjust between the two. On a bright, sunny day, at least part of the ambient light will be daylight, pouring in through a window. Even on the brightest days, however, daylight usually gets an assist from some sort of lighting fixture. It can be direct, from a fixture that scatters the light, like a floor lamp with a shade. Or it can also be indirect, thrown by a fixture onto a surface that scatters the light, like a torchiere (a type of floor lamp) shining up onto a white ceiling.

The amount of ambient light you'll need varies from room to room and depends both on the fixtures and bulbs you use. Generally speaking, however, two 60-watt incandescent bulbs will provide enough ambient light for about 60 square feet. In order to spread the light evenly, the bulbs should be in different fixtures in different parts of the room. We'll talk more about fixtures and bulbs in Tech Talk, beginning on page 20.

Task Light

Task light helps us read, write, cook, sew, build a cabinet, or paint our fingernails. It is directed specifically at the site of the activity so that the area is bright and clear of shadows.

The amount of task light required depends on the task. Reading comfortably requires about twice as much task light as combing your hair, about the same amount as you'd want for kitchen chores, and about half of what you'd want in a sewing room or workshop.

The amount of light we need and the type we prefer also vary with age. As we get older, the lenses in our eyes thicken. We need more light for any given task while at the same time we are less tolerant of glare. The amount of light and its placement become more crucial as our eyes age.

▲ The torchiere floor lamp adds ambient light to the room indirectly by throwing the light up onto the vaulted ceiling.

Accent Light

Accent light is the finishing touch that adds interest to a room. Light becomes accent light when you intensify it (it may be up to three times brighter than surrounding lights), limit it to a confined space, such as in a china cabinet, or change its color. The bright, white light from a halogen bulb, for example, provides task light if it shines down on a kitchen counter. But put it in a room otherwise lit with warm, yellow, incandescent bulbs, and, by contrast, it becomes accent light. Accent light can be a spotlight focused on a statue. It can be a strip lighting fixture inside a cabinet or a downlight that shines out from the base of a chandelier to show off a centerpiece on the table below. Accent light can be produced through special features of lighting fixtures. Track lights

▲ A trio of pendant ceiling fixtures above a counter provides task light for kitchen chores.

Ambient light sources:
- Ceiling fixtures
- Wall sconces
- Recessed and track lighting
- Hanging chandeliers and pendants
- Table and floor lamps
- Outdoor post lamps
- Outdoor floodlights

Task light sources:
- Desk, table, and wall lamps
- Recessed and track lighting
- Ceiling fixtures
- Floor lamps
- Hanging fixtures and pendants

Accent light sources:
- Track and recessed fixtures
- Curio cabinet lights
- Portable lighting aimed up into or down onto an object
- Ceiling mounted spots
- Up- or downlight landscape lighting
- Indoor or outdoor spots

▲ This upstairs hallway is lit with accent lights. The track head, upper left, drapes a pool of light onto the carpet, the middle track head lights the picture, and the third throws light onto the flower arrangement. In the background, a recessed light drapes a small table and picture in accent light.

▲ **Wall washing.** Wide-angle track lights bathe the wall above this countertop with light to bring attention to wall decorations.

(called *heads*) are available with adjustable lenses that let you focus the light tightly or with shutters called barn doors that let you direct the light. Low-voltage incandescent or halogen lighting strips or miniature units can go anywhere from inside a cabinet to above a painting. Low-voltage halogen spots with a 6-inch beam and lens for focusing have become almost standard for accenting flatware and crystal in dining rooms and home bars.

Perfecting Your Accent

Light itself can be a decoration: Purple light splashed across a vaulted ceiling becomes abstract art. A strobe light seems to suspend motion on the dance floor. A laser entertains us at a planetarium. The techniques you use in your home can be equally dramatic, but the tools are subtler, and the effects are easier to create.

Crosslighting is light applied from two sides to enhance curves and contours. Sometimes crosslighting uses lights of differing focus, color, or intensity to add further interest.

Spotlighting. An intense, controlled, and sharply defined beam that draws our attention to an object, indoors or outdoors. To accent pictures or artwork hung at eye level, install ceiling-mounted spots between 24 and 30 inches from the wall. They will shine down at an angle that lights the object fully without shadows or glare.

Moonlighting. A soft, diffuse, cool-colored downlight with a small focus area. It is especially beautiful trained on indoor plants. Outdoors, it's often used to highlight a tree.

▲ **Shadowing.** The branches of the trees in this front yard cast lovely shadows on the house thanks to outdoor floodlights.

▲ **Crosslighting,** lighting an object from each side rather than from directly above, is a good way to show off contours and texture. The pottery piece in the niche behind this bed is lit using this technique.

▲ **Wall grazing** emphasizes the texture of a brick facade.

Wall washing. A wide beam that bathes the wall in a flood of soft light. Make accent colors pop in one area, light a mural, or draw attention to a whole interior design composition with wall washing. For this effect, install recessed wall washers or wide-angle track lights on the ceiling about 2 to 3 feet from the wall and 2 to 3 feet apart.

Uplighting is lighting an object from below. A dramatic way to illuminate pictures, uplighting emphasizes the contours of architectural features, or defines large potted plants and trees. Locate light sources low, hiding them behind solid objects or tucking them into foliage, and aim them high. The fixture doesn't need to be fancy. An inexpensive, plug-in, portable light can do it.

Shadowing. A charming form of uplighting that throws light at a plant or object to cast shadows on the wall beyond. This technique is often used beautifully in landscape lighting, but can be an indoor technique, too.

Silhouetting. The flip side of shadowing, this creates drama, throwing light behind an object or plant. The light filters through, emphasizing the shape and form of the backlit object. Place the fixture behind the object and point it up at a 15- to 20-degree angle. Solid objects may be lit from directly behind the object.

Wall grazing. Uplighting or downlighting a wall emphasizes its texture. Install track lights or recessed fixtures very close to the wall—6 to 12 inches away—and aim them straight down or up. The light will appear as scallops or as one continuous arc of light, depending on how far apart you place the fixtures.

Where to Begin

Like most aspects of interior design, lighting is more art than science; there is no one right way to do it. Some people can stand in the room and decide what they need—a switch here, a different bulb there. If you're one of these people, then let your artistic sense be your guide. Need to make it brighter? Add a fixture, use a brighter bulb, or substitute halogen for incandescent. Is the room too bright? A dimmer switch or a table lamp with a three-way bulb might be the answer.

Start planning from scratch, as if there were no lights anywhere in the room. List the room's key elements and areas of activity. Find the center of visual interest—the focal point—of the room, or find a part of the room you can make the focal point with the lighting. Sketch out the room and note on it what you'd like to see: Perhaps you want to highlight some love seats, for example. Or maybe you want to highlight a wall hanging and put some reading lights beside the chairs.

Tell a Lighting Story

For a lot of people, looking at a room and deciding what light goes where isn't that easy. If you're one of them, try writing what's called a lighting story. Begin by telling a "story" that describes the room you want, and then choose the lighting that makes it work.

Start by asking yourself questions. If you were thinking about lighting an entryway and living room, for example, the questions might look something like this:

- What do I want guests to see as they arrive at night—the house? The house number? The front door? The garden?
- What do I want people to see when they enter the house?

- Where do I want to lead my guests?
- What mood am I trying to create?
- What furnishings or architectural features am I trying to highlight or mask?
- What style am I going for?

Now what? Start a collection of possible solutions. Surf Web sites and flip through brochures. Collect magazine clippings that show something you have in mind. Notice lighting at the homes of friends and analyze what you like, and what you don't. If you're working with a designer or an electrician, listen to their suggestions. Visit home improvement centers and kitchen-and-bath stores to see examples of light fixtures. Visit the demonstration area of a lighting showroom, known as a lighting lab. Ask for demonstrations of various types of light bulbs, lighting controls, systems, and fixtures.

Set a Budget

The first rule of remodeling is to know what you can spend. If every spare nickel goes into a Tiffany shade, you'll never have the reading lights you planned to put next to the bed. Watch out especially for the hidden costs—there's more to lighting than lighting fixtures:

Construction and Repair. You may need to pay for materials and labor for building soffits or a recess in the ceiling around the edge of the room. If you run new wires through existing walls, you'll have extensive plaster or drywall repair.

Electrician. There's no reason you can't do most of the work yourself using the directions in the back of this book. But if you need to add a circuit or put in a new breaker box, you may want to hire an electrician who will give you an estimate to include in your budget, as well as an idea of how long the work will take. Even if you don't hire an electrician, add the cost of cable, boxes, switches, outlets, and plugs to your budget.

Tools. If you don't already have the tools you'll need, add them onto the costs of doing it yourself. At the very least, get needle-nosed pliers, lineman's pliers, a tester that tells you if a circuit is wired correctly, and a separate tester that tells you if the power is on.

Accessories and Light Bulbs. Most fixtures don't come with light bulbs, so include the price of bulbs in your budget. Track lighting systems have feeds,

My Lighting Story

Initial Stage—General Impressions

"I entertain a lot, and I want the path from the street to be well lit, warm, and inviting. It can't be so bright that it annoys neighbors. Inside, the foyer needs soft light, almost like candle-light, and I want the guests to be drawn from there into the living room. As they walk in, I want them to notice the fireplace and the painting over it. The sculpture on the table in the corner should also be highlighted."

Middle Stage—Begin to Make Selections

"Path lights beside the brick walk provide light and lead guests to new post light at the steps. Matching wall lights at the porch highlight the doorway. Lights on dimmers light the foyer. Sconces on either side of the fireplace pull the eye—and the guest—into the room. Spotlight the painting. Table lamps beside sofa. Floor lamps behind the chairs."

Final Stage—Make Specific Choices

"Six, maybe eight mushroom-style, low-voltage fixtures beside path. Arts-and-Crafts style post lamp with matching wall lantern at steps and porch. Inside, a ceiling fixture with globe made out of mica is on a dimmer in foyer. Two recessed mini-spots on a dimmer switch crosslight the painting. Arts-and-Crafts table lamps provide warm, ambient light. Bright white light from upscale halogen reading lamp draws the guests to the chairs."

end caps, and other accessories that are sold separately. Recessed fixtures have a housing, trim, and other accessories, which may or may not be included in the price of the fixture. If you want small shades for your chandelier, you may need to buy them separately.

Permits. You won't need a permit to hang a light, but if the job involves running cable, it usually requires a permit as well as one or two inspections. Ask your local building inspector whether you need a permit, what it will cost, and whether there is a separate charge for the inspection.

Designers. Some designers specialize in lighting, and they can be a great help laying out a lighting plan. Talk to the designer up front about costs: If they're too high, lighting showroom and home center staff can also help with the design.

Go Shopping

Once you get to the store, start with the key element in your lighting design—a chandelier, a pendant over an island, a vanity light, or the post light and wall lantern beside your home's entrance, for example.

Then try to think in terms of clusters or suites of fixtures. If your foyer, living room, and dining room are all within a single line of sight, consider coordinating the fixtures by using similar styles and finishes. If the cluster falls in a single room, play matches against contrasts, color against color, shape in answer to shape.

Allow for flexibility. Consider dimmers, so that the light can be bright when you need it and subdued when you want atmosphere. Install

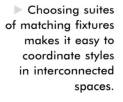

▶ Choosing suites of matching fixtures makes it easy to coordinate styles in interconnected spaces.

recessed lights so that, at one setting, the center fixture washes the wall with light all by itself and, at another setting, the lights on either side join in to "wash" the wall even more brightly. Add a small table lamp on a desk, even if there's a bright overhead light or a floor lamp nearby. You may need the extra light once in a while.

Before you buy, ask to see the fixtures when they're lit. The color of a shade can change dramatically when the lamp is on; the finish of a pendant light can look more—or less—elegant. Bring swatches of wall coverings or carpet samples to see how they look under the light of the fixture.

Ask if the fixture comes with the light bulbs or not. Most don't. Ask if the fixture will work on a dimmer. Most do; some don't. Find out about the care of the finish. Brass finishes generally have a lacquer coating to protect them. This finish can break down, allowing the brass to tarnish. Find out if there are guarantees that cover the finish.

Double-check Before Installation

When you get home with your new lights, it's worth the trouble to find a sturdy ladder and a strong assistant. Have your assistant hold your new chandelier above the table, or hold the new bracket lights above the bathroom vanity. If the match or proportion is off, you'll know before you've done the work, and before installation makes the fixture unreturnable.

Evaluating the Installation

Lighting must be seen in context to be fully appreciated. Don't try to fine-tune your lighting in a room under construction. Wait until the walls and floors are finished and the furniture is in place. Once they are, you can focus the accent lighting fixtures and program the dimmer levels. Ask those who use the room to help you evaluate it. Here are some things to look for, along with possible solutions:

Is there any glare? If so, refocus the shutters on a track head. Move a table lamp. Try a different light bulb. Rearrange some furniture.

Are there any dark areas? If so, add floor or table lamps. Add another head to your track system. Check that you are using the highest wattage capacity you can for your lamps and lighting fixture, but never exceed the recommended wattage.

Are there sharp contrasts between bright light and shadow? If so, add or adjust the dimmer. Replace a light bulb that projects a narrow beam with one that has a wider beam. Place a torchiere to even things out.

Are the colors pleasing? If not, experiment with bulbs that produce different colors of light.

How does the lighting in the room make you feel? We don't always know how to identify problems with lighting, so sometimes it helps to rely on a bit of intuition. If a lit room feels gloomy, it may be because the room is too dark or because the color of the lighting isn't working. Experiment until you find a solution.

Practical Considerations

Suppose the dream house is years away. Maybe you have only a small piece of property for your new home. Maybe you are renting. You almost certainly have to work with a limited budget. So, it's time to get practical. Read on.

New Light for Old Houses

Older buildings present special design challenges. They may have one or two outlets per room and a single light in the center of the room. Getting new fixtures and sufficient light into an old room without disturbing ceilings and walls can be tough. Here are some suggestions:

Consider swags. Most hanging fixtures are wired directly into the ceiling, but swags hang by a chain from a sturdy hook. The chain and cord

▲ Hanging fixtures like this one come ready to be direct-wired, but many can be converted into swags. Ask your lighting retailer for advice.

▶ Recessed lights are embedded in the soffit that runs around this bathroom ceiling.

are looped over to the wall, run down it, and plug into an outlet. This is great in an apartment or whenever you don't want to cut holes in the ceiling. Be sure to ask when you purchase the fixture if it can be converted to a swag. You can also buy swag kits at lighting showrooms.

Architectural features can house wiring, recessed light fixtures, or light strips. Use false columns to hide wires running from ceiling to floor. Build a box along the ceiling, called a soffit, to house lights and their wiring. Build a recess, called a cove, into the ceiling, and light it as an accent, or hide lights in it where they can't be seen. Lightweight glue-on moldings, called ceiling medallions, that imitate Victorian plasterwork can give a room a period look while hiding holes cut in the wall for wiring.

You can house lighting in a cabinet without having to rewire walls and ceilings. Work with low-voltage incandescent or halogen accent strips, and channel the wires unobtrusively behind the mullions of the cabinets and into or through the cabinet base. Be sure, however, that the lighting fixture is made for this, so it doesn't get too hot. Check to make sure, too, that it's permissible under the electrical code.

Recessed lighting systems can be installed in new or existing ceilings. Check with the lighting retailer or manufacturer for models rated and designed for a retrofit application. Low-profile recessed fixtures can fit in shallow spaces; there are specially insulated units rated for contact with ceiling insulation, as well as special units for sloped ceilings.

Attach track lighting to the ceiling. These systems consist of an electrified track and individual heads. The heads have metal connectors that turn and clip into the track at any point. The tracks carry the power to the track heads without the need for running wires through the ceiling. On most units, one end of the track wires into an existing ceiling box, or you can buy cord-and-plug accessories that enable you to plug the track into a wall outlet. (This alternative does not look as attractive as a direct-wire arrangement, though.) Track lights come in a wide variety of styles and can be used for accent, general, and task lighting.

▶ This track fixture uses a halogen bulb to create crisp, white light, which is great for showing off a treasured vase or a favorite wall hanging.

▲ The fluorescent light inside this cabinet makes rummaging easier.

▶ Sloped ceilings such as this one require recessed light housings made especially for them.

Lighting Safety and Security

Give the impression that someone is home, even when you aren't. There are no guarantees, but generally speaking lighting makes your home less attractive to intruders. Use timers and photosensitive lamp inserts to turn lamps on and off at the times you normally would if you were home. In fact, it's a good idea to have certain lights that always are run by timers or sensors, so they'll establish the same pattern whether or not you are home. Round this out with a fixture with a built-in motion detector. It installs just like a regular light and will light up automatically if someone comes near. It's great for startling intruders, but equally handy when you're coming home with a bag of groceries under each arm.

Have a good exterior lighting system. This helps family and guests to see adequately to get from the car to the door, to see keys, or the doorbell, and to get inside. Solar or low-voltage path lights are excellent for leading to the doorway, and over-the-door downlight is good for illuminating keys or the contents of your purse while you look for them.

Security lighting lets you see what's going on outside. It also lets neighbors keep an eye out for each other's houses and yards. But don't let your security lighting be any brighter than you need, and take care that it doesn't glare. Glare actually cuts your ability to see and produces shadows where trespassers can hide.

▼ The path lights and lights beside the garage show visitors where entrances are. The wall bracket between the picture windows throws soft light onto the shrubs and eliminates dark spots where intruders can hide. The landscape's textures and colors get a lift from uplighting and shadowing techniques.

Windows, Doors, Skylights, and Natural Light

Natural light has a positive effect on our mood and productivity, but because it is constantly changing, it can wreak havoc on lighting design. When developing a lighting plan, it's important to understand how daylight will affect it. In some cases, your lighting plan will call for dimmers to deal with rapidly changing light. In other cases, curtains, blinds, or even an air conditioner become an important part of your lighting scheme.

Generally speaking, the summer sun beats down on southern and western sloped roofs from midday through late afternoon. Western walls take the full force of the afternoon sun. In the winter, the sun hits southern sloped roofs and shines into southern windows at midday. It strikes the house from the southwest in late afternoon.

These factors change daily and vary depending on your latitude, but they do translate into some general design principles.

Windows and skylights on the north side of a house are the easiest to work with. They provide plenty of ambient lighting without a lot of summer heat. On sunny days, a window or two may provide all the ambient light you need. Don't make heavy curtains part of your decorating scheme. They'll block out too much light.

HIGH NOON IN A TEMPERATE ZONE

▲ The east-facing windows of this house let in morning sun during the coolest part of the day, but they won't offer much sunlight later on. The skylight on the north side provides plenty of ambient light without uncomfortable summer heat.

Windows on the eastern side of a house let in morning sun during the coolest part of the day. The room will get dark early in the day, however, at which point you'll be calling on fixtures to provide ambient light. It might be a good idea to have the lights on dimmers, or even separate switches, so you can increase the light as needed.

A southern window wall receives direct sunlight and its warmth and light in winter; it gets indirect sun in the summer, minimizing hot midday sun.

Windows facing west and skylights facing south and west collect direct sun in the hottest part of the day. You can count on them to provide good ambient light, but part of your plan should also include curtains, shutters, or blinds to control the glare. You may even want a room air conditioner to make the room more comfortable when the sun hits it hardest.

Tech Talk

2

UNDERSTANDING LIGHTS AND LIGHT BULBS

All your lights have three things in common: a light source, something to hold it, and some sort of control. Beyond that, they vary widely. Some include ballasts or starters that affect how the electricity is delivered. Others have shades or globes made of glass, or plastic shields, which influence light output. Some have transformers to reduce the voltage to an appropriate level. Still others have dimmers to gradually reduce the light level, motion detectors to react to movement, photosensors to react to daylight, or timers to turn them on and off. Understanding the components of your lighting will help you create beautiful, functional lighting design in your home.

Lighting Hardware

*T*his section offers an overview of lighting hardware—fixtures, lamps, light bulbs, and lighting
controls. You'll be amazed at the versatility and
technological sophistication of lighting today. But first,
here are a few things to keep in mind:

■ Most lights are run on an electrical current of 120 volts (line voltage),
but others are low-voltage and use transformers to reduce the voltage to
12. Transformers are built in to the fixture, the light bulb, or come as
accessories, such as in landscape lighting systems. There are incandescent and halogen bulbs, as well as dimmers made especially for low-
voltage fixtures.

■ Put the same light bulb in two different fixtures, and you will get two
different levels of light. That's because shields or diffusers, glass reflectors
and globes, shades, and even the shape of the light all affect illumination.

■ Not all fixtures work in all places. Some bulbs, for example, will not
work if mounted upside down. Indoor fixtures shouldn't be used outdoors. And if you are choosing a fixture for a damp or wet location,
you need to buy units specially made for this purpose.

A Light from Above: Ceiling Fixtures

Placing light high above the action is the most logical of design deci-
sions, and that's why lights mounted to ceilings are everywhere. They
provide general light, primarily, but they can help out with task light
and even accent light. They can be teamed with other lights for great
effects and a unified interior design. Types of ceiling fixtures include
flush, semi-flush—which extend downward 6 to 18 inches—carriage
lights, chandeliers, pendants, recessed lights, track lights, and ceiling
fans with light kits.

Recessed Lights

The housing for recessed lights is tucked up into the ceiling—recessed.
Only the trim is visible. Recessed lighting can supply task, accent, and
ambient light in any area of the house (even outdoors, under eaves).
Common decorator units are called "cans" or "high hats."

▲ A semi-flush fixture may be a suitable focal point for a foyer or a bathroom.

▲ A flush-mount fixture provides basic ambient lighting.

▷ A pendant fixture extends the light downward on a rigid stem or a chain. It is a great choice for task lighting.

▲ A chandelier is a key element in interior design.

Fixtures range from 2½ to 8 inches in diameter. The more narrow sizes tend to be for accent light applications, while the mid-sized and wider units are best for task and ambient lighting. They're available in line or low voltage and use a variety of bulbs—halogen, incandescent, fluorescent, reflector floods, and spots. If you opt for the energy efficiency of compact fluorescent bulbs, they may require special integrated ballasts and compatible dimmers. Ask at the store or lighting showroom.

A recessed light consists of two parts: the housing, which goes above the ceiling, and the trim, which is seen from below. The recessed housing you choose depends on where and how you plan to install the unit. The two most important choices are new construction and retrofit. Retrofit housings are for remodeling jobs and have a housing compact enough to slide up through the small opening you cut in the ceiling for the bulb. New construction housings are larger and are designed to be installed before the drywall for the ceiling is in place.

Beyond that, you have several choices:

■ Non-insulated ceiling (non-IC) housings are for use in non-insulated ceilings. If you try to use one in an insulated ceiling, you run the risk of damaging the insulation, or even starting a fire unless you install barriers—usually 2x6s or 2x8s—between the housing and the insulation.

In a pinch, even an ordinary A-type light bulb works in a recessed fixture, but use it only in a pinch because much of its light simply bounces around inside the can and is wasted. The best choice for recessed fixtures is a reflector or a spot bulb (R bulbs); their silver coating pushes light out the opening.

▲ Housings for recessed fixtures are available for new construction, renovation situations, sloped ceilings, and damp locations. Compatible trims include "high hats" or "eyeballs."

■ Insulated ceiling (IC) housings are designed to be safe if the housing will come in contact with insulation.

■ Energy-conserving airtight (AT) or performance-tested fixtures minimize the drafts that can come down through the light into the room.

■ Housings for wet or damp locations, sloped ceilings, shallow, or non-standard ceilings.

The trim snaps into the housing. Trim comes in black, white, silver, brass, and other finishes to match your decor, but more importantly, the trim "shapes" the light into task, general, or accent light. Baffles, a series of concentric rings inside the trim, cut glare, for instance. Eyeballs swivel around to aim at some area or piece of furniture. Lenses, diffusers, mini- and pinhole spots tighten and focus the beam. Lighting demonstration labs in showrooms and home centers can be particularly helpful for choosing trims and the lighting controls that will operate your recessed system.

Versatile Track Lighting

When you think track lighting, think flexibility. Electrical current runs through the long, electrified track unit. The lights, called heads, turn and click into the track. The heads swivel, rotate, and aim in practically any direction and you can slide the heads anywhere along the track. As a result, it's possible to generate all three layers of light: ambient, task, and accent from a single track. A newer cousin, the cable lighting system, is low voltage and its fixtures fit into flexible cables rather than rigid tracks.

In an 8-foot ceiling, space recessed can lights 5½ to 6 feet apart. In a 9-foot ceiling, space them 6 feet apart. For every additional foot of ceiling height, increase the spacing another foot. Do a little overlighting. Choose fixtures that take 75 to 150 watts. Then install a dimmer or substitute lower-wattage bulbs if you find you don't always need the maximum light they produce.

◀ This framing projector track head is ideal for highlighting four-sided flat objects such as paintings, photographs, and wall art. Like a camera lens, the projector can be adjusted to width and length of the object.

▲ Track systems offer flexibility because each track fixture can be slid along to any point on the track.

Usually, track systems are purchased à la carte—components come separately. Here's a rundown:

▪ The track itself is usually in 2-, 4-, or 8-foot lengths. Some can be cut. Most track is mounted flush on the ceiling, but some units can also be recessed, hung from the ceiling, or even mounted on a wall. Mounting hardware usually comes with the track.

▪ Electrical feed boxes and canopies provide the power to the tracks. End feeds connect to the electrical box at the end of the track; floating canopies enable the connection to be made at any point along the track. Plug-and-cord sets allow you to use an electrical outlet if you don't want to direct-wire.

▪ Connectors enable you to join track sections in different "shapes"—X, T, L, and even curves.

▪ Track heads or lamp holders range from large tubular fluorescent wallwashers to miniature, low-voltage pin spots with built-in transformers. Their finishes can be white, black, wood, or wood-tone, brass, silver, or glass. Some systems offer hanging pendants or other hanging fixtures that can snap into the track. As a retrofit, track lights are much easier to install than recessed light. Instead of stringing cable from light to light, you simply screw the track in place and put the light where you want it.

▪ Track head accessories include barn doors and framing projectors for shaping a beam to a specific size; louvers, baffles, and spread lenses to manipulate the light or cut glare; extension wands drop heads down closer to work surfaces.

Is This Enough Light?

Light levels are measured in foot-candles—the amount of light a candle shines on a surface one foot away. For something like crossing a room, you'll want 15 to 25 foot-candles. Comfortable dining requires about 20 foot-candles. You'll need 50 foot-candles for reading and 200 for difficult tasks.

You can estimate foot-candles with a simple formula. You'll need to know how much light the bulb produces in lumens, a figure you'll find on the bulb package. You'll also need to know the area a bulb lights, listed as beam spread in lighting catalogs. You can assume a couple of other things. Assume the fixture is 75 percent efficient, and that the rest of the light is absorbed by shades, baffles, and other hardware. Also assume after the light has been used for a while, it produces about 60 or 70 percent of its initial output. (This is called the light loss factor.)

The formula looks like this:

Lumens x fixture efficiency x light loss factor (LLF) ÷ square feet = foot-candles (FC)

When you do the math, the formula tells you that a fixture using a 100-watt bulb generating 1510 lumens would supply more than enough light for dining, but not enough for reading:

1510 (lumens) x .75 (fixture efficiency) x .7 (LLF) ÷ 25 square feet = 31.71 (FC)

Up Against It: Wall Fixtures

Long ago someone got tired of holding up the flaming torch and invented the wall sconce. Today, there's a whole family of sconces—wall sconces, lanterns, bath bars and channels, brackets, wall lamps with shades, picture lights, even undercabinet lights, all of which can provide either general, task, or accent light. They're usually wired directly into an electrical box and operated with a wall switch. Sometimes, they plug into an outlet, their cord discreetly hidden by a plastic cord cover.

▶ Track connectors allow you to join sections of track according to a wide variety of configurations, such as the one pictured here.

▼ Halogen track lights illuminate the work surface and make the cookware glitter.

▲ Use wall lamps like this to provide task lighting at bedsides and above desks.

▼ If you get tired of the look of the glass in this wall bracket, substitute one of the many types of replacement pieces available at home centers and lighting showrooms.

▲ Wall sconces placed on either side of a bathroom mirror or mantelpiece artwork are classic approaches to lighting design.

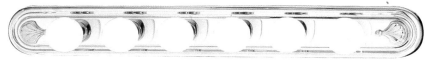

▲ Wall brackets, commonly used in bathrooms, use many, softly lit bulbs to provide even illumination.

Mount wall sconces 62 to 72 inches from the floor. The rule isn't hard and fast—vary the placement according to your particular application. Allow clearance for passersby. Covered sconces or wall lamps with shades need to be mounted so that the bulb is not visible. Vanity fixtures should distribute light evenly around a mirror.

You Can Take It with You: Portable Lights

Floor lamps, table lamps, portable piano lamps, and desk lamps are a great source of general and task lighting. Their primary advantage is their portability. Don't like how that brass floor lamp looks here? Unplug it and move it over there. Moving? Unscrew the finial, remove the shade, roll the lamp in bubble wrap, box it and put it on the truck. For an inexpensive accent lighting effect, buy a portable "can" light, plug it in, and shine it up to silhouette your ficus plant.

Shades are a critical part of a table or floor lamp. They color and filter, spread, direct and shape, and shield the light. Shades may be clear, translucent, prismatic, or opaque. They are made of metal, glass, ceramic, mica, silk, linen, paper, acrylic, and more.

Torchieres thrust light up toward the ceiling and scatter it around, creating an effective source of general lighting and, in some cases, task light.

A floor lamp offers flexibility to your lighting scheme.

Torchieres throw light upward and reflect it off ceilings and walls. Usually about 70 inches tall, they can have graceful curving bowls of glass in white or more fantastic colors such as opalescent pink or blue. Older models may have extra-wide mogul-base sockets. Many of today's torchieres take halogen "Q" type bulbs. All generate heat and should not be used near draperies or in children's rooms. For more about torchiere safety, see the discussion under halogen bulbs, page 42.

Floor lamps balance a room's brightness or boost it. They provide task lighting and most often take incandescent or compact fluorescent bulbs. Their average height is 58 to 60 inches, and they come in finishes including bright and antique brass, verdi (green), or black and white lacquer. Look for models that have a weighted or wide base so they won't tip or wobble. Many operate with three-way or dimmer switches; others have foot or touch controls. Swing-arm floor lamps are good for reading since they can be adjusted.

Picture lights are mounted onto a frame or onto the wall. If you don't want to get into track or recessed lights to light your artwork, this is a good choice.

Piano and music lights, like picture lights, have adjustable cylindrical shades that direct light downward while cutting glare in other directions. Most have a clutch that allows you to adjust the neck. They can be freestanding or attached to music stands.

Specialty lamps include adjustable-arm desk lamps with built-in magnifiers—great for needlework or graphic arts. A model that uses a fluorescent tube stays cool enough to allow you to adjust light positions without burning your fingers.

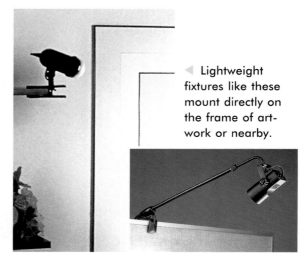

Lightweight fixtures like these mount directly on the frame of artwork or nearby.

Avoid using three-way bulbs in one-way sockets. They operate only at the highest wattage, wasting energy.

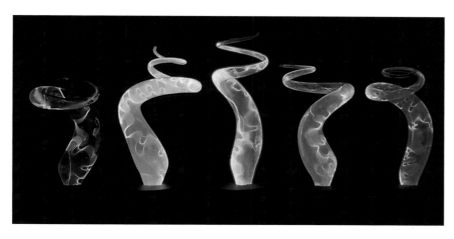

◀ Specialty lamps include models that add more to the decoration of the room than to its light level.

▶ Lamps with built-in magnifiers are great for close work and for people with low vision.

Ceiling Fans Do Double Duty

Ceiling fans are customarily sold in places where you buy home lighting. They circulate air and thereby assist your heating and cooling systems. They do double duty as a light if you attach a "light kit." Look for silent, stable operation. Stay away from fans that make noise or wobble precariously. Ask if the fan comes with a unit that allows you to control the fan speed and the light levels either with a wall switch, or by remote control. An 11- to 13-degree blade pitch, enough tilt to get the air moving, is important. Get a model with a variety of speeds. Three-speed, reversible operation allows you to circulate air up or down, slowly or quickly. For porches or patios, look for damp-location models.

▶ Ceiling fans can be used with or without light kits. They are sold in lighting showrooms and lighting departments of home centers.

More Function Than Form: Architectural Lighting

Architectural lighting can be subtle or dramatic. The fixtures are tucked away, hidden behind a bit of molding or plasterwork. These effects can be achieved with mini-tracks, strips, fluorescent fixtures, or cable lighting, depending on your installation. Installing architectural lighting can involve as much carpentry as it does wiring, but the effects are worth the extra effort. Here are a few architectural techniques:

Cove Lighting. A cove is a horizontal recess located high on the wall. Lights inside the cove shine up at the ceiling, providing good ambient light. In open areas and walkways, install a cove about 18 inches from the ceiling and at least 80 inches from the floor. Above cabinets in kitchens and home offices, reduce the distance from the ceiling to 12 inches or even less.

Valance or Bracket Lighting. A rigid valance over a window top can house lights that shine both up at the ceiling and down over the window or draperies, creating the illusion of daylight. A wall bracket is similar to a window valance, except it is mounted on a solid wall.

Cornice Lighting. Lights are hidden behind a panel, called a fascia, that comes down from the ceiling, parallel to the wall. Lighting behind the fascia is directed down. A lighted cornice works well where there is little clearance between window tops and ceiling, but be sure the light source is not visible from below or it will ruin the effect.

Soffit Lighting. A soffit is a box that runs along the wall at the ceiling. Recessed lights or fluorescent troffers in a soffit direct light downward, working well as wall-washers or for direct, task lighting above a counter.

Fixtures and bulbs create heat and can be dangerous in architectural lighting. Whenever possible use linear fluorescent tubes in architectural lighting, because they are cooler. Also, their long life reduces the need for light bulb changes.

Follow manufacturer's guidelines and local building codes whenever you put lighting near fabric, wallcoverings, or other flammable materials. As a general rule, keep bulbs a minimum of 3 inches from curtains (in lighted valances) and prevent any heat-conducting part of a fixture from touching flammables.

▲ A cove is a horizontal recess located high on a wall, such as the one at the top of these cabinets. Cove lighting subtly adds to the ambient lighting in the room.

▶ The delicate effect of lighting from behind a valance or cove will be lost unless the light fixture is hidden.

Canopy Lighting. A lighted canopy is like a soffit, but is mounted lower on the wall. It provides general illumination as well as downlight in bathrooms or dressing rooms.

Coffer Lighting. A coffer is a recessed dome or panel in the ceiling. One type of coffer lighting is hidden in coves at the base of the coffer, with the light that reflects off the cove and into the coffer. Another type conceals fluorescent tubes behind an acrylic diffuser. Either type of coffer light adds the illusion of height to a ceiling and provides general illumination.

▼ Choose light sources that won't generate too much heat if you want to place them behind canopies, valances, and panels.

▲ A coffer is a recessed dome or panel. A cove at the base of this coffer is the perfect place to hide lighting fixtures.

▶ The soffit that runs around the perimeter of this kitchen is fitted with recessed lights to create even, bright ambient light.

▲ This troffer is recessed above the center countertop in the kitchen. The diffuser hides the light bulbs, softening and evening out the distribution of the light.

Troffer Lighting. Troffers are rectangular or square recessed fluorescent fixtures shielded either by a baffle (a series of metal slats 1 inch apart), louvers (grids of 1-inch-square cells), or diffusers, which are solid prismatic lenses made of acrylic or other synthetic material. In homes, troffers are usually found in basement playrooms or workshops.

When Moonlight Isn't Enough: Outdoor Lighting

Superior outdoor and indoor home lighting share many of the same elements. Both consider ambient, task, and accent light and are designed around a focal point. Safety and security must be first, both as a design goal and an approach to installation. Glare is bad, efficiency is good, and beauty matters. Use accent lighting effects such as up- and downlighting, crosslighting, silhouetting, and shadowing.

Outdoors, you don't need task light as much except perhaps at a patio or deck table. Create enough outdoor lighting to see the path to an entrance, avoid tripping on steps, make out a house number, or find keys and keyholes. Unless you are lighting your private tennis court, you are not trying to mimic Yankee Stadium at night. Don't overlight.

Sturdiness is important outdoors too, so use outdoor fixtures. They are made with durable materials, such as cast aluminum. Special seals, gaskets, and lenses protect bulbs and keep moisture at bay. Apply car wax to maintain lacquered brass and other decorative finishes on post,

Ecology of Lighting

The consumer who wants energy efficiency has many choices today. One guide to efficiency is the bulb package. It tells you about light output and the amount of energy the bulb uses. If you want to save energy and money, keep the following tips in mind:

■ Use fluorescent bulbs. They consume electricity far more efficiently than other bulbs. Pump the same amount of electricity into a fluorescent, a halogen, and an incandescent, and the fluorescent

will produce three to four times the light. Fluorescents last longer, too. Fluorescent tubes are rated to last 20,000 hours. Compact fluorescent bulbs are rated to last 10,000 hours. That's much longer than halogen bulbs (rated for 2,500 to 3,000 hours); long-life incandescents (rated for 1,500 to 2,000 hours); or standard incandescent (rated for 750 to 1,000 hours). Many people used to be put off by the color of light from fluorescent bulbs; nowadays manufacturers are

coming up with fluorescent bulbs that mimic the tones of natural light and can rival the cozy feel of incandescent light.

■ Turn off those lights! How often you flick the switch affects greatly how long any bulb lasts. But without a doubt, all bulbs last longer if they are not left burning.

■ Use dimmers. Most dimmers don't actually save electricity, but do make the bulb last longer by reducing wear on the filaments.

wall, and hanging lanterns. No matter how good the finish, sun, grit, and moisture can do their dirty work, so be prepared to spray on some lacquer from an aerosol can after a few years. If you want to avoid re-polishing entirely, purchase lanterns made of plastic or buy finishes such as copper that are made to weather to a dark patina over time.

Check on bulb compatibility if your outdoor lantern of the wall-mount or hanging variety has a bulb that hangs downward from the socket. Some bulbs are only rated for upward installation.

▶ A coat of car wax can slow down the effects of weather on lantern lights.

▼ Superior outdoor lighting combines ambient, task, and accent lighting, just like it does inside. Low-voltage and line-voltage systems are well suited for use outdoors.

▲ Provide enough light to keep passersby from tripping. Be careful not to overlight outdoors.

Once you've aimed a track light at artwork inside, it's done. Not so with a flood or spot aimed at a shrub. Landscaping changes; plants and trees grow. Leave extra space when placing in-ground fixtures. As the plants grow, use the lights to create shadowing, silhouetting, crosslighting, or other effects.

Low-voltage Lighting

Low-voltage outdoor systems offer flexibility. As landscape grows, fixtures can be moved easily because they are staked into the ground and have a long lead wire. These systems are comprised of a 12-volt transformer, cable, connection accessories, bulbs, and fixtures, and commonly use "MR" or bi-pin halogen bulbs. The transformer can be wired directly into your house current or plugged into an outdoor receptacle. Low-voltage systems can be less expensive to operate, and they are easy to install. Because the voltage is equivalent to that of a child's toy (12-v), there's little danger of electrical shock around pools. Fixtures farthest away from the transformer aren't as bright as those close to it, however, so these systems are best for shorter runs.

Line-voltage Lighting

When you're looking for lots of light, you're looking for 120-volt lighting. The code requirements are stricter than they are for low-voltage lighting. You'll need special cable, boxes, and switches, and ground-fault protectors, but the wiring itself is really no harder than indoors.

Good lighting makes good neighbors. Check your installation for glare beyond your property line, especially if you really are lighting something

▲ Top-covered lights like the one shown on the left cut light pollution. Outdoor fixtures are made of durable materials and usually have special seals and gaskets meant to withstand the elements.

▲ A transformer, such as the black box in the center of this outdoor lighting kit, steps the voltage down from 120 to 12 volts. Transformers are wired directly into household current or plugged into an outdoor receptacle.

▲ Shrubs and gardens grow. Keep that in mind when you are planning your outdoor lighting.

like a tennis court. Outdoor lighting catalogs have charts and guides that help you calculate brightness and reach. Cut light pollution in your town by using top-covered fixtures and floods aimed downward.

Components from different manufacturers may not be compatible, and mixing them may void your warranty.

Floods and Spots

Start with a cast aluminum holder with porcelain sockets, mount it between the garage doors, screw in a couple of 150-watt spot bulbs and voila! Outdoor lighting. If you stop there, though, you're missing a lot of the fun, drama, and beauty.

◁ Outdoor fixtures embedded in the ground can light up an entrance or landscaping.

◁ When you are looking for lots of light, use line-voltage fixtures.

Bullet-shaped floods with shrouds that rotate or that sit on swivels aim the beam precisely at a statue, trellis, or tree. Lenses focus the light and protect the inside of the fixture. Well lights are mounted in a cylinder and can be buried in the ground. Use them for security, to graze a wall, or silhouette a tree. Hang lights in a shrub or gazebo to create soft light and shadow.

For extra security, throw light at entrances and windows with directional lights that attach to walls, fences, threaded pipes, or stakes.

Motion detectors, light sensors, or timers improve your outdoor systems by providing light that's on when you arrive home or when you are away on vacation. Many outdoor systems have these features built in. You can also buy plug-in versions for retrofitting your current lighting scheme.

Many models of outdoor fixtures come as either low- or line-voltage. All you have to do is specify which one you want when placing your order.

▲ Light your garden pathway with a light that resembles a tulip.

▲ Outdoor floodlights swivel for precise aiming. Shrouds around the opening, as shown here, help "shape" the light.

▲ Some fixtures are made to attach or hang in trees or to light trees from below.

▲ A "mushroom" landscape light looks attractive day and night.

▲ This brick walk is lit by a variation on the pagoda style of landscape fixture.

What Do You Want to See: The Light, The Fixture, or Both?

The path lighting you choose depends on your tastes. Tulip and mushroom shapes are naturals for path lighting. They radiate light levels close to the ground, helping you find your way, without creating glare or light pollution. Use their pools of light to create scallops on a walkway at night; the fixtures look lovely during the day. Bullet-shaped flood fixtures can be easy on the eyes, and bollards (waist-high posts) are sleek and attractive. Pagoda lights look great and do the same job. Avoid rigid parallel lines of fixtures along a straight walkway, or it will look like someone's about to be cleared for takeoff.

If you want to hide the fixtures, choose models that are designed to be embedded in the ground or set into steps and risers. Mount fixtures under benches, in bricks, or on walls. Other options include hanging the light in a tree, or hiding it under a rail or even under water. You can even buy fixtures that are disguised as rocks!

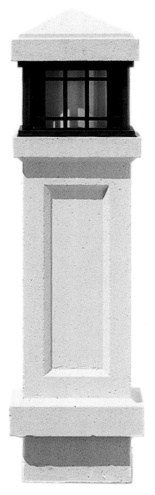

▲ A bollard is a half-post that lifts the light up, lighting a wider area than fixtures located closer to the ground could light.

▲ Light decks, steps, or rails with recessed units like this one. Fluorescent or halogen light bulbs are good choices for this type of outdoor lighting.

▲ Fixtures like this can be mounted into walls or brickwork.

▲ Some outdoor fixtures come disguised as rocks.

Lights and Lighting Controls: Changing Your Lighting

*N*o theater set would be complete without its lighting. It establishes mood, time of day, and atmosphere for each scene of a play. With today's lighting controls, it's easy to adjust mood and atmosphere at home. The discussion that follows will acquaint you with the many exciting choices in lighting control technology. You don't need to settle for a simple on/off switch.

Dimmers

The most simple wall switch offers two choices: on or off. Three-way switches offer those same options from two different locations. Dimmer switches allow you to alter the light level, vary the mood, change the light intensity, create and save light settings, and increase bulb life. They handle the power flow of high-wattage fixtures without shorting a circuit in your home, and they cut the wear on bulb filaments, making them last longer. Some dimmers even reduce electrical energy consumption. The actual control can take many forms: slide, dial, rocker, toggle, push-button, touch-sensitive, or socket mount. There are tabletop models, too. Plug the lamp into the dimmer and plug the dimmer into the outlet. These models are great for the elderly and others with restricted movement because they make it unnecessary to bend or reach at awkward angles under lampshades to adjust brightness.

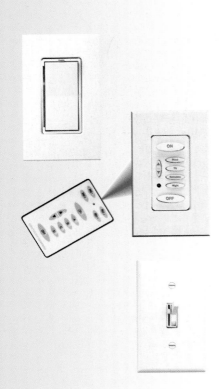

◄ Dimmers come in many varieties these days. You can choose designs that resemble the familiar toggle-style switch or models that operate with a slide or knob. Preset dimmers let you switch on the light at a favorite level of illumination. There are dimmers that can be connected to table lamps. There are others that come with remote control function. Scene control systems enable you to operate groups of lights all at the same time.

Just as your light bulb must be compatible with the socket, the dimmer must be compatible with the light bulb. Hence, 120-volt lights require a 120-volt dimmer. Low-voltage fixtures usually require their own special dimmers. Fluorescent bulbs need fluorescent dimmers. HID bulbs can't be used on dimmers.

Dimmers normally feel warm, which isn't a concern, unless you're grouping several dimmers (and/or fan controls) together. Ask your lighting specialist for advice.

Automated Controls

Timers, photosensors, and motion detectors "automate" control of your lights. They go on based on a preset designation of time or a level of darkness, or they go on because movement has tripped the switch. These devices plug into the wall, screw into a socket, replace a wall switch, or come as an integral part of a fixture or fixture systems.

Scene control is the next level of automation. It allows you to balance the intensity of lighting in a room, or focused on your house and property, just as you set the volume and balance of a music system. Instead of having three switches controlling three lights, a scene control device combines the lights at selected levels of brightness. The "good night setting," for example, signals the network of controls to change to night mode, with some lights off and others lit dimly. Fade-rate features bring the element of time into the mix by causing light to dim instantly or gradually. Timing features allow you to program when various scenes operate. "All-on" features allow you to instantly switch on all the lights, if for example, you hear a noise in the middle of the night.

Some automation systems use conditional logic. Different conditions cause different responses. For example, driveway sensors signal interior and exterior lights to turn on when it becomes dark outside, at a certain time of day, or if the motion of a car is detected. You can use your computer to program one type of controller, and then disconnect it from the computer and let it run your house. Master control systems can be tied into a home security system to turn on lights to startle and scare off intruders. And some systems even have a "vacation mode" that

It's the same kitchen at three different scene control settings. The top setting might be used for food preparation and breakfast, the middle for dining and entertaining, and the bottom for late evenings.

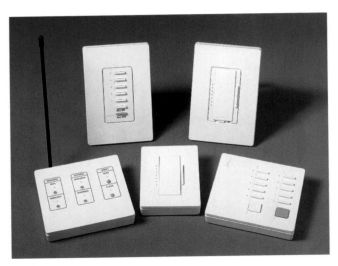

△ Scene control systems can assist you with home security by mimicking your light use patterns even while you are away.

memorizes your household's normal lighting usage patterns and re-creates them when you are away. Key-chain remotes give you the ability to turn lights on before you enter your house.

Scene control devices can use high-frequency signals sent across existing power lines to special switches or outlets. Another model uses radio frequency technology for wireless home lighting control.

These devices are available at electrical supply outlets, home centers, via mail order, or through Internet companies. Some manufacturers sell starter kits that will give you a reasonable combination of remote and automatic control. You can add to these systems as time goes on.

Contact the Home Automation Association (HAA) or the Custom Electronic Design and Installation Association (CEDIA) to find a home automation expert.

Reading the Label: Light As a Foreign Language

As you're planning your lighting scheme, remember there's more to it than just the fixture and where you put it. The wrong bulb will make even the most expensive fixture look wrong. A quick look at the label on the bulb's package will tell you an quite a bit whether or not you've got the right bulb—as long as you can translate it. Here, for example, is the label on a bright, white full-spectrum fluorescent bulb. "Average lumens 2250; Color temp 5000° K; 90 CRI."

In simplest terms, these are all measurements of something you know intuitively: Some light bulbs are brighter than others. Lumens, color temperature, and CRI are simply more precise ways of talking about it. Let's take another look at the label.

Average Lumens 2250 tells you how much light the bulb produces. A lumen is roughly equal to the light produced by a dozen candles. It would take nearly 30,000 candles to produce the light of this fluorescent bulb.

Color Temperature 5000° K tells you how white the light is. It's based on the glow of a bar of iron heated to the temperature indicated. When iron is heated to 1500 degrees on the Kelvin scale, for example, it has a color temperature of 1500° K—the same yellowish light you get from a candle. (The scale does not measure the heat produced by a light. A candle produces nowhere near 1500° of heat.) At 3500° K the bar takes on the glow of a 100-watt incandescent bulb. With a color temperature of 5000° K, our fluorescent light is an almost

pure, bright white. For the truest colors, get a bulb with a color temperature between 3000° and 4000° K.

CRI 90. When that beautiful suit or dress you bought looks wrong in the sunlight, you've experienced the true meaning of the Color Rendering Index (CRI). CRI measures how well a particular light reflects without distorting color. Bright, white daylight has a perfect CRI of 100. The highest-rated light bulbs are incandescent and halogen with a CRI of 99 or better. Some newer fluorescents and High-Intensity Discharge (HID) lights come in warm colors with good CRI ratings in the 80s. For most indoor lighting, you'll want a CRI of 75 or better. If you're lighting a room for graphic arts on the other hand, look for bulbs with a CRI of 90 or better.

Incandescent Light

The typical light bulb in your house is probably an incandescent bulb. It is vacuum-sealed and produces light when a thin, coiled filament of tungsten wire glows. The glow is caused by heat from electricity that has come through the socket, the bulb base, some lead-in wires, and finally to the filament. An inert gas slows the breakdown of the tungsten, but eventually, the heat wins and the tungsten breaks. The arcing that follows blows an internal fuse to protect the circuit.

The general-service incandescent light bulb with a medium

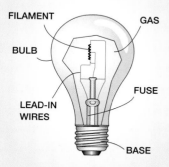

FILAMENT
GAS
BULB
FUSE
LEAD-IN WIRES
BASE

COMMON INCANDESCENT A-LIGHT BULB

▲ Heat makes the light in an ordinary bulb, and heat causes the filament to break down. When that happens, it's time to change the bulb.

base (also called standard or Edison base)—the A bulb—is the most common in the United States, available everywhere and at low cost. Incandescent light bulbs provide warm, diffuse light and a comfortable, cozy ambience. The color of their light is closest to light from the sun. Where color is critical, they are the best. Incandescents are available in many shapes and sizes and range from utilitarian to decorative.

- Some are silver-coated on the crown.
- Rough-service bulbs are made to withstand vibration, such as in garage-door openers.
- Appliance bulbs withstand extremes of temperature.
- Silicone-treated bulbs are shatter-resistant, for use around workbenches.
- Three-way bulbs have two filaments that produce different light levels.

Heat makes the light and breaks down the filament. Common incandescent bulbs, then, cost the least, produce more light but don't last as long (typically 750 hours). So-called long-life A bulbs cost more, produce less light, but last longer (1500 to 3500 hours).

Incandescents are the least efficient bulbs—90 percent of their energy is given off as heat. Near the end of an incandescent's life, its output decreases 20 percent because of the dark deposits on the inside.

Fluorescent Light

In a fluorescent bulb, cathodes conduct electrical current into fluorescent tubes and create an electric arc. The current acts on the mixture of gases, including a small amount of mercury to produce ultraviolet rays. These, in turn, cause the phosphor coating on the tube to glow and produce light. Fluorescent tubes may be straight, bent, circular, or encased in an outer bulb. They attach to sockets in fixtures in a variety of ways. Continuing development in fluorescent bulbs has made them far more versatile and their light more attractive than ever before.

Ballasts in fluorescent fixtures or sometimes in the base of the bulb itself regulate the electrical arc of the bulb. Light bulbs and ballasts must be compatible. Up to four fluorescent tubes can operate on a single ballast. Compact bulbs, with screw-in or bi-pin bases, have ballasts in their bases.

Screw-type compacts replace incandescent A bulbs. They save energy and newer models produce light much closer to the pleasing amber color of regular bulbs. Older fluorescents require a small accessory called a starter to strike an arc between the cathodes when the light is turned on, but newer fluorescent tubes have this built in.

Fluorescent light bulbs are not made for low-voltage fixtures. As a general rule, do not dim

(continued on next page)

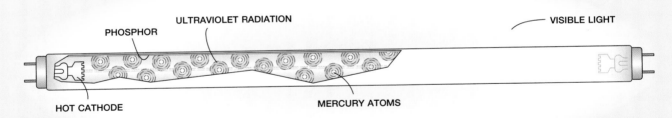

PHOSPHOR   ULTRAVIOLET RADIATION   VISIBLE LIGHT

HOT CATHODE   MERCURY ATOMS

FLUORESCENT LIGHT BULB

▲ In a fluorescent bulb, cathodes conduct electrical current in the tubes and create an electric arc. The gases in the bulb glow and produce light.

fluorescent bulbs with a regular incandescent-type dimmer. Do not use them with motion detectors, timers, or photocell devices without first checking compatibility with manufacturers. When in doubt, read the label on the packaging. Before you buy, check in a lighting lab to see for yourself how dimmed fluorescent bulbs will look.

Linear fluorescent T-12 tubes are everywhere in office buildings, schools, kitchens, and basements. Nowadays, a more efficient alternative is the T-8 bulb. You can use T-8 tubes in older fixtures, as long as you replace them with new, electronic ballasts. It may be easier to simply replace the entire fluorescent fixture with a newer model. Either way, you will see significant savings in your power consumption. (New rules govern how you may dispose of fluorescents, see the discussion of the Universal Waste Rule on page 37.)

More about fluorescents:

■ Many undercabinet fixtures take miniature tubes such as the T-5. They are ideal for small spaces.

■ Modular screw-base conversion units that hold ballast and pin-base compacts fit into medium or standard incandescent sockets.

■ Reflective compact fluorescents concentrate the light forward, although without the precise beam control of incandescents and halogens.

■ Often, compact fluorescents are bigger than A bulbs, so you may need a taller harp (the assembly that holds a lampshade) when substituting a compact fluorescent for an incandescent.

Fluorescents consume less energy and are cooler than incandescent bulbs that generate the same amount of light, and they are rated to last much longer— 10,000 to 20,000 hours. Older types of fluorescent bulbs often gave off a color of light that homeowners found was suited

best only to task lighting on workbenches or in bathrooms and kitchens. But today's fluorescent bulbs, with their improved color quality and compatibility with standard screw bases, are far more versatile than their predecessors were.

Halogen Light

Halogen light bulbs are incandescent bulbs that have a tungsten filament and are filled with halogen gas. When the filament heats up, part of it evaporates, and the tungsten molecules collect on the bulb wall. The halogen gas collects those molecules and returns them to the filament. The filament lasts longer, and the halogen bulb uses its energy more efficiently because the tungsten breakdown doesn't interfere with light output. Halogen bulbs produce almost the same amount of light at the beginning and end of their "lives"—up to four times longer than a standard incandescent.

Halogen light's conical, easily focused beam and intense, white light make it ideal for spotlights and task lighting in general. It is especially attractive for illuminating works of art or making dining room crystal sparkle.

Halogen bulbs are up to 65 percent more efficient than similar incandescent bulbs, but they are more expensive. Miniature halogen bulbs, used in low-voltage systems, are brighter and have more precise beam control than incandescents of similar wattage.

Halogen Safety

PAR 38, PAR 30, and PAR 20 halogen light sources used in recessed fixtures have hard glass outer bulbs with a small capsule inside containing the halogen tungsten burner. If the outer glass cracks or breaks, it's possible the bulb might still light—but not safely. Turn off the light, let it cool off, and replace the bulb.

Use gloves or a cloth when handling tubular halogen bulbs. Skin oils cause the quartz capsule to fail when the bulb gets hot. Also, be sure to use them only in UL-approved torchieres and other fixtures that have a protective cover in case the bulbs shatter.

Exposed, 500-watt halogens have been identified as a fire hazard. In response, Underwriters Laboratories (UL) now requires halogen light sources to have an outer cover provided either by the fixture or light bulb itself. The light bulbs cannot exceed 300 watts. Look for UL approval when you purchase freestanding halogen lamps, and follow some common-sense safety rules:

◄ Halogen bulbs are filled with halogen gas, which preserves the bulb filament longer than in incandescent bulbs.

■ Do not use scratched or cracked halogen bulbs.

■ Halogen floor lamps and table lamps, like all plug-in lamps, must be properly weighted and balanced so they cannot easily tip over.

■ Locate halogen lamps away from areas where roughhousing, high traffic, or other activities can knock them over.

■ Do not use halogen lamps in children's rooms.

■ Keep halogen lamps away from bedding or other flammable materials.

■ Do not put halogen lamps near open windows where curtains blow in the breeze.

■ Look for diffuser designs that will prevent accidental skin contact with the hot light bulb. Let the bulbs cool before you handle them.

■ Don't exceed bulb maximums for floor lamps and other lights. You wouldn't use a 300-watt regular incandescent bulb in a living room reading lamp. Don't use a 300-watt halogen bulb for that purpose, either—300 watts is very hot, whether its source is halogen or incandescent.

Running a halogen constantly at a dim level will cause the bulb to blacken. Once a week run the bulb at full brightness for 15 minutes to "clean" it.

House Tour
3

Each space in your house and yard requires a different level of general, task, or accent lighting. General lighting is different in a formal living room than it is in a laundry, and the task lighting for assembling a model airplane is different from what you need at a computer desk. Outdoors, the focus changes again. This chapter will take you on a tour of the interior and exterior of the home, offering specific ideas for lighting each area. We'll suggest types of fixtures, the layer of light (ambient, task, or accent), and the maximum wattages to use in each application. Remember that different bulbs with different wattage ratings can produce the same amount of light.

The Light Within: Indoor Lighting

When you plan your lighting, you will naturally think about style preferences. Classic? Sleek, high-tech? Down-to-earth? But whatever the style, don't forget to consider the quality of the light itself, whether it is bright and yellow, sharply focused and crisp white, or widely scattered and soft blue. The actual light from the fixtures will exert a profound influence on the look of the room.

The Kitchen: Hub of Activity

Because of the different types and levels of activity, the kitchen more than any other room requires many different types of lighting and a lot of advance planning. Think your plans through. It can be tricky to make up for a neglected lighting need later—a kitchen is not usually a good place for table and floor lamps, whose fabric shades can't stand up to grease and steam.

▶ Whether your kitchen is simple or elegant, its lighting design will require some careful advance planning.

Kitchen Task Light

Install task lighting above the stove, sink, at both front and back of counters, over islands and tables, and at kitchen desks. Here are a few popular task-lighting options:

■ Install continuous undercabinet task lights above the counters using linear mini-fluorescent systems that provide shadowless, even light and little heat. Another good alternative is low-voltage halogen systems. They provide crisp, white light and can be dimmed for mood light. In either case, choose low-profile or slim models designed to be hidden by the lip of the cabinet. Under-cabinet fixtures may be wired directly to the circuit ("hardwired") or can plug into existing backsplash outlets.

Make sure all task light comes from an area in front of the task, not behind, so people will not cast shadows on their own work surfaces.

▷ Recessed lights both above the island and in soffits along the perimeter of the cabinets provide even, well-spaced lighting for this kitchen.

Lighting designers often favor halogen for work surfaces because of the crisp, clean light they emit.

◁ Task lighting in a kitchen should put the light directly above where food preparation, eating, reading directions, and other tasks are performed. In this kitchen, undercabinet lighting keeps the countertops free of shadows, handsome pendant lighting illuminates the island and sink areas, and lighting above the cabinets highlights treasured artwork while adding to the general lighting in the room.

■ Light the front of counters with fixtures installed in soffits. Good choices are 75- or 150-watt recessed high hats or recessed fluorescent troffers that will double as general lighting for the walkway in front of the counters. Measure to be sure soffit fixtures will not interfere with operation of cabinet doors.

■ Furnish task lighting over the sink with flush-mounted ceiling fixtures that have light-softening white or frosted glass and have a capacity of up to 100 watts. Another good choice: recessed cans fitted with 75-watt halogen or 20-watt compact fluorescent bulbs.

■ Type A appliance bulbs in 25 or 40 watts in the stove hood may serve your lighting needs. But if the stove is hoodless, in a center island for example, crosslight it with track heads or recessed lights with a maximum of 75 or 150 watts and aim light at the stove from both sides. This design—or choosing fixtures with prismatic lenses—minimizes buildup from spattered grease and gushes of steam on bulbs and fixtures.

■ Dress up islands and peninsulas with pendant lights that take halogen or compact fluorescent bulbs. Hang them 30 inches above the countertop, and they'll work well for food preparation or doing homework. Models with retractable cords that let you adjust height add flexibility. Another good option is two recessed downlights with 75-watt PAR 30 halogen bulbs.

Create a cozy feel and visual variety in the breakfast area by lighting it differently from the work half of the kitchen. Choose types of fixtures and bulbs that produce a different color of light.

▲ Over islands, install lights on either side of the cooking surface rather than directly above. This keeps the fixtures out of the way of grease splatters and provides even, shadow-free light for the chef.

▶ Stove hoods with halogen or incandescent lights put the task lighting where it's needed for cooking.

■ Desks in kitchens need light like any other desks, but must also resist kitchen grease and stay clear of the clutter they tend to accumulate. Mount a single metal track head with 50- or 75-watt capacity on the wall beside either side of the desk. Aim it down, toward the center of the desktop. If there are overhead cabinets, install undercabinet halogen or fluorescent slim-design lights.

■ Eating doesn't require particularly bright light, but kitchen tables are often hobby stations and homework centers. The light over them must provide both ambient and task light. Choose a pendant fixture with an inverted bowl-shaped shade to thrust the light toward the table, or consider a modified chandelier. Decorative bulbs in the chandelier arms provide ambient light, while a downlight in the center is good for tasks. The downlights inside these chandeliers often have a separate switch that enables you to vary brightness between high and low and operate it independently. Hang a pendant or chandelier 30 inches above the tabletop, and it should clear at least 6 inches in from the table edge. Provide additional lighting in a breakfast area with matching wall sconces.

▲ The scale of this hanging fixture is just right for the small breakfast-nook table, and its simple design matches the spareness of the space.

◀ The basket-style chandelier above this breakfast table helps create a visual separation between this area and the rest of the kitchen.

Dimmers are a natural for controlling the many light sources in this kitchen—above the cabinets and the center work table, between the beams, and over the sink and stove.

Two low-voltage, halogen recessed units bathe treasured objects above a cabinet with accent light in this kitchen.

For energy savings, use color-balanced fluorescent bulbs and fixtures instead of incandescent for general lighting.

Kitchen Ambient Light

Ambient lighting in kitchens depends largely on the floor plan. You need general lighting above tables, above walkways between counters, above islands, and to see inside wall cabinets and drawers. Diffuse light sources are best for this. Linear fluorescent lighting, flush mounted, provides a high level of general lighting for the least money, but there are better ways to distribute downlight. Track lighting is acceptable but can be a dirt catcher. Recessed lights are popular choices. Space them 5½ to 6 feet apart over the walkways between the counters and the island. Use reflector incandescent bulbs because they tend to fill in better than halogen, and they're better for getting light into cabinets. Be generous with wattage-capacities— 75-watt capacity or higher is the best choice. You will often need a lot of light.

Kitchen Accent Light

Highlight collections such as cookie jars, baskets, or teapots in cupboards, on open shelves, or above cabinets and show off wall collections such as tole paintings and plates with accent lighting in the kitchen. Here's how:

■ Aim low-voltage, halogen track lights or recessed eyeballs with a 50- or 75-watt maximum capacity at the display.

■ Illuminate interesting items in open shelves or glass-front cabinets with low-voltage mini-lights. Be sure they are made for this purpose and won't overheat.

Only the Best: The Dining Room

Romance reigns in the dining room. Style, too. The lighting here should be appropriate to the gathering and flattering to guests. It should show off prized possessions and family heirlooms.

Focal Point

Traditionally, the prominent decorative lighting in a formal dining room is the chandelier.

■ Locate the fixture over the center of the table, not the center of the room. To determine where that is, arrange furniture—on paper or in actuality—before installing the fixture.

■ Select a fixture that is at least 6 inches narrower than the table so people won't bump their heads when rising from their chairs.

- Locate the fixture 30 inches above the tabletop in a room with an 8-foot ceiling—3 inches higher for each additional foot of ceiling height.

- Put the fixture on a separate dimmer. Although chandeliers are beautiful, they can become "glare bombs." They usually look best when dimmed down to a nice glow.

Table Light

Do not rely on the chandelier to light the table. Instead, use more subtle means:

- Install one recessed low-voltage downlight on each side of the chandelier, centered over each table half. Aim them toward the tabletop, not faces. The halogen light from these fixtures will make your dishes and silverware sparkle, but it can be harsh on human faces.

- Another option: Position four recessed downlights with soft incandescent light just outside the corners of the table to supplement chandelier light and illuminate faces with a flattering glow. Alternately, use low-voltage fixtures with halogen bulbs in this same pattern to make the tabletop sparkle.

- In less traditional dining rooms, try architectural approaches such as coffer lighting to echo the table shape and cast a glow on its top.

Install dimmers for all incandescent line-voltage fixtures and even consider the special fluorescent and low-voltage dimmers for those fixtures. With the ability to control a variety of light sources, you can change the atmosphere of the room at will.

▲ A traditional Williamsburg chandelier in distressed brass furnishes this dining room with a lovely focal point.

◄ Coordinating chandelier, sconces, and lamps can create the level of light you need and pull the design of the dining room together.

Adding Details

Dining rooms often have interesting little areas in addition to the table. Highlighting them can add to the charm and warmth of the room.

■ Incorporate wall sconces over the sideboard to match the chandelier. Or provide a nice glow with a pair of candlestick table lamps on the sideboard.

■ Hanging a large mirror above the sideboard to reflect the chandelier can work well as long as the fixture is dimmed.

■ Light a picture with a low-voltage recessed halogen spot. If the picture is over the sideboard and wall sconces or candlestick lamps are on either side, then you have created another point of visual interest in the room.

■ Light the interior of a china cabinet with low-voltage mini-lights installed under shelves.

■ Lighted centerpieces add interest on special occasions. Run low-voltage lights through tabletop topiary arrangements, or light the centerpiece with battery-powered miniature lights available from craft and holiday retailers.

▲ Light the interior of a china cabinet to create dining room accent light.

▲ A mirror reflects the brilliance of the crystal chandelier.

▶ Mount a chandelier about 30 inches above the table and be sure it is at least 6 inches narrower than the table so that guests don't bump their heads when they rise from their chairs.

The Living Room: Where Mood's the Thing

In homes with separate family rooms, the living room is often a formal parlor reserved for entertaining, contemplating art objects, conversing quietly, or reading. In this kind of living room, there will be less emphasis on task and general lighting and more emphasis on accent lighting.

Start with Accents

To create drama, start with the accent lights in a living room. Highlight pictures, plants, or an architectural feature.

▪ Define the perimeter with low-voltage, halogen accent lighting. Spotlight wall art with recessed downlights or track lights that blend with the interior design of the room. Fixtures with a capacity of 50 or 75 watts are a good option.

▪ Uplight a potted tree in the corner to create interesting ceiling shadows, or graze a brick wall to bring out its textures.

▪ Bring some highlights into the center of the room, too. Spotlight a flower arrangement on a coffee table or shower a baby grand piano with soft light.

▽ In living rooms, atmosphere counts big-time. Graze a stone wall with recessed or track lighting. Throw light on indoor plants or artwork. Warm things up with table lamps.

Recessed eyeballs accent the painting above the fireplace, make the glass shelves glisten, show off display objects, and bounce light around the room.

Fill In

Fill in the living room lighting with table and floor lamps for general illumination and for reading. Provide an adjustable piano light for pianos. In a room that is large or has high ceilings, consider adding an ambient glow with coffers, coves, or wall brackets illuminated with dim, warm-colored bulbs.

This approach creates a great combination of light sources. Light only the accent lights, and you'll have a dramatic contrast between light and dark. If you want more light to read by, turn on a lamp with a 3-way bulb or a lamp dimmer to the brightness you need. You can change the lights to suit your mood.

Recessed eyeballs splash the artwork and bookshelves with light and create indirect lighting perfect for lounging in front of the TV.

Life on the Leisure Side: The Family Room

Family rooms are a mixed bag of informal activities. Some, such as TV and computer games, require glare-free ambient lighting. Others, such as jigsaw puzzles or reading, require good task lighting.

Focal Point

Fireplaces, common in family rooms, can be accentuated with dramatic lighting.

■ Graze the brick or stone on either side of the fireplace opening with track lights or recessed eyeballs mounted 6 to 12 inches from the wall and aimed downward. Use 75- or 100-watt capacity models.

■ Aim a low-voltage track head or recessed halogen accent light on artwork above the mantle. Or, light it with a frame-mounted picture light.

■ Add decorative wall sconces on either side of mantelpiece art to add ambient glow and reinforce the room decor.

Entertainment Center

For watching television, you'll want ambient lighting that does not compete with the TV or reflect off the screen into viewers' eyes. Following are approaches for rooms with ceilings up to 10 feet high:

■ Provide indirect light from architectural coves or cornices around the perimeter.

■ Position 150-watt recessed incandescent floodlights in the ceiling or use 23-watt compact fluorescent reflectors.

■ Install miniature low-voltage lighting in the entertainment center shelves, hiding the bulbs behind moldings or shades.

The light behaves differently in rooms with very high ceilings, so you must adjust your approach in these spaces. For two-story family rooms:

■ As a general rule, avoid recessed downlights for general lighting. With reflector or compact fluorescent bulbs, these fixtures light the top half of the room more than the bottom, and with halogen bulbs, they are too harsh for ambient lighting. Besides, in either case, it's difficult to change bulbs.

■ Install metal or wood 300-watt halogen uplight sconces about three-quarters of the way up the walls. Choose fixtures that are the same color as the walls or paint them. For a focal point like a center fire-

▲ Select a pair of decorative sconces for the mantelpiece to add an ambient glow to your fireplace area.

◄ The illumination levels of recessed lights in this entertainment room can be adjusted for games or TV viewing. Miniature halogen units accent prized possessions.

Pendant fixtures are a natural for a pool table, but don't install them above a Ping-Pong table. They will interfere with play.

place, put two sconces on each of the side walls. Or install them on the walls on either side of the television wall. This will bounce bright halogen light off the ceiling and around the room without glare. A white ceiling reflects back about 80 percent of the light that hits it. One disadvantage: This type of lighting emphasizes flaws in walls.

■ Suspend a track-lighting system on cable from the ceiling, 8 to 10 feet above the floor. Aim fluorescent wall-washers at the walls adjacent to the television wall. Add large incandescent track heads to fill the room, making sure the heads are not pointed toward the television screen.

Game Tables

Game and hobby tables need bright, diffuse overhead lighting, such as you get with incandescent or fluorescent bulbs.

■ Suspend two metal-shade pendants 3 feet above a rectangular pool table. You'll need only one pendant over a circular card table.

■ An elongated pendant hung from two chains is also a good choice for a pool table. Fluorescent is a good choice here because it produces less heat than other bulbs and so will make a more comfortable playing environment for pool players leaning over the table during a game.

■ Pendant lights will interfere with play at a Ping-Pong table. Instead, try track lights or recessed downlights over each end of the table.

Bars

Light bars in family rooms with a combination of accent lighting and low-level mood lighting.

■ Hang miniature low-voltage incandescent pendants over the bar to create a warm amber pool of light at each stool. Pendants should be suspended high enough so a person seated at the bar can see the bartender's face.

▶ Bars and snack centers need plenty of light when you're cleaning up spills, but they are a great place for accent lighting, too.

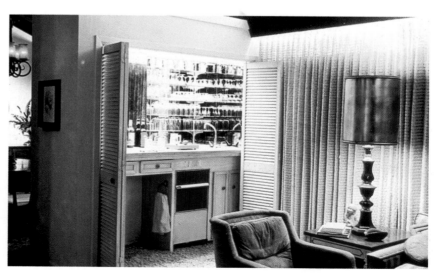

■ Light the bottles and glasses on shelves with two or three small, low-voltage halogen track heads or adjustable recessed spots to make the glass sparkle.

■ On a separate switch, provide fluorescent or incandescent general light to use for cleanup behind the bar. The overall general lighting in the family room might be enough for this.

Additional Task Light

Provide task lighting as needed for favorite activities.

■ If your household is sedate, floor lamps and table lamps make excellent task and fill lights to complement the other lighting in the room.

■ If your household is rambunctious, you should try to minimize the use of floor lamps and table lamps that can be knocked over, or whose cords are an attraction for puppies and young children. Instead, use monopoint adjustable track heads mounted on walls near the task. Another option: Suspend adjustable mini-pendants over task areas that can be pushed up out of the way when not in use.

Bedrooms: Easy Does It

In the bedroom, most adults are happy with portable lamps next to the bed and maybe on the dresser. Light on a picture over the bed or sifting softly from indirect lighting in cornices or coves are nice touches.

Successful lighting is a combination of directions of light and contrast between light and dark.

▲ The halogen floor lamp with the adjustable arm and the table lamp's soft glow create a contrast in bedside lighting.

◄ Good bedroom lighting doesn't require a ceiling fixture in the center of the room.

Practical Matters

We've all seen a single, flush-mounted fixture in the center of the bedroom ceiling, but this approach has fallen out of favor. Designers say this approach almost never creates the right ambiance and means that the early riser either has to wake up the spouse or fumble in the dark. There are alternatives:

■ With downlights on separate switches above bureau or dresser, your spouse can choose socks from the drawer on a dark morning without waking you.

■ Put in closet lights. The National Electrical Code (NEC) recommends that you use only incandescent fixtures with completely enclosed light bulbs or fluorescent fixtures, either surface-mounted or recessed. It recommends against pendants and open or partially open incandescent fixtures. It also recommends you locate fixtures on the wall above the door or on the ceiling. There must be clearance of at least 12 inches between surface-mounted incandescent fixtures and the nearest point of storage, and 6 inches for fluorescent or recessed incandescent fixtures. Check with local officials for variations regarding closet lighting codes. Avoid these issues by installing spotlights on the ceiling near closets with sliding doors.

▼ Wall-mounted lamps on each side of the bed can be pulled out for reading and pushed aside when it's time for sleep.

Reading for Two

Sometimes one person likes to read in bed, while the other wants to sleep. There are solutions without the inconvenience of marriage counseling.

■ Select adjustable gooseneck table lamps for nightstands. They provide both reading and general light.

■ Install individually controlled recessed low-voltage fixtures with a maximum capacity of 50 watts in the ceiling above each side of the bed. Their focused beams are like airplane reading lights and have little spill.

■ Install wall-mounted, swing-arm lamps on either side of the bed above or beside the headboard. They can be pulled overhead for reading and pushed out of the way when it's time to sleep.

Sitting Room

Some bedrooms are like hotel suites, with a separate sitting area. Light sleeping and sitting spaces differently to create clear visual boundaries.

■ Hang wall sconces in the sitting area. They will add soft, general light, good for watching television. Metal or wood half-moon sconces cast light up and reduce glare.

■ For master bedroom ceilings with varying levels of height (as in vaulted or tray ceilings), install cornice or cove lighting to create a nice mood and provide some of the indirect, even light for watching television or viewing a computer screen. Be careful this light doesn't spill too much into the sleeping area.

■ For reading in a comfortable chair, place a floor lamp beside it or recessed downlight above.

■ Desks in a sitting area should have well-shielded task lights that do not spill out of the desk area. Banker's lights with cased-glass, green shades, piano lights with adjustable metal shades, and gooseneck lamps with deep conical metal shades are appropriate. But if there is a computer on the desk, be sure you can add some soft ambient lighting around the spot to prevent eyestrain.

Child-centered Lighting: Children's Rooms

Portability can be a drawback in a child's room. Plug-in lamps can tip over during play, leaving broken glass and creating a fire hazard. Finding that other sneaker or a lost retainer requires bright light. Computers require balanced light. And, unlike adults, children grow. Choose a system that accommodates these needs:

■ Track lighting offers flexibility, allowing you to keep light sources out of harm's way, provide variations in brightness as needed, and giving you and your child the option of changing the lighting configuration. Install tracks either parallel to one another on the ceiling, 2 to 3 feet from opposite walls, or around the perimeter of four

▲ Use a simple floor lamp to provide reading light beside a comfortable chaise lounge in a bedroom seating area.

Consider lights on timers in children's rooms. You can program them to switch off at night after the child is asleep.

▼ A single sconce mounted above the bed provides light for bedtime reading. Be sure to install its switch within reach of the bed.

walls. Use heads that take at least 75 watts and up to 150 watts for larger rooms, and add a low-voltage track head or two to aim at stuffed animal collections or into closets. Reflector flood bulbs will fill in lots of general light, but compact fluorescent bulbs can help you combat higher energy costs our dear little ones incur when they forget to turn off the lights.

■ Recessed downlights are also a good lighting solution for young children's rooms. Combine them with desk lamps that have solid, weighted bases, clip-on headboard lamps, or wall lamps with retractable arms.

Bathrooms: From Simple to Spectacular

Simple powder rooms to full-scale spas, bathrooms vary widely—and your lighting choices do, too. Local electrical codes for bathrooms are usually very strict. Have a local code official review your plans before proceeding.

Vanity Lights

Light at the grooming mirror is the most important in the bathroom. The light should be even, free from glare and shadow, and, for the sake of makeup application, it should be as close to natural light as possible. Check the bulb package; bulbs with CRI numbers that are close to 100 will do this.

■ Wire mirror lights on a separate switch.

■ To disperse the light evenly, choose fixtures with white, translucent globes or diffusers, or fixtures that take frosted decorative bulbs. These are available in incandescent and fluorescent and in many wattages.

■ Locate fixtures on both sides of the mirror if there is room. Mount decorative wall sconces or color-enhanced vertical fluorescent linear fixtures 60 inches on center from the floor.

■ If side lighting won't work, mount horizontal fixtures along the top of the mirror, 78 inches off the floor.

■ Hollywood-style strip lights with exposed globes are most effective as makeup lights when they have many relatively dim white bulbs close together. The wider the mirror, the longer the strips should be. Use 15- or 25-watt incandescent bulbs and line both sides and the top of the mirror with the strips. Add a dimmer to accommodate individual preferences.

■ Augment mirror lights with downlights recessed in canopies or soffits. These fixtures should be centered front to back over the countertop and spaced 3 to 4 feet apart.

▼ These sconces are mounted directly on the mirror, high above and to the side of the sink, to furnish even, shadow-free light for primping.

Powder Rooms

Half-baths or powder rooms are most often used by guests. Make their lighting cozy and inviting.

■ Fit the mirror lights with soft incandescent pink bulbs to bathe guests in a flattering glow.

■ Keep wall sconces subtle and not garish with 15-watt decorative bulbs.

■ Install an illuminated switch plate directly inside the door so that it's easy for unfamiliar hands to find.

Fast and Functional

A modest-sized, contemporary bathroom with a shower-tub, toilet, and vanity mirror/sink combination needs functional lighting on a small scale.

■ Good vanity lighting lines the top and, if possible, the sides of the mirror with low-level, even light. Pick fixtures with as many bulbs as you can to create many soft points of light rather than one, bright source.

■ Provide general light with a center ceiling light. Many lights combine exhaust fan, general light, and nightlight or include infrared heat lamps. Be sure you can control each function separately. There will be times you want the light without the fan, or the nightlight by itself and so on.

■ People who shave in the shower or bath will appreciate additional task light there. Use fixtures designated for damp or wet locations, and

▲ The two-light fixture above this mirror provides ample light for a guest who wants to check her lipstick before she returns to the party.

▼ Recessed lights provide general illumination around the vanity and up on the platform where the tub is located. Operate vanity and tub light separately and install dimmers so that you can create just the atmosphere and level of light you want in the bathroom.

be sure to follow codes. For example, there will be strict guidelines regarding the proximity of switches to protect against electric shock. For step-by-step instructions about wiring switches, see page 136.

■ Provide night light either in the ceiling fixture (see page 61) or with strip lights or mini-fluorescent tubes under toe spaces. Consider using a light sensor that will turn on automatically when the room darkens. You can buy plug-in nightlights that have light sensors, too.

Bathroom Spas

Fancy master baths with platform tubs should be illuminated like the luxury spas that they are. Go for a little atmosphere and drama.

■ Create pools of light with recessed low-voltage halogen downlights aimed into corners of a platform hot tub. They will provide enough light to find soap and a relaxing, softly lit atmosphere.

■ Consider tub lighting near or under the water, but buy only fixtures made for this purpose. Consult a professional and your local code official before you begin, and have them professionally installed.

■ For large bathrooms, add decorative flush or semi-flush ceiling fixtures and coordinating wall sconces.

■ Recessed downlights made for damp or wet locations are a good alternative for general lighting. Stick to wattages from 75 to 150 watts, un-

▲ Fluorescent lights mounted vertically beside the mirror furnish light that is even and shadow-free.

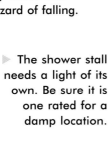

▲ It is important to light changes in floor level, especially where wet floors add to the hazard of falling.

▶ The shower stall needs a light of its own. Be sure it is one rated for a damp location.

less it is a small bathroom. Space them so that the beams overlap to create even lighting, or separate them for dramatic variations in light and shadow.

■ Create the impression of a skylight with a lighted coffer shielded by a lens. Line the perimeter of the opening of a real skylight with cove lighting to mimic sunlight.

■ Bathroom readers will appreciate a focused low-voltage halogen reading light, especially if the toilet is in a private niche.

■ It is important to light changes in floor level, especially in a bathroom where wet floors add to the hazard of falling. Recess louvered lights into the risers on steps, or be sure the ambient lighting amply illuminates the step or stairs.

■ Plants like the bathroom's moisture. Add an artificial growing light in your recessed fixtures to make plants feel at home even if there is no natural light. For more about plant bulbs, see page 75.

■ Step up the ambient light in an exercise area. You'll need to maneuver past exercise equipment and read digital readouts on machines.

You Can Get There from Here: Foyer, Hallway, Stairwell

Builders seem to think that entrance halls, corridors, and stairways require little more than general light, and often make do with a skimpy fixture. These areas need layers of light just like other rooms, to bring out their true beauty and enhance their function.

Foyers

Entrance halls create the first impression of your home. They predict the furnishing styles of the rest of the house and set the tone, whether casual or formal. Lighting typically revolves around a ceiling fixture whose style offers a transition between outdoors and indoors. Do not make the foyer light too bright—you don't want to blind people entering from the dark.

▶ Hang fixtures in grand foyers so that they are framed by the window from the outside.

You can't see your lighted chandelier in its finished installation, and that makes planning tough. Here's a trick to help you:

1 Make a paper mobile or buy a kite with the rough dimensions of the fixture you are considering.

2 Hang it by a string in the foyer.

3 Adjust the template's height as needed. Check to see if it is the right scale for the space.

4 Order a fixture matching size and shape of your model.

■ In small entryways, give flush-mounted ceiling fixtures ample clearance for the opening of the door. Make them decorative, but don't let them overwhelm the space—8 inches in diameter is a good size for a 5- x 8-square-foot space. Fixtures that have clear glass and decorative globes or flame bulbs are cozy and welcoming. Keep the wattages low—15, 25, or 40 watts maximum, particularly in fixtures that take three or more bulbs.

■ In a grand, multiple-story foyer, suspend decorative fixtures about 10 feet above the floor. Choose a fixture in scale with the space—a wide floor visually balances a large hanging fixture or chandelier up to 30 inches in diameter. If the ceiling is tall but the floor area small, choose a tall, narrow fixture, 12 to 18 inches in diameter. Birdcage-style fixtures are popular choices here.

■ Grand 1½- or 2-story foyers usually have windows above the front door. Hang foyer fixtures in these spaces so that they are framed by the window from outside. Passersby should not see the top or bottom of this key design element cut off like a badly cropped photo. Ask if the foyer fixture comes with extra chain and cord to accommodate your grand foyer—such fixtures usually do. Or ask your lighting dealer to rewire the fixture with longer chain and cord.

▶ A foyer fixture should be of a scale that is proportioned to the space.

■ Use decorative wall sconces and small table lamps on foyer tables to blend and fill the light in the space. Recessed low-voltage pin spots or frame-mounted picture lights highlight art and add interest to an entrance hall.

Hallways

Hallways are either a dull route from here to there or a pleasing visual experience. To make your hallways interesting as well as safe, try some of these ideas:

■ Shallow wall sconces, mounted high enough not to interfere with passing traffic, provide beautiful uplighting in hallways and can break a long expanse of wall into shorter visual sections.

■ Treat your hallway as a gallery, highlighting wall art or photographs with low-voltage halogen track lighting or recessed spots and eyeballs.

■ Install flush-mounted ceiling fixtures that match those in adjoining foyers, dining rooms, or stairways. Space them at least 10 feet apart.

Stairways

Light all changes in floor level, whether it's a single step or a full staircase. Stairway lighting should clearly define the dimensions of the risers.

You'll have switches at either end of a hallway, but if the hall is long, you may also consider placing switches in the middle near bedroom doorways so that occupants don't have to backtrack to one end or another to turn off the lights.

◀ Stairway lighting should clearly define the dimensions of the risers.

◀ The lighting in your hallways should complement the decor, just as it should in any other part of the house.

For safety at night, install dimmers on hall lights, plug in soft nightlights with photo sensors that will switch them off at dawn, or replace switches with timers that reduce or turn light off at the times you select.

■ A classic stairway lighting plan provides ceiling downlights at the top of the steps, on landings, and at the bottom of the stairs, all controlled by three-way switches at top and bottom.

■ Shield the fixtures on landings and at the lower part of the stairs so they don't shine into the eyes of people descending.

■ Use a combination of intense, directional light and soft, diffuse light to define the depth and height of risers, to help stair users maintain their footing. For example, use a halogen PAR in a line-voltage downlight at the top of the stairs, and use compact fluorescent or incandescent A bulbs in surface-mounted fixtures on the landing and at the bottom of the stairs.

■ For open stairwells with no landing, suspended foyer fixtures can take the place of stair-bottom fixtures to cast a soft glow on the risers.

■ Other ways to safely and beautifully define stairs include crosslights, louvered recessed lights set into the risers, strip lighting or fiberoptic cable outlining the edges of steps, and architectural lights hidden in stair moldings.

Work Lights: The Home Office

Eyes get a pretty intense workout in offices. In a home office, go out of your way to provide a well-lit, glare-free environment for reading, studying, drafting, writing, graphic arts, or computer tasks. Enhance the environment with accent lighting on pictures, diplomas, and other signs of your accomplishments.

▼ Light desks and computer work areas with undercabinet lighting. Its indirect lighting won't reflect on the screen and is great for reading and paperwork.

General Illumination

For general, eye-friendly office illumination conducive to high-energy intellectual work, tailor one of these methods to your situation:

■ Install architectural wall brackets or cove lights with bright white fluorescent bulbs to furnish indirect light, important for minimizing glare.

■ Wood or metal halogen uplight sconces or halogen torchieres can bounce off a white ceiling with little or no glare.

■ Two rectangular fluorescent ceiling fixtures installed parallel to each other, 1 to 3 feet apart, provide better shadowless light than a single fixture. Position the desk perpendicular to the fixtures, but not directly underneath, so that the light will shine over your shoulders at the desk, but won't glare directly on the work surface.

■ Recessed downlights spaced 5½ to 6 feet apart on an 8-foot ceiling provide good general light. Use incandescent, halogen, or compact fluorescent floodlights. In critical viewing areas, such as where computers are used, recessed lights with lenses or louvers soften the beam and reduce glare. Avoid placing a desk directly under a downlight, which can create glare from the surface.

Desktop Lighting

Don't create too much contrast between the work surface and the rest of the room. To prevent eyestrain, balance the ambient and task lighting; work surfaces should be no more than three times brighter than the surrounding area. To light a desktop, consider these ideas:

■ Use fluorescent or low-voltage halogen undercabinet fixtures above the desk to light the writing or reading surface directly below. This is a good way to light computer desks so the light won't reflect in the monitor.

■ Choose an adjustable table lamp with a conical metal shade and a weighted or clamp base. This will allow you to direct the light wherever you wish. Better yet, use two desk lamps—one on each side of the desk—so you can crosslight the work area, eliminating shadows and glare.

■ Look for table lamps with adjustable light levels, or get the same flexibility with a dimmer control on the outlet.

■ Use an adjustable-height pendant to spread light over a desktop, keeping the surface clear for projects.

Laundry and Workbench

A ceiling-mounted fluorescent fixture is usually adequate for doing laundry and won't add to the heat from the appliances. Add a swing-arm wall lamp or wall-mounted track head nearby for mending or ironing. Covered fluorescent shoplights, suspended on chains, are a classic approach to lighting a workbench. Or attach a 2x2 wood strip horizontally about 15 inches above the workbench. Then you can move clip-on work lights along the strip as needed.

▲ Eyes work full time in the home office. Make sure you have adequate light.

◀ Track lights are a good alternative to fluorescent shop lights at the workbench.

Living Outdoors, Lighting Outdoors

*W*ell-designed lighting outdoors has a lot in common with its counterpart indoors. It combines ambient, task, and accent light and is designed around a focal point. Safety and security must be first, both as a design goal and an approach to installation. Glare is bad, efficiency is good, and beauty matters. Outdoors, use accent lighting effects such as up- and downlighting, crosslighting, silhouetting, and shadowing. You don't need task light as much except perhaps at a patio or deck table. Install enough outdoor lighting to see the path to an entrance, avoid tripping on steps, make out a house number, or find keys and keyholes. Show off the beauty of your garden.

General Considerations

Don't light too brightly. Unless you are lighting your private tennis court, you don't need to imitate high noon. Don't overlight. Outdoor floodlights create a big contrast between the lit area and surrounding darkness. Ironically, this actually interferes with night vision and provides shadowy places where intruders can hide. Low-contrast lighting is more relaxing and improves night vision. Use low-wattage bulbs and shielded fixtures that don't cause glare or waste their light up in the night sky.

Decide what to light. Obvious places include driveways, paths, steps, doorways, decks, and the exterior walls of the house itself. Also light landscaping features such as shrubs, trees, sculptures, fountains, and pools. Decide which one will be the focal point. Draw a plan, just as you did for your indoor lighting scheme. See *Where to Begin* on page 12.

Line-voltage or low-voltage? You may start out with some preferences for either line-voltage or low-voltage lighting outside, but what you end up with will depend a great deal on the lighting design and the types of areas you want to light.

Line-voltage (120-volt) systems, those that run on normal household current, are recommended for permanent installations in areas larger than 25 feet and more than 30 feet from the light source. The cable must be protected in conduit and/or buried according to strict local electrical codes. You can install outdoor line-voltage receptacles and fixtures on the side of the house without burying cable, though, as long as the cable isn't exposed.

A low-voltage system, which uses a transformer to convert a regular 120-volt to 12, is good for lighting small areas close to the ground. Because the electrical shock risk is so minimal, they are easier to install. The cables can be above ground or buried shallowly, and you can move the fixtures as your landscape grows and changes.

The best solution may be combining the two lighting systems, using line-voltage for the distance runs and 12-volt branch circuits with transformers for garden and path lighting. Since many outdoor fixture models come in line- or low-voltage, you can maintain visual continuity and style throughout the yard, even if you use both types of systems.

The House

Show off your home's beauty, make it inviting, and give people a sense of security when you light your house from outside. Here are some ideas to consider:

■ Light front door entrances with wall lanterns mounted about 5½ feet above the landing on both sides of the door. Choose fixtures that complement the style of your home. For a porch or overhang, add a damp-location ceiling fixture flush-mounted, semi-flush, or chain-hung. Be

Especially when aiming floodlights, check the angles from the road out front, from property lines, or even from your neighbor's porch to be sure you are not shining light where it is not wanted and where its glare could cause an accident.

▶ Lighting outside your home combines ambient, task, and accent lighting, just as it does indoors.

▶ Post lanterns and the posts
they sit on are usually purchased
separately.

sure you have enough light to see the house number from the street
and so that you can see the keyhole when you're at the door. Start out
with 40 watts incandescent or its equivalent in fluorescent, and increase
the wattage only if necessary. Hang floodlight fixtures from soffits and
crosslight the front entrance. This is a good place for compact fluorescent bulbs, whose light will illuminate the heads and upper bodies of
visitors without glaring in their faces.

■ Light side and rear entrances with a single fixture overhead or a wall
lantern on the side of the door with the handle. Start out with 25 or 40
watts and increase that as needed. Decorative incandescent or compact
fluorescent bulbs are the likely choices here.

■ Post lights are a great way to light the front yard. Posts come in wood
and a variety of metal finishes. The lanterns that sit on top are usually
purchased separately. You can purchase post and wall lanterns manufactured in coordinating styles.

■ Aim floodlights on the garage facade at an angle low enough to light
the driveway without glaring into drivers' eyes. Try fixtures with long-
lasting, energy-efficient, high-pressure-sodium bulbs if the lights are
on all night. Many outdoor floodlights come with motion sensors built
in. Outdoor halogen PAR bulbs are the most popular choice for these
fixtures.

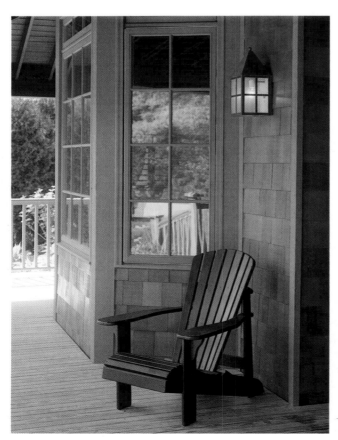

◀ Mount wall
lanterns about
5½ feet above
the walkway.

▼ Define decks
and level changes
with outdoor light-
ing that mounts
on rails, steps, or
benches.

■ Light decks and patios with spots recessed in roof soffits or surface-mounted floodlight units. Metal housings on flood and baffles in recessed fixtures will cut glare. Consider wiring units into separate switches. If this space is an outdoor room, there will be occasions such as parties when you want all the lights on, and other times when a low level of deck light is most appropriate.

■ Define deck railings, steps, and benches with low-voltage mini-lights or louvered recessed lights. Post lights at the corners make an attractive visual boundary between a patio and the yard. Use yellow bug-light bulbs in fixtures near seating areas, doorways, and windows to avoid attracting pests. String miniature specialty lights around the perimeter to create a festive look.

■ Wash or graze house walls with wall-mounted spots aimed down over interesting architectural features, or with in-ground uplights tucked behind shrubs. Aim uplights so their beam ends at or before the roof edge—there's no point in sending light up into space.

Paths and Driveways

Dark paths and driveways can be frightening and confusing at night, especially for those unfamiliar with the layout. Lighting them not only helps to keep people from tripping or getting lost, but also makes us feel safer. Path and driveway lighting is generally inconspicuous during daylight, low to the ground, glare free, and softer than front-door lighting.

■ Line short, narrow paths with low-voltage pagoda or spread lights mounted directly on the ground. For longer, wider, or winding paths, mount the lights on bollards, which are waist-high posts, or full-sized posts. This increases the width of the lit area. Alternate the lights along sides of the path to add interest and widen the area of illumination.

■ Line driveways with lights mounted on bollards that are positioned 1 or 2 feet from the edge. Light a single-lane driveway on either edge, but light multiple-lane driveways on both edges.

■ Clearly light all changes in level. Install recessed louvered downlights in concrete, brick, or wooden risers or in walls beside a staircase. Where this is not practical, position lights at the corners of a step to gently illuminate risers. Don't shine the light upward, or it will blind someone descending.

Buy fixtures rated for high-wind or damp locations. They are made to withstand these forces. Copper, brass, and bronze with less than 20-percent nickel content resist corrosion in saltwater conditions.

▼ Guide guests through your garden at night with path lighting.

Landscapes

Although it provides light, landscape lighting is almost entirely decorative. Allow your creativity and taste to guide you. Especially with the landscape, don't overdo it. Overlit landscapes are garish. Think of moonlight—it is soft and without glare. That's the goal. Experiment with lighting technology you might not try indoors. Mercury-vapor bulbs flatter greenery. It may be worth the investment to try a new fiberoptic system because of its flexibility and generous light output. Here are a few of the possibilities:

■ Highlight flowers and small shrubs with miniature spotlights that throw a controlled, tight beam. Make sure these lights are well shielded with louvers or metal shades to prevent glare. For fixtures that use MR-type halogen bulbs, choose those marked narrow flood or spot for the tightest beam.

■ Illuminate garden benches, flower beds, and other small scenes with fixtures that create wide beams. Choose flood PAR bulbs or MR bulbs marked flood. These aim pools of light downward. The higher you mount them, the wider the pool of light will be.

■ Consider gardens outside your living room picture window or beside your deck focal points and give them the attention they deserve. Lighted gardens expand the feeling of the room or deck they adjoin.

If you are mounting lights in trees, be sure the material in the fixture isn't toxic to the tree.

MR-16 bulbs come with and without lenses. Outdoors, use the models with lenses to keep moisture out.

▼ A tree is a fine choice as a focal point in landscape lighting.

▼ Light gardens and make them a focal point to make the inside area or deck adjoining them feel roomier.

■ Uplight trees or shrubs using spotlights with louvers or in-ground floodlights. This is an especially nice technique for lighting statues. Uplighting is not seen in nature, so it is a dramatic attention-grabber. Be especially careful not to overuse this technique, though, and use relatively dim bulbs to avoid light pollution. A little light goes a long way here.

Timers often can be purchased as accessories to low-voltage lighting systems.

▶ Graze the facade of your home with floodlighting.

▽ Floodlight placed high above a deck can ensure safe footing at night.

Many outdoor floodlights come with knockouts that enable you to retrofit motion sensors later on.

◼ Graze a stone wall or picket fence horizontally with a flood concealed behind a bush. You can also graze tree trunks, walls, and fences with uplights or downlights positioned close to the surface. Use spotlights with a louver or metal shield, and hide the light source in the foliage.

◼ Silhouette a plant by lighting it from behind and below. Near the house, this technique works well combined with wall grazing.

◼ Shadowing lights the object and casts a shadow against a fence or wall behind it. Floodlights positioned at ground level close to the object make a nice effect. Aim the light up at the object to cast the shadow.

◼ Spotlight prized landscape features. Like indoor accent lighting, spotlighting trains a focused beam of light to accent a specific item. Spotlights can be mounted high, out of the line of sight, and aimed down at a 30-degree angle.

◼ Aim spotlights or floodlights straight down through the branches of a tree to create a moonlighting effect. (Check local codes regarding tree-mounted fixtures.)

◼ Decorate a tree with many fiberoptic cable lanterns for a charming, festive look.

◀ Uplighting is a dramatic effect wherever it is used.

Controls

Timers, motion, and photo sensors are almost indispensable with outdoor lighting. Include them throughout your outdoor lighting plans to increase security and convenience. Lights that are controlled and timed to respond to your needs will be less likely to be left on for hours on end, unnecessarily, and that will reduce your electricity use.

Timers and sensors are built in much more than they used to be, but you can also replace on/off switches with many models. Timers and motion sensors are built in to many models of outdoor lights, but you can replace on/off switches that operate your outdoor lighting with timers and sensors that you purchase separately.

Most low-voltage systems offer timers as part of the kit or as an accessory you can buy separately. Consider units with remote-control capacity and units that combine motion, light, and timed controlling. Garage door openers usually have built-in lights; otherwise, wire your garage lights to the same circuit.

Decide which fixtures or sets of fixtures will require dedicated switches. Think of arriving home at night, and think of which lights you'll want on first—the driveway floods? The path to the side door? The post lantern and the front entrance lights? Is there an inside light you want to switch on at the same time, or one you want to be on already? Can you use a power-line carrier control to turn on lights when you enter your driveway?

Aim motion sensors at a height that will make them less likely to be tripped by small animals. This may take a little trial and error. Choose models with override switches. There will be times when you want the garage floodlight on, and you don't want to have to walk out into the dark to make that happen. The override switch will enable you to turn the light on from inside if you need to.

Outdoor lighting offers an ideal situation for scene controls and power-line carrier switches. See *Tech Talk,* page 32, for additional information.

Locate controls at all entrances, including the garage, and use three-way and remote switching. Adjust timers and light sensors to the changing routines of your family or the changing patterns of dusk and dawn.

Lighting Indoor Plants

If you can't light your plants with sunlight, use ordinary bulbs or special types made for plants. Specialty bulbs cost more. Remember to give plants intervals of darkness and light—they need both! Cool or warm white fluorescent tubes are good sources of the light from the blue end of the spectrum. Boost the level of red light with incandescent bulbs, placing them at a ratio of 3 incandescent to every 10 fluorescent bulbs. Or, combine fluorescent plant bulbs with ordinary fluorescent tubes at a ratio of 1:1 or 1:2 plant bulbs. Metal-halide HID bulbs are good for leafy, green plants, and high-pressure sodium HID bulbs emit rays good for flowering and fruit stages. If you do choose these bulbs (which are more common in commercial applications), consider combining them to encourage both types of plant growth.

Outdoors, fixtures with sealed lenses are a good choice, especially at ground level. Sprinkler water could cause exposed bulbs to shatter.

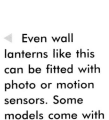

▶ Program outdoor timers to give you light when you arrive home on a dark winter evening and to create a lived-in look when you are away.

◀ Even wall lanterns like this can be fitted with photo or motion sensors. Some models come with sensors built in.

Home Electricity

4

Even some of the most experienced do-it-yourselfers blanch when it comes to electrical wiring. Wiring has the reputation of being tricky, difficult to understand, and yes, even dangerous. In truth, however, electrical wiring is very straightforward, quite easy to do, and safe— provided it is done correctly. The first step in becoming proficient at electric work is to understand the basics of electricity and how it is distributed throughout your house. Once you have an understanding of the overall system, you'll be ready to tackle the components that make it work—switches, cables, receptacles, and the like. After that, wiring itself is simple screwdriver and plier work; wires are screwed in place or twisted together. It doesn't get more basic than that.

Understanding Your Home's Electrical System

That tangle of wires leading to an ominous gray box in your basement or garage is not nearly as mysterious as it might appear. It seems complicated because of the sheer number of wires. But what you have to realize is that each of those wires serves the same function as its neighbors—supplying electricity to a certain part of your house. There are a lot of wires because there are a lot of different parts of your house.

Getting Power into the House

The big gray box, called the service panel, connects your household wiring and the utility company's wiring. Outside your house, the utility company's wires run from their pole (or underground service in some areas) to your electric meter. The meter keeps track of the amount of electricity you use so the utility company can charge you. It measures electrical consumption in units called kilowatt-hours. Ten 100-watt light bulbs (for a total of 1000 watts or 1 kilowatt) lit for one hour use one kilowatt-hour of electricity. Your electric bill states how much the utility company charges for each kilowatt-hour.

From the meter, the wires enter your house and run into the service panel. Here they are connected (through fuses or circuit breakers) to the various wires that run inside your walls. Actually, those "wires" are called cables. They contain several individual wires and are known as branch circuits because they branch off from the main source of electricity.

Branch Circuits

There are essentially two kinds of branch circuits in your house: 120-volt circuits, which carry current to small electrical devices such as lamps, TVs, and toasters; and 240-volt circuits, which supply power to bigger appliances such as air conditioners, water heaters, and stoves. The voltages listed here are nominal—the actual line voltage may be somewhat different depending on how far away from the actual power plant (or substation) you are, and how far away a given receptacle is from the service panel. The difference isn't a problem as electrical devices are designed to operate with up to a 10-percent variation in voltage.

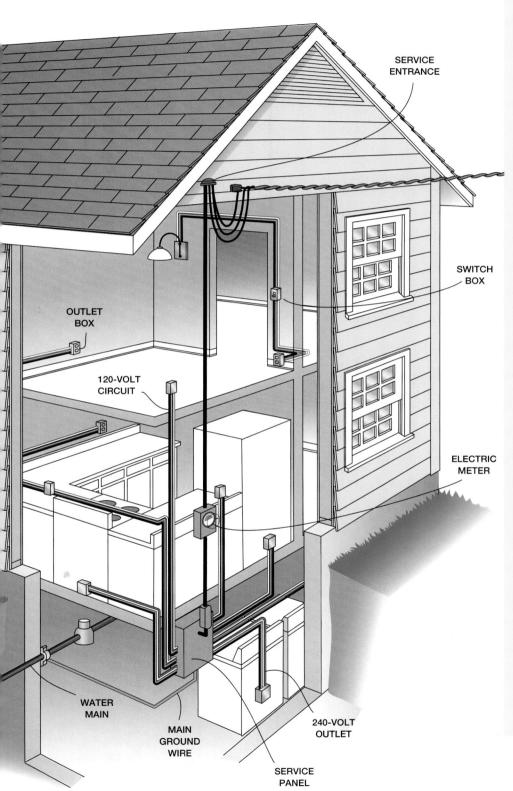

SERVICE
ENTRANCE

SWITCH
BOX

OUTLET
BOX

ELECTRIC
METER

120-VOLT
CIRCUIT

WATER
MAIN

MAIN
GROUND
WIRE

240-VOLT
OUTLET

SERVICE
PANEL

Electrical work is more closely regulated than any other
building trade. With good reason: Shoddy electrical work
can be deadly.

As a safeguard, most com-
munities have electrical codes
that govern the installation and
the size and type of electrical
equipment allowed. These
codes also dictate who may
perform electrical work and
what (if any) inspections are
necessary. The basis for many
local electrical codes is often
one of the national codes de-
veloped by various trade asso-
ciations. One of the most
widely used is the National
Electrical Code (NEC) pub-
lished by the National Fire
Protection Association.

Because your local code
may be stricter than the NEC,
you should check with your local code enforcement officials
before starting any of the work
discussed in this book. You
may discover, for example,
that only licensed electricians
are allowed to work on household wiring or that you have to
pass a test before performing
the work yourself. Keep in
mind, while code and the local
bureaucracy may sometimes
seem ridiculous, they're based
on safety and that cutting corners while doing electrical
work is just not worth the risk.

The Heart of the Electrical System

The Service Panel

Your service panel serves two main functions: It is the interface between your household wiring and the utility company's wires, and it guards your house against electrical overloads. To understand what's going on inside the panel, it helps to understand a little bit about how electricity works.

For electricity to flow, it must travel in a complete circuit. That is, there must be a path leading from the source of electricity to whatever you want to operate, and a path leading back to the source. If either of these paths is broken, no electricity will flow. The utility company accomplishes this by running three wires to your house. Two of these wires are considered "hot" and the third is a neutral or ground wire. If you connect something between either of the hot wires and the ground wire, you will have a 120-volt circuit. If you connect something between the two hot wires, you'll have a 240-volt circuit.

If you unscrew the cover of your service panel, you'll see three fat wires (usually two insulated and one bare) and a number of thinner ones all connected to various places inside the panel. The three fat wires come from the utility company's lines. The two with insulation are the hot lines, while the third is the neutral. The thinner wires run to various parts of your house. Of these, the black and red lines are hot, while the white and the bare lines are the neutral and ground, respectively. For more about the differences between the ground and the neutral wires in your house, see *The Importance of the Ground Wire* on page 88.

The incoming hot lines from the utility company are connected to the hot lines in your house through either fuses or circuit breakers. These are safety devices designed to shut off the current should a circuit try to use more electricity than it can handle. When a fuse blows, it must be replaced with a new one, whereas circuit breakers are switches that can be reset to restore power.

Causes and Cures

Tripped circuit breakers and/or blown fuses are always signs of some sort of problem with your electrical system. Don't simply replace the fuse or reset the breaker without investigating why the circuit is overloaded. The most common problem (and the easiest to fix) is having too many things plugged into a circuit. Before restoring power, unplug some of the devices that were on before the problem occurred. If you cannot find a source of the overload, check to be sure all your appliances are functioning properly—an overloaded electric motor can draw a lot more current than usual. Malfunctioning appliances are often warm to the touch and may smell hot or even burned. Unplug anything you are suspicious of before restoring power.

The worst-case scenario is an actual short circuit, where bare wires are actually touching each other, or some other grounded object. These problems are harder to find and may require some careful investigation. Look and smell for traces of smoke around outlets and switches. Call in a licensed electrician if you cannot find the source of the problem.

Safety

Keep in mind that fuses and circuit breakers are designed to protect the wiring in your house from overloads; they won't necessarily protect you. If you accidentally touch live wires, the resulting short circuit may not trip the breaker or blow a fuse fast enough to save your life. Only GFCI-protected circuits work this way. (See *An Ingenious Safety Device* on page 150.) Be sure to turn off the power to the circuit you are working on before you begin. Do this by throwing the breaker or pulling the appropriate fuse.

> **CAUTION!** Never try to fix an overloaded circuit by replacing the fuse or breaker with one of a higher rating. This can allow the wires feeding the circuit to overheat and start a fire.

> **CAUTION!** Tripping the main breaker or pulling out the main fuse block will shut off power to your entire house, but it will not completely cut off the power inside your service panel. Only the utility company can do this. Exercise extreme caution when working inside the service panel.

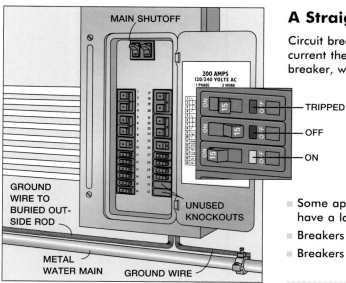

A Straight-Bus Circuit Breaker Panel

Circuit breakers look like switches. They are rated by the amount of current they can safely handle. At the top of the panel is the main breaker, which controls the flow of current to the entire house.

Most newer houses have at least a 200-amp main breaker, while some older systems have considerably less (60 to 100 amps). Inside the panel, the two incoming hot lines are connected to two metal strips that run down the center of the box. Individual circuit breakers then connect to these strips.

- Most of the circuits in your house will be protected by 15- or 20-amp breakers.

- Some appliances, such as an electric range or water heater, will have a larger breaker.

- Breakers that handle 120-volt circuits connect to one strip.

- Breakers for 240-volt circuits attach to both strips.

A Straight-Bus Fuse Panel

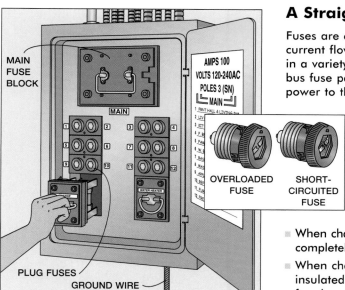

Fuses are electric devices that are designed to melt when the current flowing through them exceeds their capacity. Fuses come in a variety of shapes and sizes as described below. A straight-bus fuse panel has a main block of fuses at the top that controls power to the entire panel. Turning off the power requires pulling this main block.

- Below the main block are plug fuses that control the individual 120-volt circuits in your house.

- Blocks toward the bottom of the panel control the various 240-volt circuits.

- Before removing a fuse, make sure there is no current flowing through it by turning off all devices plugged into the circuit.

- When changing cartridge-type fuses, be sure to pull the block completely out of the panel.

- When changing plug fuses, unscrew them by touching only the insulated rim. Also, do not stand on damp ground and keep your free hand in your hip pocket to avoid accidentally touching a potential ground in the panel.

A Split-Bus Panel

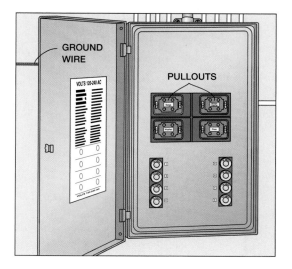

Split-bus panels have no main shutoff. Instead, high-capacity breakers or fuses control portions of the panel. All of these must be removed or tripped to shut off the power. This style of panel has been banned in new construction since 1984, but still exists in some older homes.

> Bus is an electrical term for a conductor that carries current to many separate items. In a straight-bus service panel (with fuses or circuit breakers), there are two metal bars (or buses) down the center of the panel that are connected to the incoming lines from the electric company. The breakers (or fuses) for all the circuits are connected to these buses.

Removing Cartridge Fuses

Circuits of 240 volts are protected by cartridge-type fuses. These can be housed in blocks in the main service panel or in a separate panel attached to the main panel. Before removing the fuse block or pulling an individual fuse, make sure the device the fuses are protecting is turned off.

- For cartridge fuses in a separate panel, simply pull them with a fuse puller *(right)*. Be careful of the metal ends. They may be hot.
- To remove fuses in a block, pull the block free from the panel with its attached handle.
- Then remove the fuses from the block with a fuse puller.

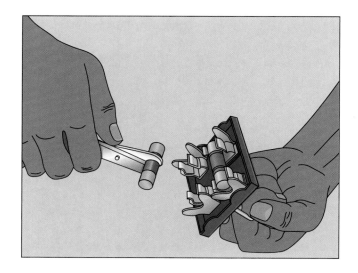

Testing Cartridge Fuses

You can tell when a plug fuse has blown by looking at it. But to determine whether or not a cartridge fuse is good, you'll have to test it.

- Set a multitester to the Rx1 scale. Touch the probes to either end of the fuse. A good fuse will register 0 Ohms (no resistance), while a blown one will show infinite resistance *(right)*.
- If the fuse is good, it can be reinstalled.
- If the fuse is bad, replace it with one of the same type and capacity.

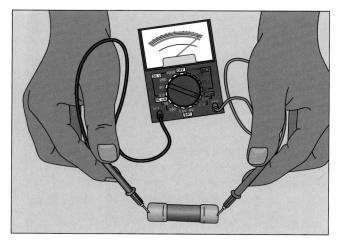

Types of Fuses

It pays to investigate what kind of fuses your service panel uses and have some spares on hand for use when needed. If you have to change a fuse, replace it with one of the same type and capacity, never higher.

Ferruled-cartridge fuses are used to protect higher-powered circuits (up to 60 amps) such as those for a water heater or an electric clothes dryer.

Knife-blade-cartridge fuses —rated for more than 60 amps— are used as the main fuses in a service panel.

Standard plug fuses come in 12-, 20-, and 30-amp capacities.

Time-delay fuses are available for circuits that power electric motors. Motors often draw extra current when they start— a time-delay fuse withstands this temporary overload, but will blow if the increased current flow doesn't return to normal.

Type-S fuses fit into an adapter that prevents the installation of higher-capacity fuses.

Mapping Your Electrical System

Before you begin an electrical project, find out what you have to work with. Start with a map of your home's electrical system so you know which breaker or fuse controls which lights and outlets.

- Sketch each floor of your house, marking all the switches, lights, and outlets as shown.

- Take one room at a time and turn on all the lights and other devices plugged into receptacles. (It may be easier to do this with a helper.) Plug a test light or radio into unused receptacles. You don't have to test the 240-volt appliances that have their own circuits.

- At your service panel, trip breakers or unscrew fuses until you cut the power to that room.

- Note on your plan which circuit breaker or fuse controls which outlets and switches.

- Keep in mind some circuits may extend into adjacent rooms.

- List the rooms controlled by the various breakers/fuses on the door of the service panel.

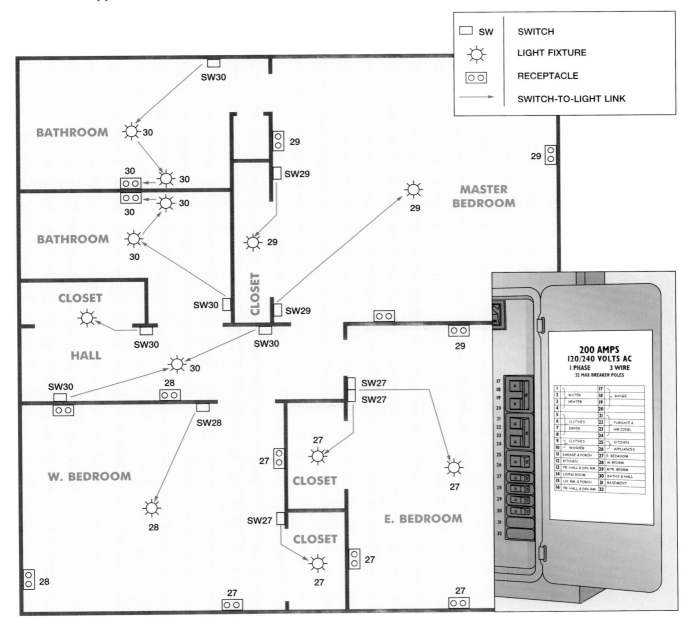

Calculating the Load on a Circuit

If you intend to add lights or receptacles to a circuit, it is a good idea to calculate the existing load on the circuit. This can also help you check for an overload if you have a circuit that is continually tripping breakers or blowing fuses. The continuous load on a circuit—the total of all the devices that are plugged into it all the time—should not exceed 80 percent of the circuit's rated capacity, which is listed on the breaker or fuse. This leaves a 20-percent margin for temporary loads—things that are not plugged in all the time. Thus, a 20-amp circuit should have no more than 16 amps on it (12 amps for a 15-amp circuit). To calculate the load on a circuit:

■ Add up the wattage of all the things powered by the circuit. These numbers can be found on the Un-

derwriters Laboratory labels on each device, or printed on the bulbs in the case of a lighting fixture, or in the unit's owner's manual.

```
TYPE LISTED
605 | 639F          (U L)
120V AC ONLY 60 Hz 1500W   (GF)
MADE IN USA
DO NOT IMMERSE IN ANY LIQUID
```

■ Once you have the total wattage, divide the result by 120 (the voltage). Watts divided by volts equals amps.

■ Check your results against the figures listed above. This will tell you if you can safely add on to a circuit (or it may tell you to unplug a few items).

Electrical Units

There are a number of different terms used when trying to quantify electricity. The three most useful for household wiring are *volts*, *amps* (or *amperes*), and *watts*.

Electrical Emergencies

There are a number of emergencies that can arise when electrical devices malfunction or people make mistakes. Review these instructions periodically, so you'll know what to do in an emergency.

A person who comes in contact with a live wire or other charged item can appear to be stuck to the source. DO NOT touch the person, or you too, may become stuck. Instead, shut off the power to the house at the service panel, or unplug the appliance or lamp, if you can do so safely. If this isn't possible, use a broomstick or other nonconducting object to knock the person free (upper left).

Should a switch, receptacle, or other fixture snap, crackle, smoke, spark, or burn, immediately turn off the power to the

entire house and call the fire department. Get everyone out of the house, immediately.

If a lamp or other appliance feels hot, sparks, shocks you, or is burning, unplug it immediately. Use a thick, dry towel or a heavy work glove to protect your hand (upper right).

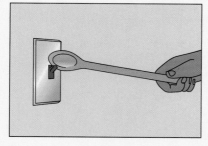

And never touch a burning power cord or switch. Use a wooden spoon to shut it off or disconnect it (lower right).

To help understand them, think of a wire conducting electricity as a hose carrying water. Voltage represents the force in the wire or the pressure in the hose. Amperage represents the amount of current flowing, or the volume of water flowing out of the hose. Wattage indicates how much energy a device consumes or how much work is being done by a waterwheel driven by the stream of water.

The units are closely related. This relationship can be expressed as a mathematical equation known as Watt's Law:

Volts x amps = watts

For example, an electrical device designed to work on 120 volts and which draws 4 amps would use 480 watts of electricity.

$$120 \times 4 = 480$$

You can also use the formula in reverse to calculate how much current a device needs when you know how many watts it consumes:

Watts/volts = amps

A toaster rated for 1500 watts requires 12.5 amps of current.

$$1500/120 = 12.5$$

With household electricity, the voltage is fixed— you're either going to use 120 volts or 240 volts. For the most part, the people who made your appliances make this choice for you—generally things that plug in operate on 120 volts. So what you are left with is deciding how many amps a circuit will require. Here again, you have essentially two choices: 15 or 20 amps. Most general household circuits are 15 amps, with one or two heavy-duty 20-amp circuits run to places like the kitchen where high-wattage appliances are used. What this choice affects most is deciding what size wire to use—15-amp circuits can use 14-gauge wire, while 20-amp circuits require heavier, 12-gauge wire. For more on wire, see *Wires and Cables* on page 86.

The Hazards of Aluminum Wiring

Soaring copper prices in the early 1960s prompted manufacturers to look for another conductor to use for electrical wiring. They settled on aluminum. It was relatively cheap, it conducted well, and it was easy to form. Two types of aluminum wire were produced: pure aluminum and aluminum covered with a thin layer of copper. The copper cover aluminum wire has proved safe, but there are some real dangers with the pure aluminum variety.

In 1972, after these hazards came to light, manufacturers modified the way they made aluminum wire, making it much safer. However, there are about two million homes that were wired with aluminum wire between 1962 and 1972. Many of these houses have not had their wiring updated. If your house has aluminum wire, you should leave your electrical work to a professional. (Aluminum wire is dull gray and the sheathing is marked AL.)

The hazards of aluminum wire stem from corrosion, which occurs in two ways: The first is when the aluminum is exposed to air—as it will be when connected to switches and outlets. The second occurs when dissimilar metals are in close contact with each other, as might occur where aluminum wire joins the copper alloy terminals of a lighting fixture. Both types of corrosion increase the resistance of the wire. Increased resistance means the wire will heat up when in use. If it gets hot enough, it can cause a fire.

Both types of corrosion can be prevented if the aluminum wire is installed according to the process laid out in the National Electrical Code. Exposed aluminum must be coated with a special antioxidizing coating, and all switches, receptacles, and other devices must be marked (CO/ALU) as acceptable for use with aluminum wire. The terminals on these devices are designed to prevent dissimilar metals from coming in contact with each other.

CAUTION! If your home is wired with aluminum wire, you should be especially alert for electrical problems. Avoid using high-wattage appliances, especially in rarely occupied rooms. Watch for warm cover plates, devices that fail to work for no apparent reason, and strange electrical odors or smoke. Leave all electrical work to a licensed electrician who has been specially trained to deal with aluminum wire.

Wires and Cables

Wires are individual conductors for electricity. Most of the wires in a household electrical system are solid, although some are made up of smaller strands. Cables consist of several wires bundled together. Most of the wiring in a house is done with cables, as circuits require two wires to make a complete loop.

Wires

Wires vary in diameter depending on how many amps they are meant to carry. The larger the diameter, the more current a wire can handle. A wire that is undersized for the current in a circuit can over-

heat, melt its insulation, and cause a fire hazard. Wire diameter is stated in gauge numbers according to the American Wire Gauge system (AWG). In this system, the smaller the number, the larger the wire. The most common wire gauges used in household wiring are #12 and #14. Circuits that are 20 amps require #12 wire, while 15-amp circuits use #14 wire. Some heavy-duty appliances such as electric ranges and large air conditioners may require even heavier wire. The wire gauge is usually marked on the wire's insulation.

There are also different types of wire. Most of the wire used today is known as TW wire. The T means the wire has a thermoplastic insulation and the W means that it is weatherproof. If your house is old enough, it may contain wire that is rated type T.

Cables

The most common type of household cable is non-metallic cable, called NM. It is often referred to as Romex cable, although Romex is a brand name. NM cable contains several individual insulated conductors within a plastic sheathing. It is often specified by the diameter of the wires and the number of individual conductors it contains. Thus 14-2 with ground is a cable containing two insulated #14 wires along with a bare ground wire. This information is embossed into the cable's plastic sheathing.

There are three types of NM cable that are commonly used for residential wiring:

■ Type NM-B is basic, everyday cable used for running circuits throughout the walls of a house. Until the late 1980s this was known simply as NM cable.

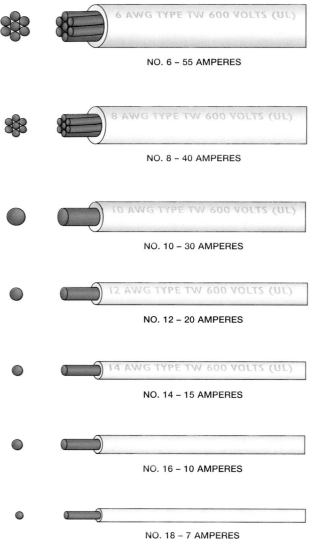

NO. 6 – 55 AMPERES

NO. 8 – 40 AMPERES

NO. 10 – 30 AMPERES

NO. 12 – 20 AMPERES

NO. 14 – 15 AMPERES

NO. 16 – 10 AMPERES

NO. 18 – 7 AMPERES

WIRE SIZES

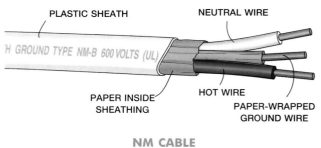

NM CABLE

PLASTIC SHEATH | NEUTRAL WIRE | PAPER INSIDE SHEATHING | HOT WIRE | PAPER-WRAPPED GROUND WIRE

■ Type NM-C is cable used in damp locations such as basements and outbuildings.

■ Type UF (Underground Feeder) is for outdoor use. It can be buried, although it should not be embedded in concrete or aggregate without being encased in a protective conduit. A special type of UF cable with UV-resistant sheathing is made for exposed exterior wiring.

Armored Cable

This type of cable has a flexible metal jacket. It is most commonly found in houses built before the early 1960s, although it is still required by some local codes. With its steel sheathing, it is tougher than NM cable, but it is also more difficult to work with. It is referred to as AC cable or sometimes by its older designation BX. Most of the time, AC cable only contains the insulated conductors and a light aluminum bonding wire. The steel sheath serves as the ground.

When the cable is being attached to a junction box, the bonding wire is bent back against the steel sheathing and crimped in place with a cable clamp. This ensures good electrical contact between the sheathing and the box, maintaining a solid ground.

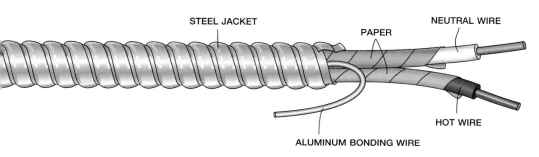

STEEL JACKET   PAPER   NEUTRAL WIRE

ALUMINUM BONDING WIRE   HOT WIRE

ARMORED CABLE

Hot, Neutral, and Ground

When you start working with household wiring, most of the circuits you'll be dealing with will have three wires—a hot, a neutral, and a ground. You'll be able to tell them apart by the color of the insulation that surrounds the actual wire. The hot side of a circuit will be black, red, or occasionally blue. These wires run to the circuit breakers or fuses in your service panel. The neutral wire (known in the NEC as the "grounded conductor") will be white or gray. Neutral wires run to the grounded terminals in your service panel. In a circuit, both the hot and the neutral wires carry electrical current.

The final wire is the ground, which is usually bare, or sometimes sheathed in green insulation. Ground wires run to the grounded terminals in the service panel like the neutral wire does. They normally carry no current, but are there for safety. Should a short circuit occur, the ground wire provides an alternate route for the electricity to follow back to the ground.

When you are attaching wires to various fixtures, it is important to make sure the right wires are attached to the right terminals on the fixtures. This is known as maintaining polarity. In receptacles and fixtures, the hot wire should be attached to the brass terminal, the neutral wire goes to the silver terminal, and the ground wire goes to the green terminal. If you are installing a switch, it should interrupt the hot line, so that when the switch is off, there won't be any power in the wires beyond it.

The Importance of the Ground Wire

When people first started wiring houses for electricity, there was no such thing as a ground wire. Electricians simply ran two wires to receptacles and other fixtures where electricity was needed. This works very well, as long as everything stays connected the way it should. The problem occurs when electricity from the hot (black) wire "leaks" to some other conductor, say a metal light fixture, making that fixture hot as well. Now a person who comes in contact with that fixture has the potential to become a conductor, at best getting a little jolt, at worst being electrocuted. Electrical "leaks" can also cause fires.

As an answer to this problem, people started running a ground wire along with the hot and the neutral conductors. This extra wire connects all the receptacles, switches, junction boxes, and other components in a circuit and offers a path for electricity to flow to the ground should something malfunction.

At face value, this ground wire seems to be a duplicate of the neutral wire. And in fact, the two are connected to the same place in the service panel, but their functions are very different. The neutral wire is part of the circuit and provides a path for the flow of electricity back to the source. The ground wire only conducts electricity in case of an emergency.

Methods of Grounding

In the most common type of household electrical cable (NMB), the ground wire is a separate, bare wire that runs along with the hot and the neutral wires inside the plastic casing. Occasionally, you'll find ground wires that are insulated with green or green and yellow striped insulation. In circuits that use metal conduit, or armored BX cable, the metal housing itself serves as the ground.

Grounding Appliances

Power tools and other appliances with metal cases generally have a three-pronged plug that connects the tool to the household's ground wire. This guards the user against a shock should a wire work loose inside the case. Other appliances may have a specially designed plastic case, which protects the user against shocks. This type of tool is known as double-insulated and requires only a two-pronged plug.

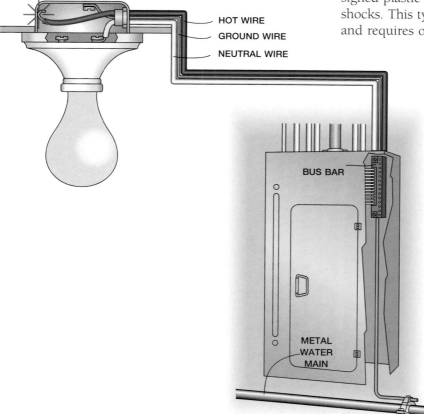

HOT WIRE
GROUND WIRE
NEUTRAL WIRE

BUS BAR

METAL WATER MAIN

The Ground Wire in Action

Should a connection come loose and the hot wire come in contact with a junction box as shown, the ground wire will direct the resulting current leak back to the service panel. The ground wire is connected to a bus bar in the panel that is also connected to the ground (in this case, a metal water main). If the current flow is strong enough, the breaker to which the hot wire is attached will trip, cutting power to the circuit.

Limits to Safety

The ground wire system in your house is an excellent safety feature, but it is not foolproof. A large current leak from hot to ground will probably trip a breaker or blow a fuse, but a small leak may not. And a small leak can still have enough power to deliver a fatal shock. In places where the risk is highest (outdoors or inside near water), code now requires circuits to be protected with ground-fault circuit interrupters (GFCI). (See *Installing a GFCI Receptacle* on page 151.) These relatively new devices work with the ground system in your house to provide an even safer level of protection against shock.

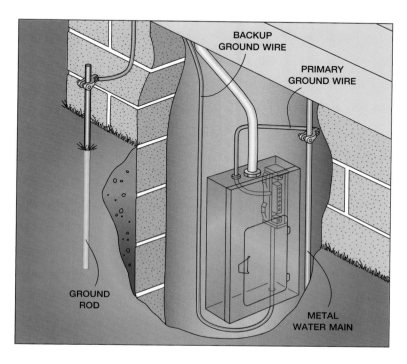

BACKUP
GROUND WIRE

PRIMARY
GROUND WIRE

GROUND
ROD

METAL
WATER MAIN

The Actual Ground Connection

In the past, most electrical systems used a cold water line as a ground. This worked well as the pipes were metal and made good contact with the ground as they ran out to meet the larger, feeder lines. Now, with the advent of plastic water pipes, most codes require a backup ground (or two). These are usually metal rods at least 8 feet long driven into the ground and connected to the bus bar in the service panel. They should be driven into the ground slightly away from the foundation of your house.

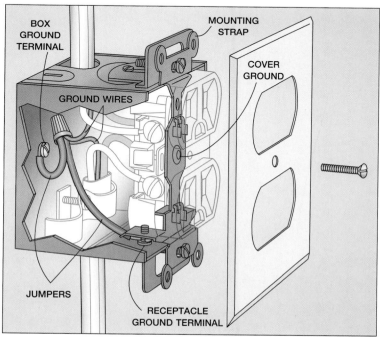

BOX
GROUND
TERMINAL

MOUNTING
STRAP

COVER
GROUND

GROUND WIRES

JUMPERS

RECEPTACLE
GROUND TERMINAL

Grounding an Electrical Fixture

When installing a fixture in a metal junction box, both the fixture and the box must be attached to the ground wire system. Most fixtures have a screw terminal (colored green) for this purpose. Wrap the ground wire around this terminal clockwise and tighten the screw to make a good solid connection. Tying the wire to the box isn't quite as easy. Many of the stricter electrical codes require you to connect all the various ground wires to a separate wire, called a jumper or pigtail, which is then connected to the box. The connection to the box should be made with a green-colored grounding screw.

Basic Electrical Wiring

TOOLS AND TECHNIQUES

As with most trades, electrical work has its own tools, techniques, and even vocabulary. But, fortunately, most of the tools are relatively inexpensive, and the techniques are fairly easy to learn. Unlike many trades, electrical work is based more on knowledge than actual skill, so you needn't have the nimble fingers of a pianist to do a good job. More important are patience, thoroughness, and attention to detail. Take your time, work slowly and double-check what you're doing against the directions in this book. Experience is the hallmark of a good pro. Your work won't be as fast, and you'll probably never climb a power pole, but with care and patience, your final product can be just as good.

The Home Electrician's Tool Kit

*C*hances are, you already have a lot of the tools needed for electrical work in your toolbox. Some of the tools, like hammers and screwdrivers, are used in a number of other trades, while others, like the cable ripper, are specific to wiring.

Start Simple

Pictured here are a few tools that will allow you to accomplish all of the projects in this book. But keep in mind that many electrical jobs can be accomplished with little more than a screwdriver and a pair of long-nose pliers. Rather than rushing out to purchase all of the items here, wait until you have a job that requires the item in question, then add it to your collection. In time you will build a collection tailored to the sort of electrical work that appeals to you.

▲ **Cable Ripper.** This inexpensive tool is a real timesaver. A sharp tooth on one end of the tool slits the plastic jacket on cable quickly, without damaging the insulation on the wires within.

▲ **Voltage Tester.** This tester is used to check whether or not a circuit is live. After you turn the power off at the service panel, you can use it as a double-check before you begin working on a circuit. Do not check with your fingers!

◀ **Multipurpose Tool.** With three key functions, this tool deserves a premium space in your toolbox. It will cut wire, strip the insulation from it, and squeeze crimp fittings in place.

▲ **Fuse Puller.** One of the few tools that benefits being made from plastic (plastic is an insulator), the fuse puller is needed to extract cartridge fuses from your fuse panel.

Receptacle Analyzer. When plugged into a receptacle, this tester will tell you if the receptacle has been wired properly.

Continuity Tester. With its built-in battery, this unit is used to check circuits to make sure that current can flow from one point to another. Use it only when the power to the circuit is turned off.

Diagonal Wire Cutters. Called "dikes" by those in the trade, these cutters have a narrow tip and angled jaws, making it easy to reach into tight spaces to trim wires to length.

Lineman's Pliers. The square jaws on these pliers are ideal for grasping wires and twisting them together. The built-in wire cutter combined with the long handles makes quick work of cutting cables to length.

Long-nosed Pliers. The long, thin jaws of these pliers are handy when working in tight places. You'll also use them for bending wires to fit around screw terminals.

Other Tools You May Need

Some of the tools you'll need, you may already have. Others will make the job easier. Here are some of the tools to consider:

Utility Knife. A sharp utility knife will come in handy for cutting through all sorts of material, from drywall to plastic cable sheathing.

Claw Hammer. Carpenters aren't the only ones who need to drive nails. Electrical work sometimes demands a good hammer—to drive in staples or the nails that attach junction boxes into studs, among other reasons.

Four-way Screwdriver. A four-way screwdriver will handle all the screws you are likely to come across when installing electrical fixtures.

Tool Pouch. Many companies make tool pouches especially for electrical work. They feature a holder designed to hold a roll of electrical tape.

Drill and Auger. When running new cables, you'll have to drill a lot of holes through various parts of your house. A heavy-duty drill (½ inch) and a self-feeding power auger will make this task much easier.

Fish Tape. Similar in appearance to a tape measure, a fish tape is used to pull or "fish" wires through walls, ceilings, and other enclosed spaces.

Circuit Testing Techniques

Whether your intent is repair or extension, before you start working on electrical circuits, there are some basic tests you can do so you know what you're dealing with. At the very least, you should check the fixtures with a voltage tester to make sure that the power is off. Use your circuit map as a guide so you are sure to switch the proper breaker or pull the appropriate fuse. If the tester's light glows at any stage of your testing, it indicates you have a live wire. Stop working until you can figure out how to cut power to that wire.

Checking a Receptacle for Power

Start every job by turning off the power at the box. Then double-check that power is really off:

■ First, push the probes of the tester into the receptacle's vertical slots.

■ Then remove the cover and touch the probes to the two screw terminals on either side of the receptacle *(right)*. (On dual receptacles, check both pairs of terminals.)

■ Finally, touch one probe to the hot (black) wire and the other to the ground wire to guard against problems with the neutral side of the circuit.

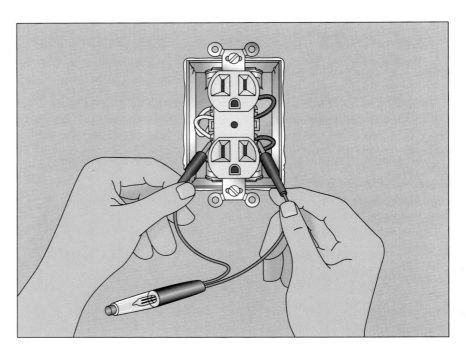

Checking a Light Fixture

With the power off and any wall switches turned off:

■ Detach the fixture from its box and gently pull it to allow you access to the wires.

■ Undo the wire nuts connecting the fixture to the household wiring.

■ Touch the probes to the ends of the black and white wires—the tester should not light *(right)*.

■ Check for voltage between the hot wire and the ground wire by touching them with the probes.

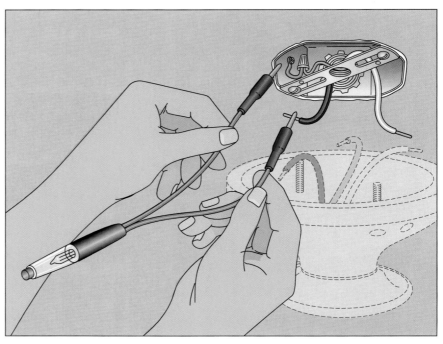

Checking a Switch for Power

Starting with the power off:

■ Remove the cover plate and detach the switch from its box.

■ Hold one probe in contact with the ground wire or electrical box, if it's metal *(right)*. Touch the other probe to the screw terminals on the switch, one at a time.

■ If the switch only has push-in terminals, insert the probe into the release slots.

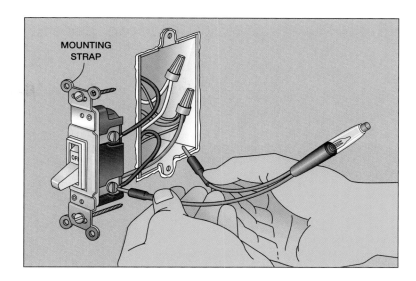

MOUNTING STRAP

Double-checking Receptacle Wiring

A quick way to make sure a receptacle is wired properly is with a receptacle analyzer. This handy tool will verify whether a receptacle is live, is properly grounded, and has the black and white wires attached to the appropriate terminals. To use the tool, plug it into a live receptacle. On most models, all the lights will glow if the receptacle is wired properly. Follow the key printed on the unit to determine what faults other combinations of lights indicate.

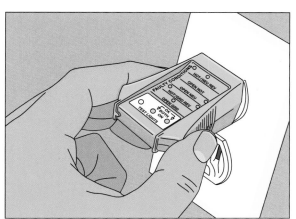

Finding the Feed Wire

Many times when you open an electrical box, you'll find it has two or more cables leading into it. One of these cables will be the one that comes from the service panel, while the other(s) lead to other fixtures farther along the circuit. You can determine which wire is the feed fairly easily with a voltage tester:

■ Turn off the power.

■ Pull the fixture out of the box and disconnect all the black wires. (Mark them with tape if you have trouble remembering where they go.)

■ Arrange the bare ends of the wires so they are not touching anything.

■ Have a helper turn on the power.

■ Hold the probes by touching only the insulated plastic grips.

■ Touch a probe to the ground wire or metal box and check each black wire in turn *(right)*. The one that allows the light on the tester to glow is the feed wire.

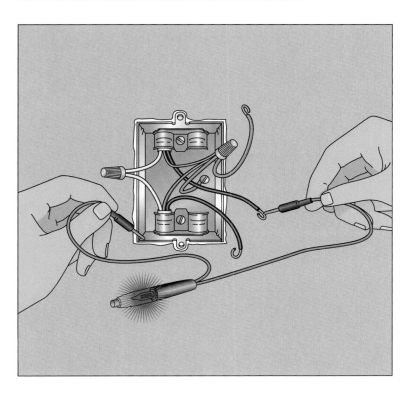

Basic Skills

*T*here are a few basic electrical skills common to almost every wiring project. These include stripping cable sheathing and wire insulation, joining wires together, and joining wires to screw terminals. These skills are not difficult to master, and you can learn them as you go along.

Follow the Rules.

Don't risk disaster. The key rule to follow when working with wire and cable is to avoid damaging the insulation that covers the metal conductors. Even the smallest nick can create a shock hazard and possibly cause a fire. If you accidentally cut through the insulation, replace the cable rather than risk disaster.

You should also be careful not to mangle the bare ends of the wires themselves. A few scars are unavoidable as you twist and shape the wires, but major damage can lead to trouble. Connections between badly marred wires don't conduct electricity especially well. This can lead to a buildup of heat, which can cause a fire.

Allow some slack. When running new electrical lines, allow an extra foot or three of cable between junction boxes, especially on long runs. This will provide you with some room for error. Should you accidentally nick a wire, you can cut off the damaged section and proceed without having to run a totally new cable. A couple of feet of cable isn't that expensive and won't affect the function of the circuit in the least.

No bare wires. When you are finished with your work, there should be no bare wire exposed (with the exception of the ground wire). This includes places where wires attach to receptacles and switches as well as places where two or more wires are twisted together. If you can see even a hint of bare metal away from the connection, undo the wires, trim the ends, and try again.

Clockwise hooks. When you attach wires underneath fixture screws, put a hook in the wire so that it will fit around the screw. When you attach the wire, position it so the hook goes clockwise around the screw. This assures that, as you tighten the screw, it will tighten the hook around the screw shank. Sounds like a small thing, but believe it or not, it's code.

1 Expose the wires in the cable.

To slit the sheathing of NM-B cable, slip the cable into a cable ripper until the tooth in the tool is about 10 to 12 inches from the end of the cable. Squeeze the ripper so the tooth penetrates the sheathing. (Try to keep the tooth in the center of the cable.) Pull on the cable with one hand and the ripper with the other, slitting the sheathing *(right)*.

Stripping UF cable isn't as easy as stripping NM-B because the sheathing is much thicker and is formed around the wires. Start by cutting a 2-inch slit along the ground wire. Then grasp the ground wire with a pair of long-nosed pliers and the end of the cable with lineman's pliers. Pull on the ground wire, splitting the sheathing for 10 to 12 inches. Repeat the process to free the other conductors.

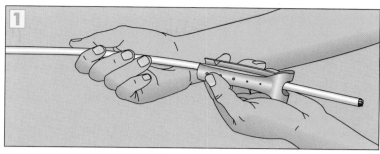

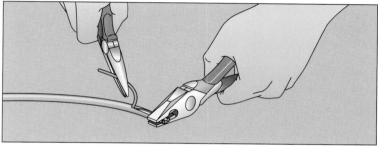

2 Remove the excess sheathing.

For both NM-B and UF cable, pull the excess sheathing back away from the exposed wires. (With NM-B cable, also peel back the paper that surrounds the ground wire.) Cut the sheathing with a utility knife or tin snips *(right)*.

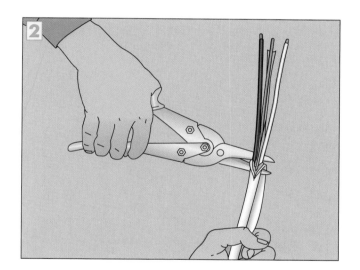

3 Strip the insulation.

Slip the wire through the appropriate size hole in your multipurpose tool or wire stripper. If you are not sure which hole to use, look closely at the tool. The wire gauge sizes should be stamped next to the holes. Then check the wire gauge on the cable—it should be embossed on the sheathing.

Close the multipurpose tool ½ to ¾ inch from the end of the wire and give it a quarter turn in each direction. This will cut the insulation cleanly.

Without opening the tool, pull the wire through the tool, removing the insulation *(right)*.

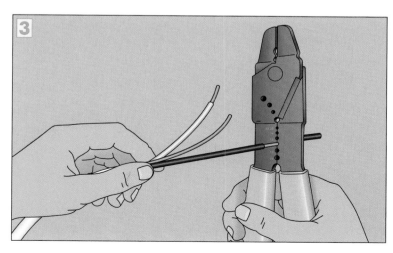

Connecting Two (or More) Solid Wires

- Strip an inch of insulation off each wire to be connected.
- Hold the wires side by side and grab the ends with lineman's pliers. Twist them together clockwise, as viewed from the pliers' perspective *(upper right)*.
- Clip the twisted connection to leave about ¾inch of bare wire exposed *(lower left)*.
- Twist a wire nut on to the connection to cover the bare wire *(lower right)*. No bare wire should be left exposed.

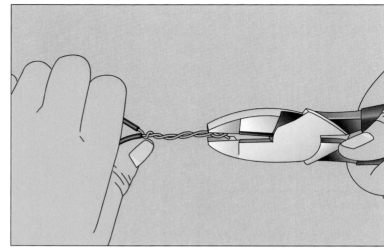

Wire nuts are cone-shaped, plastic connectors made to twist over a wire connection, locking it together and covering the bare ends of the wire. They come in various colors, which represent different sizes. Which size to use depends on the quantity and size of the wires involved. Check the box when you purchase the nuts—it should tell you what size wires the nuts are made to cover. Keep a variety of sizes on hand so you'll have the right size when you need it.

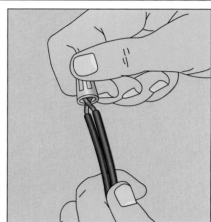

Joining Stranded Wire to Solid Wire

Joining stranded wire to solid wire is tough because the stranded wire tends to slip loose. The method shown here should make a good, solid connection.

- Strip an inch of insulation from each wire.
- Twist the stranded wire around the solid wire with lineman's pliers *(upper right)*.
- Bend the connection in half and squeeze it flat with the pliers *(lower right)*.
- Twist on a wire nut of the appropriate size, leaving no bare wire exposed.

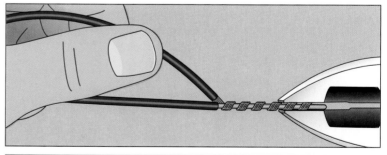

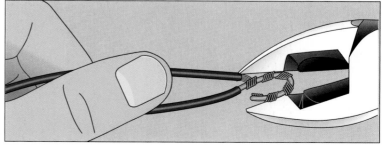

Connecting Ground Wires

Wire nuts make fast, solid connections. But occasionally you'll end up in a situation where you have to join more ground wires than a wire nut can handle. In this situation you can use a piece of hardware called a crimping barrel. This round bit of copper tubing slips over a twisted bundle of ground wires and is squashed (or crimped) into place with a squeeze from your lineman's pliers.

There are three other things to note about connecting ground wires:

■ The code requires them to be joined with some sort of connec-

tor. Simply twisting them together isn't enough.

■ Crimping barrels only work with bare ground wires, not ground wires with green insulation.

■ In addition to connecting the ground wires to each other, you also need to attach them to the fixtures (receptacles, switches, etc.) and metal junction boxes, using an extra wire, called a jumper. Most fixtures have a ground terminal. The connection to the box should be made with a green grounding screw.

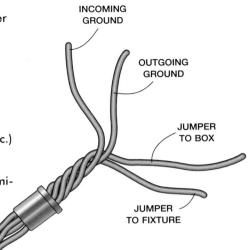

INCOMING GROUND

OUTGOING GROUND

JUMPER TO BOX

JUMPER TO FIXTURE

Electrical Fixture Connections

For the best possible connection between wires and fixtures use the screw terminals connected to the fixtures. While they take longer to hook up, this kind of junction is better than a push-in connection because it allows more metal to metal contact between the wire and the fixture. More metal to metal contact means the fixture will stay cooler, especially if you're using an appliance that draws close to the maximum amount of current.

Push-in connections are legal, and they are fast to connect. However, many professional electricians consider using them a sign of lesser quality work.

Screw Terminals

■ Form a hook in the end of the wire with long-nosed pliers.

■ Loosen the screw and slip the hook under it. The hook should wrap clockwise around the screw so as you tighten the screw, it will also tighten the wire.

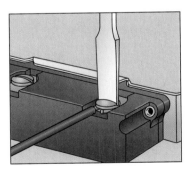

■ Pinch the hook into a loop around the screw with your pliers.

■ Tighten the screw down on the wire (above). Check to make sure the insulation runs right up to the terminal.

■ On fixtures such as receptacles where both the black and white wires connect to terminals, the terminals are usually color coded—the black wires attach to the brass terminals, and the white wires connect to the silver terminals.

Push-In Terminals

■ Strip the insulation from the wire. There should be a gauge on the fixture showing how long the bare conductor should be.

■ Push the bare end of the wire into the terminal as far as it will go (below). There should be no bare wire exposed.

■ If you need to release a wire from a push-in terminal, use a small screwdriver to push in the release button.

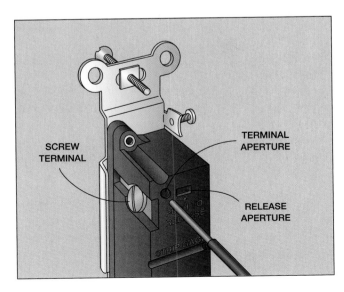

SCREW TERMINAL

TERMINAL APERTURE

RELEASE APERTURE

Rough Wiring

6

To people unfamiliar with the construction process, the term "rough wiring" might be misleading. Unlike the rough draft of a letter, which will get rewritten into a final copy, the wires placed during the process of rough wiring are there to stay. Rough wiring is the process of putting in the junction boxes and wires that connect to switches, lights, and outlets. In new construction, rough wiring or "roughing in" occurs when the walls are still open, so it is easy to route the wires where they are supposed to go.

During remodeling, rough wiring still involves running wire, but it is more complicated because the drywall is usually in place, and you'll have to cut—and patch—holes in walls and ceilings to gain access for wiring.

Adding and Extending Circuits

When adding to your house's electrical system, one of the first things to decide is how you are going to tie the new wiring into the existing system. If you are adding a new light or two or just a couple of new receptacles, you can probably extend an existing circuit—a relatively easy task. However, if your project is fairly extensive, involving a number of new receptacles and lighting fixtures, it is better to add a whole new circuit, starting right from the service panel. This is more difficult, but not impossible. Probably the best approach here is to do all the wiring except actually connecting the new circuit to the service panel. When everything else is ready, hire a licensed electrician to check your work and make the final hookup.

The Basic Process

Regardless of how you choose to tie in the new circuit, the overall process is the same:

- Plan where the receptacles, switches, and other fixtures will go.
- Cut holes for the new boxes.
- Run the cables.
- Attach the new boxes.
- Install the fixtures.
- Attach to power.
- Patch any access holes.
- Keep in mind your local building inspector may want to check your work at various stages along the way.

Planning Your Project

Take out the circuit map you drew when you were investigating your electrical system (see page 83). Draw in the new receptacles, switches, and light fixtures. Look to see where you might be able to tie into the existing wiring. Calculate the load on that circuit and add in the additional load from the fixtures you'll be installing (see page 84). If this new calculated load exceeds the circuit capacity, look for a different circuit to tap into. If you can't find a nearby circuit with enough free capacity, you'll have to run a new line from the service panel (and add an additional breaker or fuse).

Once you have decided where to get power, use your circuit map to help you develop a more detailed diagram that shows the location of all studs and joists near where you want to add junction boxes. This will help you plan the route for the cables you'll be running. After planning the route, you can estimate how much cable you'll need to purchase.

To estimate how much cable to buy, measure the distance from box to box. Add in 10 inches of cable for each box and an additional 20 percent to give yourself some wiggle room, in case things don't go exactly as planned. For example, if the boxes were 10 feet apart, you'd need 10 feet (120 inches) of cable plus 20 inches (10 inches for each box), for a total of 11 feet, 8 inches of cable (140 inches) plus 20 percent (28 inches), for a grand total of 14 feet (168 inches). Be sure to buy cable with wire that is the appropriate gauge for the circuit and has the right number of conductors.

Finding a Source of Power

When you start searching for a source of power for your new wiring, take a peek inside any nearby electrical boxes. (Turn off the power first, of course.) A close inspection of the way the fixtures are wired will tell you whether the box is a good place to connect or not. Boxes containing receptacles are almost always a good place to tap into new wires, as long as a switch does not control the receptacles. Fixture boxes that are not controlled from a separate switch are another good place to tap into existing wires. Avoid fixture boxes that are controlled by a separate switch—these will only supply power when the switch is on.

To double-check your choice, detach the fixture from the box and pull it out to expose the terminals. Turn the power back on and touch the probes of your voltage tester to the white and black wires/terminals. It should glow to indicate there is electricity flowing to the fixture.

Switch boxes can also be good places to connect, provided the switch falls in the middle of a run. (There will be two cables running to the switch, one coming in, the other going out.) End-of-the-run switches, where one cable with both wires is connected to the switch, are not good places to connect because there is no true neutral line in this type of installation and the switch would control your new circuit.

One final thing to check is whether there is room in the box to make the necessary connections. (Check the chart on page 105.) If necessary, install a bigger box or gang another one alongside to create the necessary space. Ganging is an electrician's term for coupling one box to another. Many electrical boxes have removable sides so you can expand them to suit.

Tying into Existing Boxes

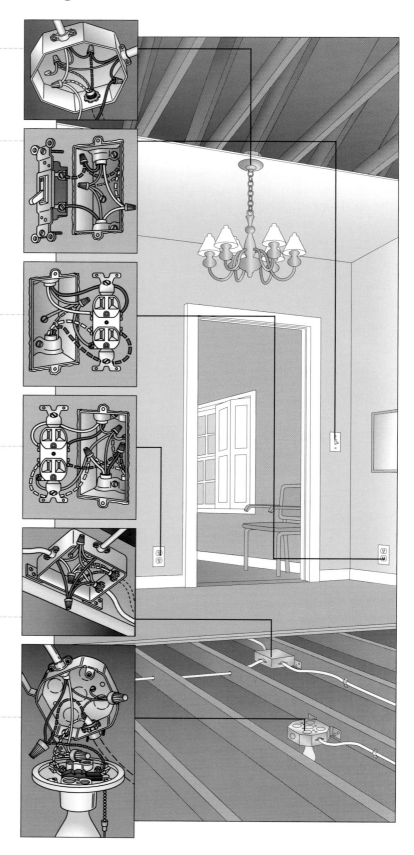

Middle-of-the-Run Ceiling Box

Connect the new black, white, and ground wires (dashed lines) to the corresponding wires that run to the box from the service panel.

Middle-of-the-Run Switch

Detach the incoming black wire from the switch. (Use a voltage tester if you aren't sure which is the incoming wire. The incoming wire will still be live when the switch is off.) Connect the new black wire and a new jumper wire (dashed lines) to the incoming black. Attach the jumper wire to the switch and attach the new white and ground wires to their existing counterparts.

End-of-the-Run Receptacle

Connect the new black and white wires (dashed lines in inset drawing) to the unused terminals on the receptacle. Connect the ground to the existing ground. Make sure the existing ground is also connected to the receptacle and to the box (if the box is metal).

Middle-of-the-Run Receptacle

Remove one set of black and white wires from the receptacle terminals. Attach them to the new black and white wires (dashed lines) and a new pair of black and white jumper wires. Attach the new jumper wires to the receptacle terminals. Attach the new ground wire to the existing ground wires. Make sure the ground wires are attached to both the receptacle and the box.

Junction Box

Attach the new black and white wires (dashed lines in inset drawing) to the corresponding wires in the box.

End-of-the-Run Pull-Chain Light Fixture

Disconnect the existing black and white wires. Attach them to the new black and white wires (dashed lines) along with a new set of black and white jumper wires. Attach the jumper wires to the terminals on the fixture. Connect the existing ground and the new ground along with a jumper. Attach the jumper to the ground screw in the box.

Choosing and Locating New Boxes

Electrical boxes are a key part of any wiring project. Not only do they provide support for fixtures such as switches and receptacles, but code requires that any connection between two or more wires occur inside a box. (Code also requires that the box be accessible so you can get at the wires if necessary.)

When you go to the hardware store, you may be faced with a bewildering array of box shapes and sizes. To help sort them out, keep in mind that boxes are made to standard shapes and sizes. Those that are destined to hold receptacles, switches, and wall-mounted light fixtures are almost always rectangular. Those meant for ceiling fixtures are octagonal or round. Junction boxes, where two or more cables join, are square.

The other choice you will be faced with is between metal and plastic. Both materials are perfectly acceptable. Plastic is less expensive than metal and installs quickly in new construction. Metal is probably the better choice when expanding a system with metal boxes or when working with armored (BX) cable or thin-wall conduit.

What Size Box to Use

As you are deciding which type of boxes to use in your project, keep in mind that the size of the box limits the number of connections that can be made within. The following chart, based on the NEC, will help you determine what size boxes to use depending on the number of wires that you'll be running. It can also help you determine whether you have room in an existing box to tie in a new cable, or whether you'll have to replace the box or add an extension to accommodate the new wires.

To use the chart, start by determining the gauge of the wire you'll be using. Heavier wires take up more space; therefore, you can fit fewer of them in a given box. Then calculate how many connections have to occur in each box. The term "connection" doesn't necessarily mean what you might think it does in this situation. The NEC counts connections like this:

- Each individual wire that enters the box counts as one connection; ignore jumper wires and ground wires for now.
- Add one connection for all the ground wires in the box.
- Add one connection if the box contains a light fixture stud.
- Add one connection if the box contains any internal clamps (metal boxes only). Two-part clamps do not count, nor do clamps in plastic boxes.
- Add one connection for each switch or duplex receptacle in the box.

After you calculate the total number of connections, find where it falls on the chart under the proper wire gauge column. From there you can find the appropriate box size.

For example, if you want to wire a new series of receptacles, the first box will have two cables entering it for a total of four connections (2 wires per cable, 1 connection per wire). Add another connection for the ground wires plus one for the internal clamps in the box and one for the receptacle itself. This gives you a total of seven connections. If you are using 14-gauge wire, you'll need a box that is 2¾ inches deep.

Selecting Appropriately Sized Boxes

	Box Depth (in inches)	Maximum Number of Connections		
		14-ga. Wire	12-ga. Wire	10-ga. Wire
Wall Boxes	2½	6	5	5
	2¾	7	6	5
	3½	9	8	7
Ceiling Boxes	1¼	6	5	5
	1½	7	6	6
	2⅛	10	9	8
Junction Boxes	1¼	9	8	7
	1½	10	9	8

Wall Boxes

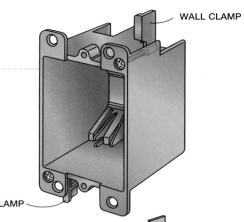

WALL CLAMP

Plastic Wall Box

This type of box will work in any type of existing wall. After an opening is cut in the wall, the box is slipped in place. With a twist of a screwdriver, built-in clamps at the top and bottom of the box rotate out and pull the box tight to the wall.

WALL CLAMP

Box with Ears and Brackets

For plaster walls with wooden lath, simply cut an opening and slip the box into place. The ears will keep it from falling through the hole. Screws driven through the ears into the lath will anchor the box securely in place. With drywall or plaster over metal lath walls, use the mounting brackets shown to anchor the box in place. More details about these brackets follow on page 123.

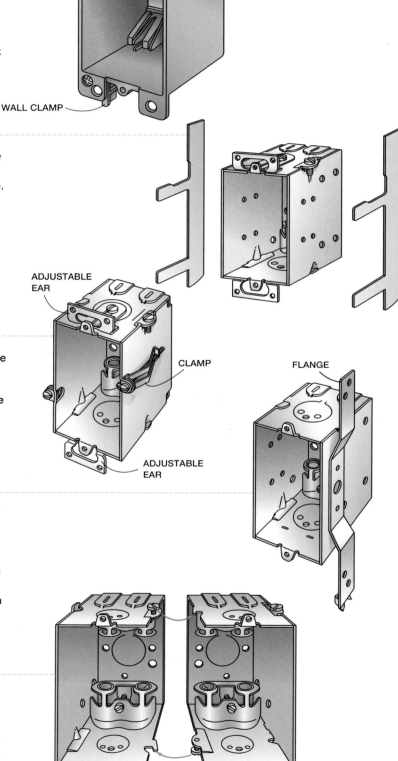

ADJUSTABLE EAR

CLAMP

FLANGE

ADJUSTABLE EAR

Box with Side Clamps and Ears

Here is yet another type of box designed to be placed in an existing wall. After the hole is cut, insert the box into the wall until the ears make contact. Then turn the screws to engage the clamps that will hold the box tight in the opening.

Box with a Flange

With new construction you have the option of installing the electric boxes before the wall surfaces go up. This means you can nail the boxes directly to the studs. Some metal boxes have built-in flanges for this purpose. Position the box with the front edge about ½ inch in front of the edge of the stud so it will be flush with the surface of the drywall.

Ganged Wall Box

When you need space in a wall box for more switches, you can gang two or more boxes together. Remove the right side from one box and the left side from the other. Hook the two boxes together and fasten them with the original screws.

Ceiling Boxes

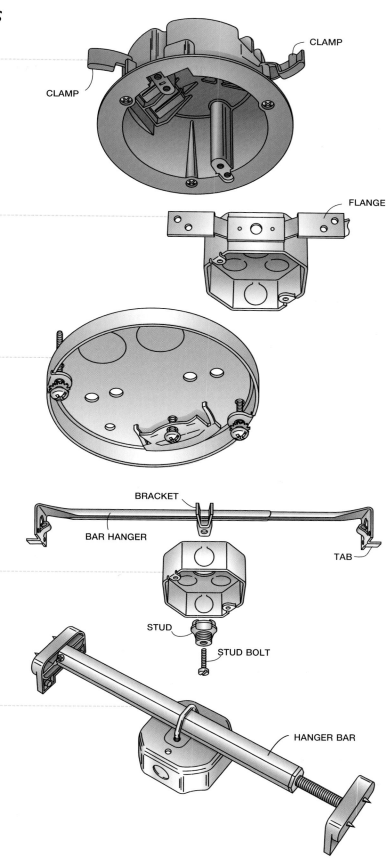

Plastic Ceiling Box

Designed to hold ceiling fixtures weighing five pounds or less, this style of ceiling box is supported directly by the drywall. Cut a hole in the ceiling that is ⅜ inch less in diameter than the outer rim of the box. Push the box through the hole, then turn the screws that engage the clamps. Tighten the clamps to lock the box in place.

CLAMP

CLAMP

Box with a Flange

Like the flanged wall box on page 106, this box is best installed in new construction where you still have access to the framing. It can support up to 30 pounds of weight. Screw the flange to a joist with the rim of the box hanging down to match the thickness of the finished ceiling.

FLANGE

Pancake Box

Flat boxes are too shallow for connecting wires unless the attached fixture has a domed cover built into it. These boxes are usually screwed directly to the joists—often for hanging ceiling fans. (Check with your local code officer to see what type of support the local code calls for.) To mount a pancake box, find a joist with a stud finder. Position the box where you want it along the joist. Trace around the box, then cut away the drywall with a utility knife, exposing the joist. Screw the box directly to the joist in the hole you just created.

BRACKET

BAR HANGER

TAB

STUD

STUD BOLT

Box with an Extendable Hanger

This setup is designed to support a heavy load (such as a ceiling fan) between joists. Install the box on the bar first. Then position the bar between the joists where you want it. The flanges on either end will help keep the bar level. Screw the bar to the joists.

A Screw-type Bar Hanger

Like its cousin above, the screw-type bar hanger is designed to hold a heavy load (50 pounds). It can be installed in an existing ceiling without having to cut more than the hole for the octagonal box itself. Cut the hole, then slip the hanger up into the ceiling. Position the hanger so it is perpendicular to the joists. Slowly twist the barrel of the hanger until its ends bite into the joists.

HANGER BAR

Cutting Box Holes in Wood or Drywall

1 Make a stencil.

Place the box open-side down on a piece of heavy paper.

Trace the outline of the box on the paper *(right)*. Be sure to include all the various nubs that protrude from the box except the ears that will keep it from falling into the wall.

Cut out the shape with a utility knife to make a stencil. Mark the face of the stencil (the side you drew on) with an X.

Hold the marked side of the stencil against the wall where you want the box and trace the opening onto the wall.

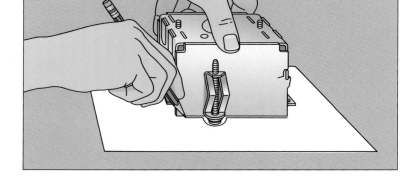

2 Cut the opening.

Drill eight holes around the outline with a ⅜-inch spade bit *(right)*. Cut around the outline with a drywall saw (for walls clad with drywall) or with a keyhole saw (if the wall is made of wood or plaster on lath). Push gently so you don't accidentally damage the drywall or plaster on the other side.

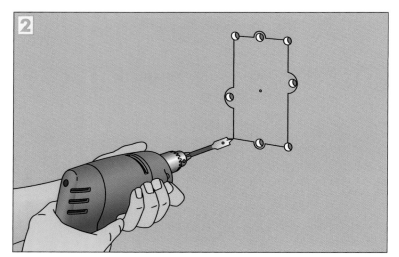

CAUTION! *Walls built before 1978 may contain lead paint or asbestos. Consult your health department for ways to protect yourself and family from the dust created by remodeling.*

Self-patching Holes

When running new wires in an older house you'll often have to cut a small hole in a wall just to gain access to the inside of the wall cavity. In these situations, cut the drywall in such a way that it becomes its own patch.

Instead of cutting straight through the wall, make the cuts at an angle (right), with the saw handle tipped away from the layout line. These beveled edges will keep the plug from falling into the hole when you replace it. When you are ready to fix the hole, butter the edges of the patch with joint compound and press it into place. Then tape over the cuts and trowel a thin coat of joint compound over the whole mess. When the compound dries, sand the area and apply a second coat, if necessary.

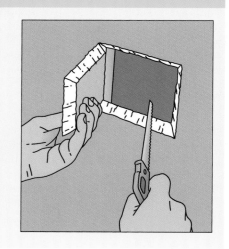

1 Expose a lath.

Mark the approximate center of the opening for the box on the wall. Chip away the plaster at this mark with a cold chisel and a ball-peen hammer to expose the lath underneath *(right)*.

Plaster over lath is fragile. Strike with short, sharp blows, and hold the chisel at an angle, as shown, to avoid damage.

Carefully enlarge the hole until you find the top and bottom of a single lath strip.

Mark the center of this strip.

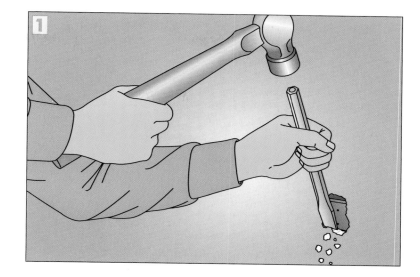

2 Lay out the hole.

Make a stencil to match the box you are installing (page 108). Do not use a box with side clamps.

Cut a hole in the center on the stencil. Align this hole with the mark you made on the lath.

Trace the stencil to lay out the box outline on the wall *(right)*.

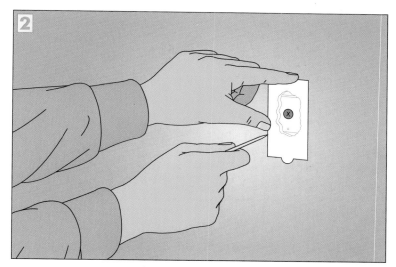

3 Cut the hole.

Adhere masking tape to the wall above the layout lines. This will help keep the plaster from chipping as you cut.

Score the layout lines heavily with a utility knife. Drill six ⅜-inch holes around the outline—one at each corner and one at the midpoint of the top and bottom lines.

Cut along the lines with a drywall saw *(right)*. Don't apply a lot of downward pressure on the saw; try to make your strokes smoothly. Heavy, jerky movements can cause the plaster to crack.

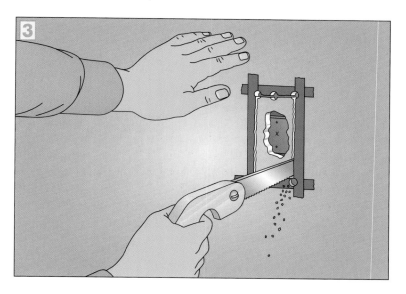

Cutting Holes in Plaster on Metal Lath

1 Chip away the plaster.

Choose the location for the new box and lay out its outline on the wall with a stencil (page 108).

Tape along the layout lines with masking tape, then score the lines heavily with a utility knife.

Chip away at the plaster within the outline with a cold chisel and ball-peen hammer. Hold the chisel at an angle, as shown *(right)*, and strike with short, sharp blows to avoid accidentally enlarging the hole. Remove the plaster right down to the metal lath underneath.

CAUTION! *Walls built before 1978 may contain lead paint or asbestos. Consult your health department for ways to protect yourself and family from the dust created by remodeling.*

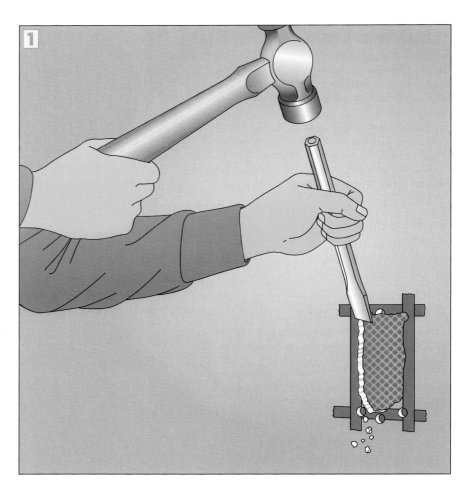

2 Cut away the lath.

Cut away the metal lath with a set of aviator's snips.

Try to cut as gently as possible. If you flex the lath, it may cause the surrounding plaster to crack and crumble.

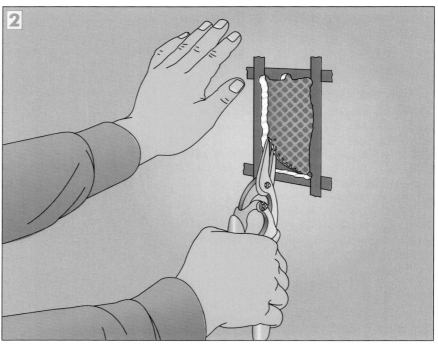

Cutting Box Holes in a Ceiling

1 Position the box.

Choose a location for the new box, checking with a stud locator to see that it is at least 4 inches away from any joists. Drill a 1/8-inch locator hole that goes just through the ceiling to mark the spot.

If you cannot see the ceiling from above, check for obstructions with a piece of coat hanger bent into an L-shaped section. Put it in the locator hole and turn it to find obstructions.

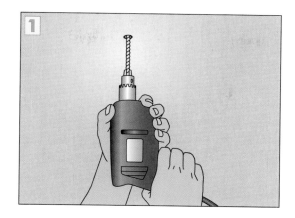

2 Bore guide holes.

Work from the attic, if possible. Center the box over the locator hole. Trace the box outline onto the surface of the ceiling below.

Drill a 3/8-inch hole at each of the outline's eight corners *(right)*. If you can't reach the ceiling from above, lay out the box and drill the holes from below.

3 Cut the hole from below.

For drywall ceilings, simply cut along the outline defined by the drilled holes with a drywall saw.

If the ceiling is plaster on wood lath, score the outline first with a utility knife. Then apply masking tape along the scored lines as shown.

Cut along the scored lines with a keyhole saw, bracing the plaster with a scrap of wood held close to the cut *(right)*.

For ceilings of plaster on metal lath, proceed as described for cutting holes in walls (page 110).

Running Cable to New Locations

Before you install your new electrical boxes, you'll have to run the new cable that will bring electricity to them. This involves snaking the cable through the structural framework of your house—along the joists and through the studs. As you plan the cable's path, choose a route that calls for the least amount of cutting and drilling through finished surfaces. Even if you end up using more cable than a direct route would require, a roundabout path that avoids damage to ceilings and walls will pay off when it comes to the labor involved in patching these surfaces.

An Advantageous Route

Whenever possible, run the cable through an unfinished basement or attic where the studs and joists are exposed or at least readily accessible. Here you can either staple the cable directly to the exposed framing, or drill holes and thread it through.

When running cable to a wall box in a finished room that is located just above the basement or below the attic, you can often gain access to the inside of the wall by drilling a hole through the plates at the top or bottom of the wall. If you have many holes like this to drill, it will pay to invest in a heavy-duty electric drill and a self-feeding bit. After

pushing the wire through the hole, use a fish tape (essentially a wire with a hook on the end) to pull the wire through to its final destination.

Opening Hidden Paths

To run cables through walls and ceilings that are not accessible from the basement or attic, you'll have to cut access holes into the cavities between the studs and joists along the intended route. Once you have access to the inside of the walls and ceilings, pull the cable through with fish tapes.

Code Requirements

The NEC provides a few general rules for running cable. Cable running along an exposed joist or stud must be supported (usually with staples) at intervals no greater than 4½ feet. Holes drilled for cables to pass through framing members must be a minimum of 1½ inches in from the edge, or the holes must be protected with a metal "kickplate" to protect the cable from nails and screws used to attach the wall surface. Exposed cable must be supported within 12 inches of a metal or plastic box with an internal clamp, or within 8 inches of a plastic box with no internal clamp.

Running Cable through an Attic

1 Drill down into the wall.

Drill a ⅛-inch locator hole up through the ceiling above the existing box you want to tap. Push a length of wire up through the hole to make it easier to find in the attic.

In the attic, drill a ¾-inch hole down through the wall plate into the wall below (*right*).

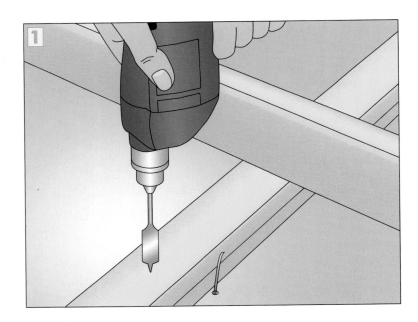

2 Fish the cable.

Turn off the power and detach the fixture from the existing box. Pull it out of the way—there is no need to unfasten the wires.

Punch a knockout slug from the top of the box with a hammer and a nail set.

Have a helper drop a lightweight chain down through the hole in the attic. (A chain works better than a fish tape in this situation.) Push a fish tape through the hole in the box, hook the chain, and pull it into the box *(right)*. You may want to protect your hands with gloves.

Tape the end of the fish tape securely to the chain, and then have your helper pull the fish tape up to the attic. Your helper should then attach the end of the cable to the fish tape, and pull the cable down to the box.

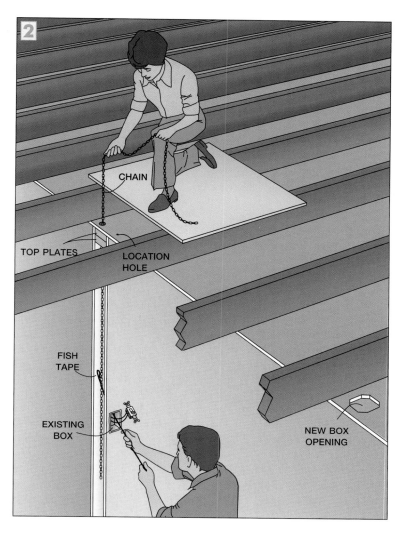

3 Notch a fire stop.

You may discover the chain can't be lowered all the way from the ceiling to the electric box. If you hit an obstruction, chances are it is a piece of framing called a fire stop. Fire stops help keep fires from spreading quickly. Without the stops, the stud bays can act like miniature chimneys, sucking the fire from one floor to another.

Measure the chain to see how far down the wall the blockage is.

Mark this distance on the wall; then remove a small piece of wallboard to uncover the stop.

Chisel a notch in the stop to allow the cable to pass *(right)*. After fishing the cable past the stop, cover the notch with a protective steel plate (often called a "kickplate"). Fill any gaps between the cable and fire stop with caulk to seal off the wall in the event of fire. Patch any holes in the wall.

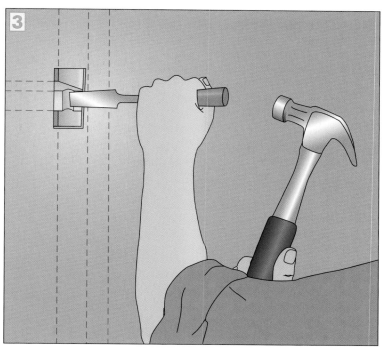

1 Access an existing box.

Bore a ⅛-inch hole through the floor directly in front of the box you plan to tap *(inset)*.

Poke a thin wire down through the hole, then go down into the basement and find this marker.

Drill a ¾-inch hole with a spade bit up into the wall adjacent to the marker. Drill at a slight angle if necessary *(right)*.

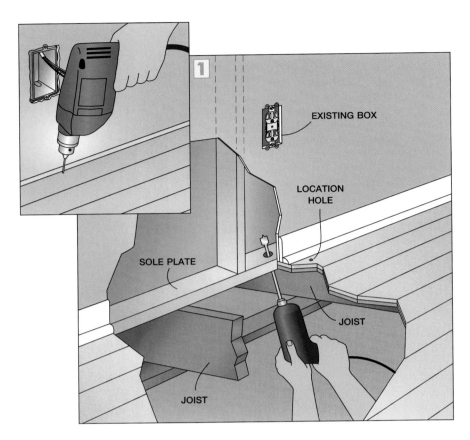

2 Fish a tape down into the basement.

Turn off the power. Unscrew the existing receptacle from the box and pull it out of the way. There is no need to disconnect the wires.

Use a hammer and a nail set to remove a knockout from the bottom of the box. (To make it easier to feed cables into metal boxes, they have removable pieces, called knockouts, in their backs, sides, tops, and bottoms.)

Feed the end of a fish tape down into the wall through the hole in the box.

Have a helper in the basement push another fish tape up into the wall through the hole you drilled. Manipulate the two tapes until they hook together. Pull the end of the upper tape down into the basement *(right)*.

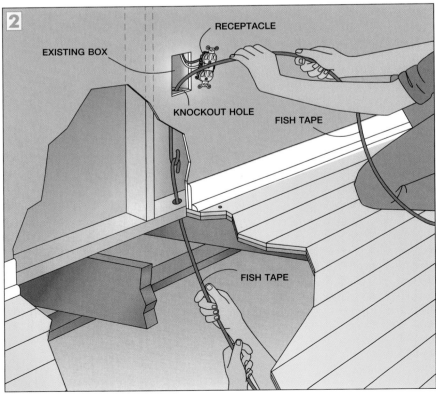

3 Pull the cable up to the box.

Strip about 3 inches of sheathing from the end of the cable. Hook the wires through the end of the fish tape *(inset)* and bend them over so they stay put—add a turn of electrical tape as added ensurance.

Pull the cable up into the box. You may need to have your helper feed the cable from below as you pull *(right)*.

Leave about 10 inches of cable projecting from the box.

4 Secure the cable.

Run the cable across the basement ceiling. Ideally you can run it along one of the joists, stapling it in place every 3 or 4 feet. (Be careful not to damage the sheathing as you drive the staples.)

If you have to run the cable across the joists, drill ¾-inch holes at least 1½ inches in from the edge and pull the cable through *(inset)*.

When you reach the place where you want the new box, repeat the process to pull the cable up into the wall *(below)*.

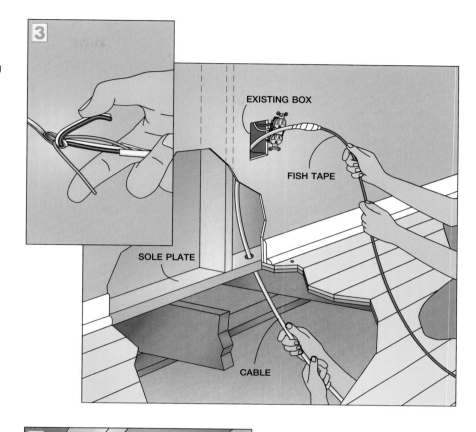

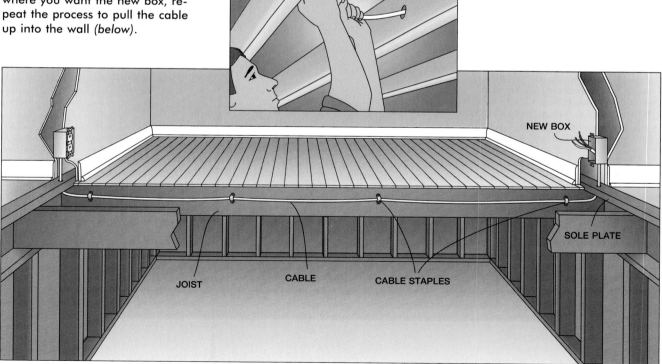

Running Cable within a Wall

1 Expose the studs.

Locate and cut an opening for your new box.

Use a stud locator to find the studs between the new box and the existing box you want to tap into. Mark the locations on the wall.

Cut away the wall surface to expose the studs (*right*). Make the holes 3 inches tall and wide enough to extend 2 inches on either side of the studs.

Drill a ¾-inch hole through each stud. Position the hole so there's at least 1½ inches between it and the back wall. (If the space is smaller, you run the risk of driving a nail through it by accident.) Drill at a slight angle if necessary.

STUD HOLES

NEW BOX OPENING

EXISTING HOLES

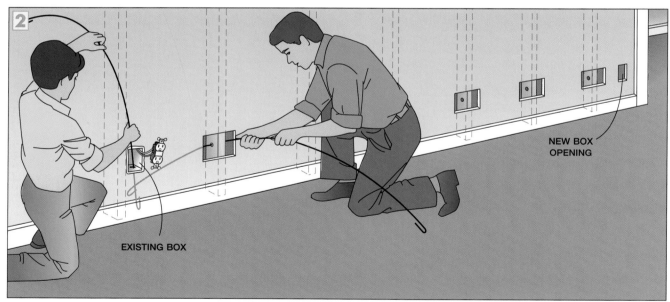

EXISTING BOX

NEW BOX OPENING

2 Thread the cable through the studs.

Turn off the power. Detach the existing fixture from its box and push it out of the way—no need to detach the wires.

Punch a knockout slug from the box with a hammer and a nail set.

Thread a fish tape into the wall through the hole in the box. Have a helper snare this tape with a second fish tape, as shown (*above*).

Work your way along the wall, until the first tape stretches from the existing box to the hole for the new box.

Attach the cable to the tape securely and pull the cable from the new opening back to the existing box. You may want to have a helper feed the cable as you pull it.

Hiding Cable behind a Baseboard

1 Pry off the baseboard.

If you have baseboards that are more than 2½ inches tall, you may be able to hide a new cable behind them. This can cut down on the patch work later.

Begin by cutting through any caulk between the baseboard and the wall or floor with a sharp knife. Then drive a thin pry bar between it and the floor. Use a slip of cardboard to keep from marring the floor.

Drive the bar down between the baseboard and the wall to free the molding (right). Use a wooden shim to protect the wall from the bar.

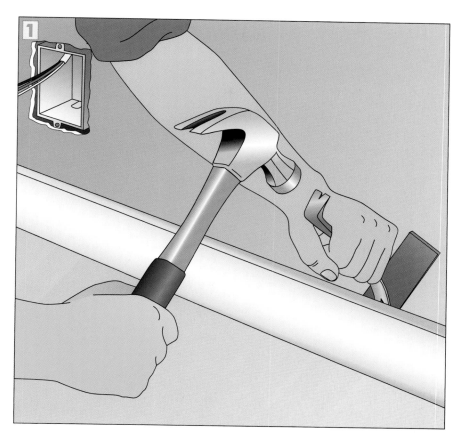

2 Cut the channel.

Start the channel by making a cut in the wall surface 1½ inches above the floor. Make a second cut about 1 to 1½ inches above the first cut, but below the top of the baseboard (right).

Remove the wall surface between the two cuts, then drill ¾-inch holes through the center of each stud.

Run the cable through the holes and fish it into the various boxes as described on page 116.

Nail metal kickplates over the notches in the studs to protect the cable from nails you may drive later. Fire code requires you to fill the channel with drywall, and then caulk the cracks to seal them. Replace the baseboard when you are finished.

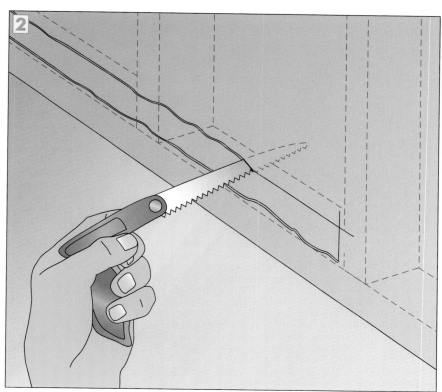

Feeding a New Ceiling Box

1 Make access holes.

Cut an opening for the new box between two joists.

Follow the joists over to the wall where you will run the new cable. Cut a 1½-inch wide by 4-inch-long access hole in the ceiling between the joists where the ceiling meets the wall. Also cut a 1½-inch-wide by 6-inch-wide opening at the top of the wall, exposing the wall's top plates.

Notch the plates by cutting them with a keyhole saw and chiseling away the waste *(right)*. The notch should be about ¾ inch wide and ½ inch deep.

Use a stud locator to find any fire stops blocking the stud bay. Cut through the wall surface and drill a ¾-inch hole through the stop to allow the cable to pass.

Cut access holes around any studs you'll have to pass through horizontally to gain access to an existing box.

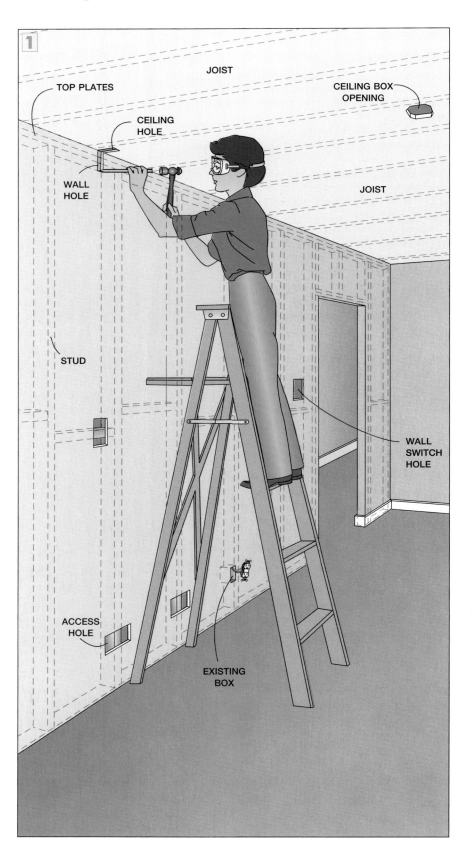

JOIST

TOP PLATES

CEILING BOX OPENING

CEILING HOLE

WALL HOLE

JOIST

STUD

WALL SWITCH HOLE

ACCESS HOLE

EXISTING BOX

2 Fish the cable to ceiling level.

Have a helper feed a fish tape up through the wall from the lowest access hole *(right)*. (If the existing box happens to be directly below the notch in the top plate, run the fish tape through a knockout hole in the box.)

Insert a second fish tape into the wall from the access hole at ceiling level. Hook the first tape and pull it through the upper access hole.

Attach one end of the cable to the first fish tape and pull it down through the wall and out the lower access hole. If you have to run the cable horizontally from this point, pull enough cable down to make this horizontal run.

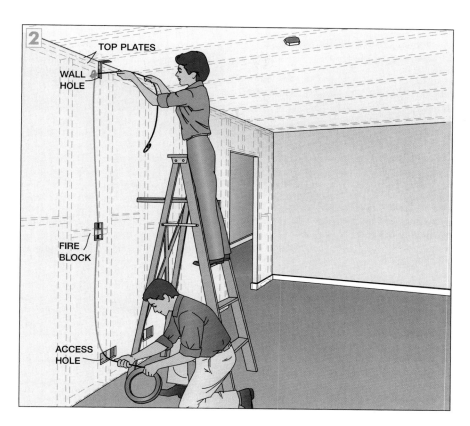

3 Fish the cable across the ceiling.

Have a helper run a fish tape from the opening for the ceiling box to the access hole you cut at the top of the wall.

Use a second tape to catch the end of the first and pull it into the room.

Attach the end of the cable to your helper's tape. Feed the cable into the opening as your helper pulls the tape (and the attached cable) back to the ceiling opening *(right)*.

Staple the cable in place in the notch cut in the top plate. Be careful not to damage the cable sheathing as you hammer.

Nail a steel protection plate over the notch to protect the cable from errant nails and screws. Fill any gaps between the cable and fire stop with caulk to seal off the wall in the event of fire. Patch any holes in the wall.

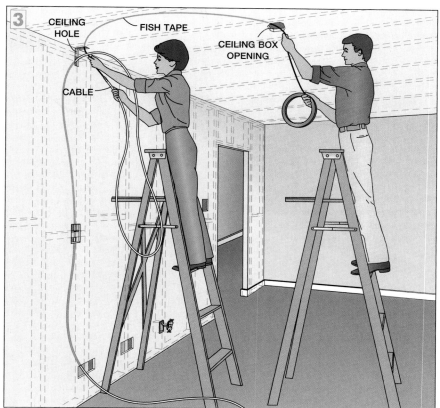

Another Way to Access a Ceiling

1 Fish the cable across the ceiling.

Cut an opening for the new ceiling box between two joists. Mark the top of the adjacent wall midway between the two joists.

Transfer the marked point to the opposite side of the wall by measuring out from a corner or doorway.

In the adjoining room, use a stud locator to find the bottom edge of the wall plate. Just below the plate and centered between the joists, cut an access hole 2 inches tall and 1 inch wide.

Drill a ¾-inch hole up through the plates, angling the bit toward the new ceiling box opening.

Feed a fish tape up through the new hole and over to the new box opening.

Secure the end of the cable to the fish tape, then pull the tape and cable across the ceiling and through the hole in the plate *(right)*.

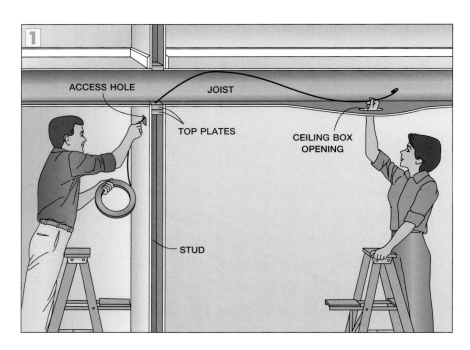

2 Fish the cable to the wall box.

In the room being wired, make a path for the new wire to connect to an existing box, cutting access holes as needed. You'll need at least one hole near the floor in the stud bay where the wire runs through the plate.

Have a helper feed a fish tape from the lower access hole to the upper one. Hook the end of the tape with a second tape and pull it out through the hole in the adjacent room.

Attach the end of the cable to the first tape and pull the cable down the wall to the lower opening. Finish running the cable to the existing box as described in *Step 2, Thread the cable through the studs,* on page 116.

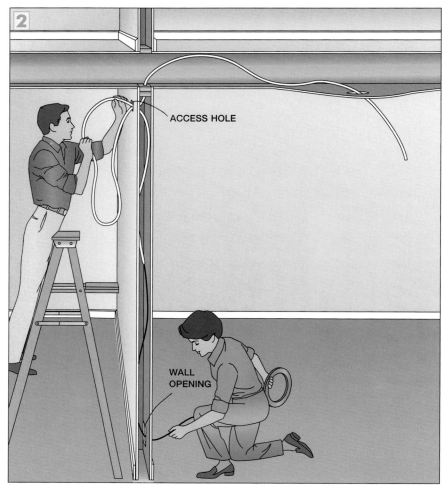

Installing New Boxes

The central element of any electrical installation is the outlet box. Boxes provide structural support for switches, receptacles, and lighting fixtures as well as protection for their wiring. When you go to purchase the boxes for your project, however, you may be slightly overwhelmed by the sheer number of choices that are available. There are a couple of things to look for that will help you make sense of the array.

Boxes for New Construction

Electrical boxes that are meant to be installed before the wall surfaces go up will have some means of fastening them directly to the studs or joists. Plastic boxes will often have nails already attached. Metal boxes for new construction will often include a nail-ing flange or other attachment point. When adding electrical boxes to new construction, the boxes often are installed before any cable is run.

Boxes for Existing Construction

Adding new electrical boxes to existing walls and ceilings is a little trickier. In order to provide adequate support for the contained fixture, the box must be securely attached to the wall or ceiling. But, without doing major damage to the wall or ceiling surface, it is nearly impossible to attach boxes directly to the framing. Instead, such boxes are usually supported by the wall surface itself. Boxes designed for this type of installation will have built-in flanges to keep them flush with the outer wall surface, and some sort of clamping mechanism to pin them to the wall.

Using Metal Boxes with Built-in Clamps

1 Remove the knockout.

A U-shaped knockout is the common choice for most wall boxes, although round knockouts are also prevalent.

To remove a U-shaped knockout, insert a screwdriver into the slot and pry the knockout loose *(right)*. Bend it back and forth until it breaks free.

To remove a round knockout, break one side free with a hammer and nail set, then twist the slug free with lineman's pliers.

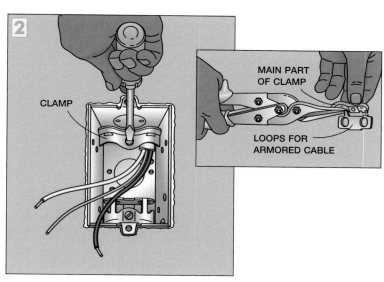

2 Clamp the cable.

Many wall boxes have built-in cable clamps. Some are made for securing both plastic-sheathed (NM-B) cable as well as armored (BX) cable. If you get this type and you're using NM-B cable, you'll need to cut away the part of the clamp intended to be used with BX cable *(inset)*.

Remove the clamp from the box and modify it, if necessary.

Screw the clamp loosely inside the box.

Cut about 8 to 10 inches of sheathing from the cable. Insert the cable into the box.

Tighten the clamp over the cable so that it squeezes down on the end of the sheathing *(right)*.

Attach the box to the wall.

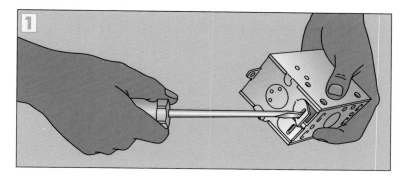

CLAMP

MAIN PART OF CLAMP

LOOPS FOR ARMORED CABLE

Using Built-in Clamps in Plastic Wall Boxes

How a Plastic Box Works

Plastic wall and ceiling boxes have built-in, flaplike clamps that tighten their grip on a cable in proportion to the amount of effort being made to pull the cable loose.

To install cable in one of these boxes:

■ Press on the clamp with a screwdriver to break one end of it free from the box.

■ Cut 8 to 10 inches of sheathing from the end of the cable.

■ Insert the cable into the box until the sheathing just shows inside. Press on the clamp from inside the box to ensure a good grip.

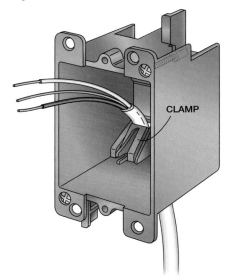

CLAMP

Using Cable Connectors in Metal Wall Boxes

1 Fasten the connector to the cable.

Cut 8 to 10 inches of sheathing from the end of the cable and strip the ends of the wires.

Slip the clamp part of the connector onto the cable, with the threaded portion facing the stripped wires.

Tighten the clamp in place so just a little sheathing shows past the end (right).

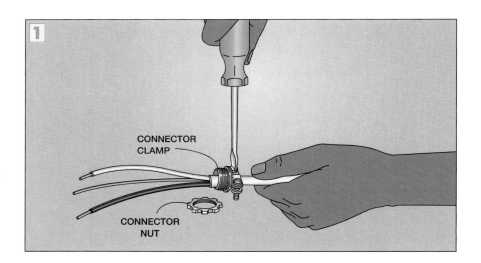

CONNECTOR CLAMP

CONNECTOR NUT

2 Fasten the connector to the box.

Insert the cable and connector through a knockout in the box.

Slip the nut over the wires and thread it onto the connector.

Fasten the box in place. Then tighten the nut by tapping one of its protrusions with a nail set (right).

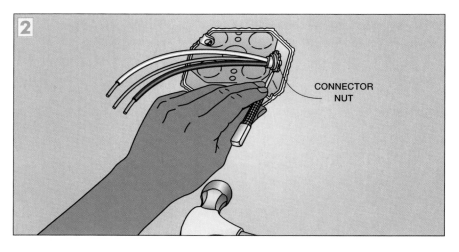

CONNECTOR NUT

Anchoring Boxes in Wood or Drywall

1 Clamp the box in place.

Ease the box and cable into the opening in the wall. Trim the opening if necessary for a good fit.

Adjust the ears on the box to make the front of the box flush with the surface of the wall.

Tighten the clamp screws on the box, expanding the clamps and drawing the box tight to the wall (*right*). Tighten just enough to hold the box snugly in place. Overtightening may break away part of the wall.

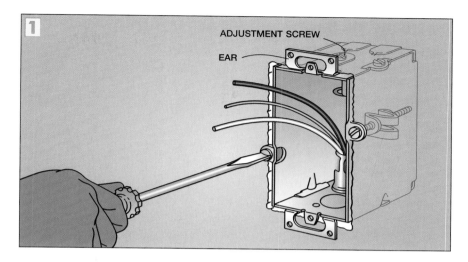

2 Hold the box with brackets.

Check the fit of the box in its opening as mentioned above. Adjust the ears to make the front of the box flush with the wall surface.

Hold the box in place and slip a bracket into the opening beside it. The longer end of the bracket is the top. Install it first, then install the bottom end (*right*).

Pull the bracket toward you, putting pressure against the inside of the wall. Fold the arms into the box to hold the box in place.

Repeat with a bracket on the other side of the box.

This process also works well with walls made of plaster over metal lath.

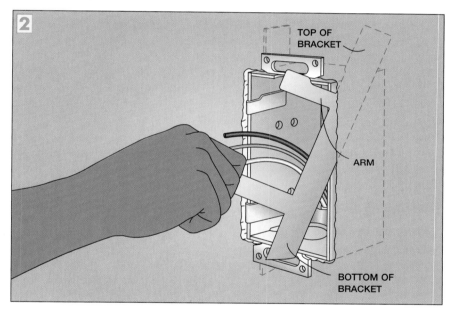

Fastening a Plastic Box

■ Fit the cable and box into the opening.

■ Tighten the clamp screws in the upper right and lower left corners of the box by turning them clockwise (*right*). This will engage the built-in clamps, which will hold the box in place.

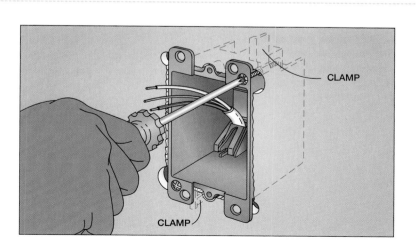

Anchoring Boxes in Plaster Walls

Installing the Box

- Hold the box in its opening and trace the outline of the ears on the plaster.
- Chisel away the plaster within the outlines to expose the underlying lath.
- Adjust the ears so the front of the box is flush with the wall surface when the ears are against the lath.
- Drill pilot holes in the lath, then fasten the box in place by screwing it through the ears *(right)*.

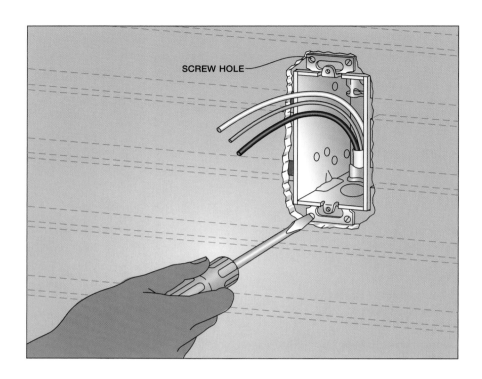

SCREW HOLE

Hanging a Ceiling Box from Above

Installing the Hanger

- Attach the box to the hanger bar.
- Drop the box into its hole. Have a helper hold it from below so the bottom edge is flush with the ceiling surface.
- Extend the hanger arms until they contact the joists on either side of the box. Screw the hanger arms in place. If you're driving the screws by hand *(right)*, make it easier by first drilling pilot holes where you want the screws to be. The pilot holes should be slightly smaller and shorter than the screws.

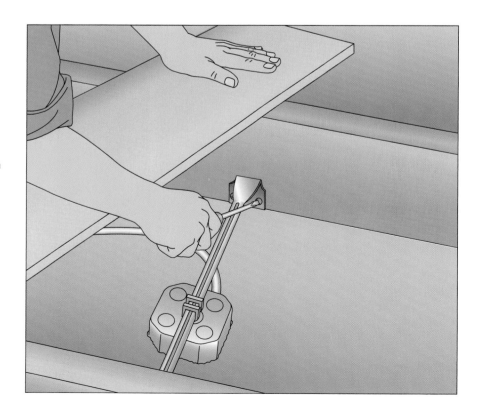

Installing a Ceiling Box from Below

1 Place the bar.

Slip the bar up into the ceiling through the opening you cut for the box.

Center the bar over the opening and extend it until it just contacts the joists on either side of the opening *(right)*. Make sure the bar is perpendicular to the joists.

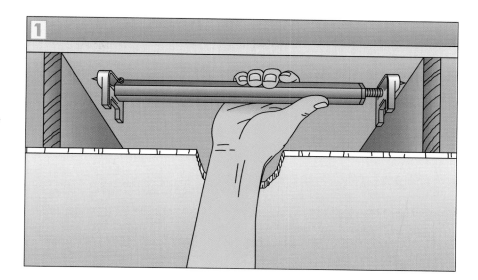

2 Tighten the bar.

Tighten the bar with an adjustable wrench until the ends bite into the joists *(right)*.

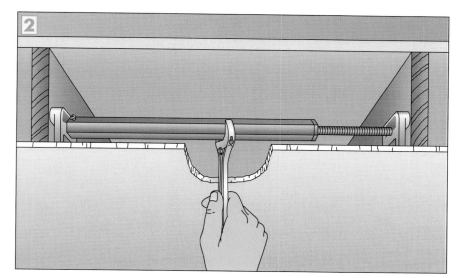

3 Add the box.

Connect the cable to the box before you put the box in the ceiling.

Hang the U-shaped bolt over the bar, and fasten the box to this bolt with lock washers and nuts.

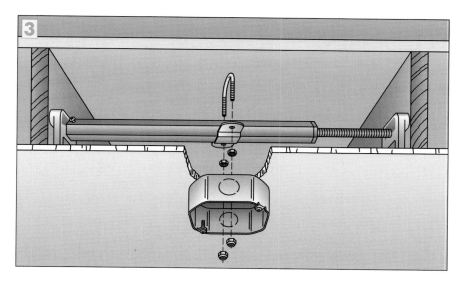

Patching Holes in Drywall and Plaster

Installing new wiring often leaves a series of holes in the walls and ceilings of your house. Fortunately, these holes are usually easy to patch.

The method to use depends on the size of the hole and the composition of the surface. Hide small test holes with Spackle or wood filler. Larger holes will require a little more effort. The methods shown on these two pages will take care of 95 percent of the holes that you are likely to make. The one main exception is a large hole in a plaster wall (18 inches or so across). Large expanses of plaster are quite tricky to apply and are best left to professionals.

Repairing Holes in Drywall

Cutting a Filler Piece

- Cut a piece of drywall about ⅛ inch smaller than the opening you want to patch.
- Screw the patch in place over the hole *(right)*.
- Put joint compound over the screwheads.
- Apply drywall tape and joint compound over the seam between the patch and wall. Let the compound dry. Apply a second coat to the seams and screwheads.
- When the second coat dries, apply a third coat. Let it dry, then sand with a drywall screen to remove irregularities.

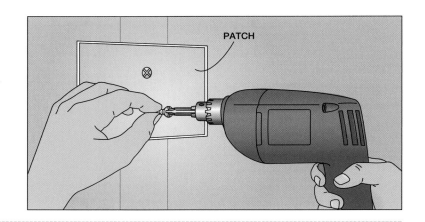

Extra Support for Large Holes

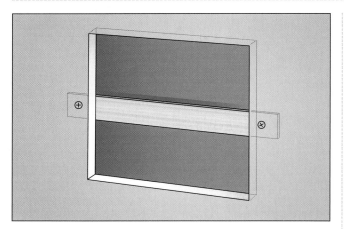

For large patches or patches without any framing nearby to attach the filler piece to, you can add your own support.

- Slip a length of wood into the opening, then screw it in place through the intact drywall surrounding the opening *(above)*.
- Insert the filler piece and screw it to the wood with drywall screws.

Patching with Drywall Clips

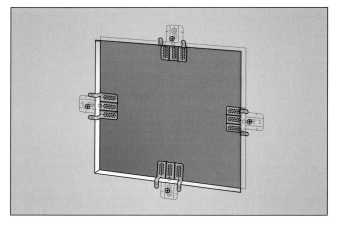

A relatively new way to hold drywall filler pieces is to use drywall clips along the edges to anchor the patch.

- Slide a clip onto each edge of the hole. Drive a drywall screw through the wall and into the portion of the clip behind it *(above)*.
- Cut the patch to fit and screw it to the clips. Tape the seams and apply compound over the seams and screws.

A Special Fix for Plaster

Supporting a Plaster Patch

- Cut a piece of metal window screen or hardware cloth 2 inches larger than the opening. Tie a length of string to the center of the screen.
- Reach inside the wall and spread plaster all around the opening.
- Hold the free ends of the string while you flex the screen and slide it into the opening.
- Pull the string to embed the screen in the plaster you just applied to the inside of the wall.
- Tie the string to a pencil and give the pencil a couple of twists to draw the screen tight.
- Moisten the edges of the hole and apply patching plaster to them *(right)*.
- Fill in the hole with more patching plaster.
- When the patch dries, sand it and apply a second layer if necessary.

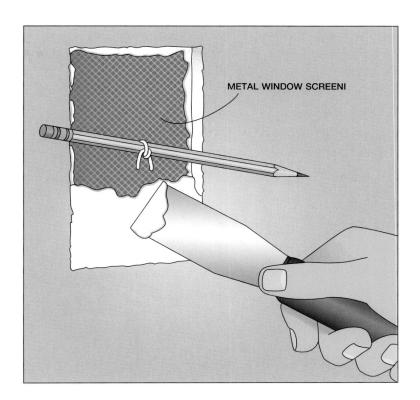

METAL WINDOW SCREEN|

Filling Gaps Next to an Electrical Box

A Steel Wool Backing

The NEC requires a space of less than ⅛ inch between the wall surface and the edge of an electrical box. If you end up with larger gaps, here's what to do:

- Pack a wad of steel wool into the gap between the box and the wall. Be careful that it doesn't fall into the wall *(right)*.
- Moisten the wall edge and apply patching plaster over the steel wool working in toward the center of the box. Stop about ⅛ inch from the edge of box and score the wet plaster with a series of lines. These lines will provide a second coat with something to grab onto.
- After the patch dries, fill the final ⅛-inch gap with some joint compound.
- After everything is dry, sand the patch to smooth and level it. Apply another coat if necessary.

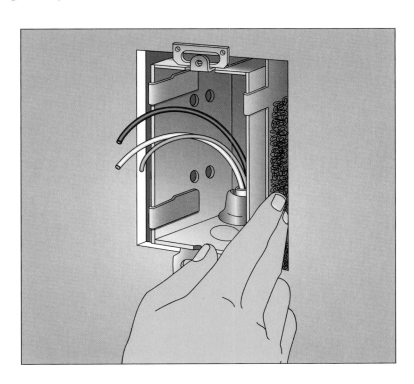

Finish Wiring

7

SWITCHES AND RECEPTACLES

*F*inish wiring is the second stage of wiring, the stage where you start attaching things to all those boxes and wires you ran during rough wiring. The process is simple—you're hooking wires to screws—but the details are important.

They seem like little things: Always ground the circuit properly. Interrupt the hot line with a switch, not the neutral line. Put the wire under a screw so that it wraps clockwise around the stem. It's easy to ignore details like these. But don't. The directions in this chapter make it just as easy to do things the right way. And each detail is there for one reason only—your safety.

Switches for New Circuits

*M*ost light fixtures and the occasional outlet are controlled by at least one switch. Its purpose is to interrupt the flow of current in the circuit's hot wire, enabling the user to turn a device on and off from some remote location. Note that the switch is wired into the hot side of the circuit—never the neutral side. This is a safety precaution. If the switch were in the neutral side of the circuit, the device would still be hot (and be, therefore, a potential shock hazard) even though it was "off."

Types of Switches

Most switches are variations of the four basic types shown on the following pages. By far the most common is the single-pole switch that performs basic on/off operations. Many specialized switches, such as timer or motion detector switches, are designed to replace a single-pole switch. Three- and four-way switches control a device from more than one location. Double-pole switches control devices that operate on 240 volts, cutting off power to both legs of a 240-volt circuit. (In a 240-volt circuit, both legs are hot.)

Switch Configuration

If you are adding on to an electrical system, you may need to be a little bit creative when it comes to fitting new switches into old boxes. As you are planning your project, it is worth a trip to your local home center or electrical supply house to see what is available. The wide variety of switch configurations available today will all accomplish more or less the same thing in different amounts of space. You can get double switches that will fit into a single box, switch-outlet combinations, and even miniature switches for very tight places. It pays to ask what is available. Chances are, your situation isn't unique. And make sure your box has enough room for all the wire ends you intend to connect—inspectors frown on overcrowded junction boxes.

CAUTION! *If your house has aluminum wiring, be sure to use switches that are approved for CO/ALR wiring.*

Choosing New Switches

Wall switches are among the most reliable devices in your house. A good quality switch will often last for 20 years or more—without your having to do anything to it. When you go to choose new switches you'll be faced with several choices. The first is largely aesthetic—do you prefer the traditional toggle switch or the flatter, more contemporary style (sometimes called rocker or paddle switches)? Beyond that, you may also have several grades or quality levels to choose from. Home centers often have bins of loose switches and receptacles available for as little as a quarter apiece. You can then move up to the individually packaged "professional" and "commercial" grades, which can cost several times as much as the bargain-bin units. While all of these devices will get the job done and all are safe, the more expensive units will last considerably longer and will have a nicer feel to them when you use them.

Four Basic Switches

Single-pole Switch

This is the most common type of switch found in household circuits. It is a basic on/off switch, controlling a light or receptacle from one location. It has two brass terminals and a green ground terminal. The words ON and OFF appear on the toggle.

Double-pole Switch

This is another on/off switch like the single-pole switch. Unlike the single-pole switch, however, the double-pole switch has two sets of terminals along with a ground terminal. The two sets of terminals allow the switch to control both of the hot legs in a 240-volt circuit. Double-pole are distinguished from four-way switches by the words ON and OFF on their toggles.

Three-way Switch

This kind of switch is used in conjunction with a second three-way switch to control a light fixture (or fixtures) or a receptacle from two locations. It has two brass "traveler" terminals, a darker common terminal, and a green ground terminal. The words ON and OFF do not appear on the toggle.

Four-way Switch

When added to a circuit containing a pair of three-way switches, a four-way switch allows a device to be turned on or off from a third location. Four-way switches have four traveler terminals and a green ground terminal. Like the three-way switch, no words appear on the toggle.

Reading a Switch

You'll find important information about each switch stamped right on the switch itself. On the front will be the switch's operating specifications and its safety certification. A switch stamped 15A-120VAC is designed to handle a maximum of 15 amps and 120 volts of alternating current. The approval stamp means an independent safety laboratory has tested the device. In the United States, look for UL (Underwriters Laboratory) certification—in Canada, the stamp will be CSL (Canadian Standards Association).

On the back of the switch will be specifications about what type and size wire will work with the switch. "ALR/CU" means the switch will work with aluminum or copper wire. "#12 or #14 solid wire only" means the switch is meant to be used with 12- or 14-gauge solid (not stranded) wire.

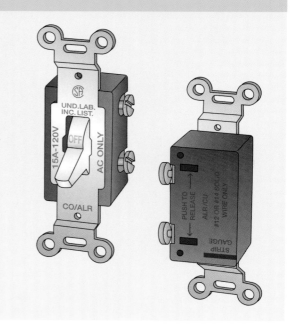

Side-wired Switch

The most common switches have their terminals mounted on the side of the switch body.

Front-wired Switch

Occasionally you may need to wire a switch that has its terminals on the front of its body. This configuration is appropriate in shallow boxes where it would be difficult to maneuver the wires around the switch.

Back-wired Switch

Instead of screw terminals, this type of switch has holes into which you can simply push the bare end of a wire. Inside is a spring-loaded clip that secures the connection. The wires can be released by pushing a thin screwdriver into the release slots. A variation of this type of switch has screws on the sides that are tightened to hold the wire. On either type, a strip gauge is molded into the switch body to show how much insulation should be removed for a proper connection.

While back wiring is fast, most electricians agree that securing wires under screw terminals gives you a better, more trouble-free connection.

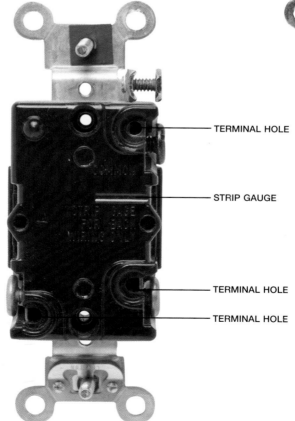

TERMINAL HOLE

STRIP GAUGE

TERMINAL HOLE

TERMINAL HOLE

Dimmer Switch

A dimmer switch controls the amount of voltage that reaches a light fixture, allowing you to vary the amount of light produced. Some dimmer switches include a separate on/off switch; with others the on/off function is built into the dimmer itself. Note: Most common dimmer switches only work with incandescent lights, not fluorescent fixtures or fixtures with motors such as fans. If you need to use a dimmer to control something other than a regular light bulb, consult with your electrical supplier.

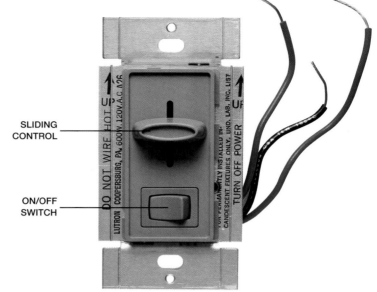

SLIDING CONTROL

ON/OFF SWITCH

Manual Timer Switch

Timer switches feature a spring-driven timer that allows you to turn a fixture on for a certain amount of time. They can be used to control exhaust fans, bathroom heat lamps, indoor and outdoor lighting, closet lights, TVs, and air conditioners. This can be a real convenience—you can set the timer to turn off your outside Christmas lights after you've gone to bed or to shut off your whole house fan after it has done its job. Different models can count down from a few minutes to several hours.

Time-clock Switch

This is a different sort of a timer switch than the manual one shown above. A time-clock switch automatically tracks the time of day and can be set to turn an appliance or lamp on and off at certain times. These switches are often used to control lights for security purposes. This kind of switch is also available as a plug-in unit, which can be moved from receptacle to receptacle. Some of the more advanced models can be programmed to operate randomly, giving your house a lived-in look, even when you are not there.

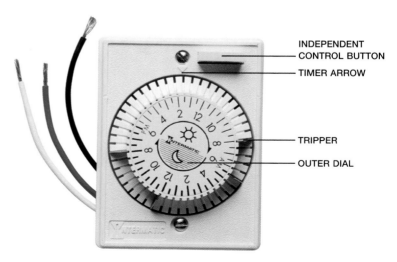

INDEPENDENT CONTROL BUTTON

TIMER ARROW

TRIPPER

OUTER DIAL

Pilot Light Switch

Pilot light switches include a small neon bulb that glows to show when the switch is on. Often these switches are used to control lights in a separate room, such as an attic or a garage, where one might forget that the lights are on. Another type of pilot light switch glows when it is off, making it easy to find in the dark.

Motion-sensor Switch

This switch uses an infrared detector to sense motion. When something moves within the switch's field of view, it activates whatever device the switch controls—generally a security light. These switches usually have sensitivity controls and also can be adjusted to remain on anywhere between a few seconds and several minutes. Some motion-sensor switches also have an on/off/automatic switch so you can control the device manually.

INFRARED SENSOR

FACEPLATE COVERING CONTROLS

ON/OFF/AUTOMATIC SWITCH

Wiring Switches

As mentioned earlier, switches should be wired so they interrupt the hot side of a circuit. There are essentially three ways to accomplish this, depending on where the switch falls in the circuit.

Two Basic Switch Alternatives

For most circuits, the switch will fall either between the power source and light or after the light. If the switch is in between, it is said to fall in the middle of a run. In this situation, you'll run the cable feeding the fixture to the switch box and then on to the fixture itself. In the switch box, you'll tie the two white wires together, while the two black wires are connected to the switch terminals.

When the switch must be located beyond the fixture, you'll have to run a cable (known as a traveler) to create a switch loop. In a switch loop, the incoming power cable is run right to the fixture's box. There, the white wire is connected to the fixture and the black wire is connected to the white wire of the traveler cable. The white traveler wire should be marked with a piece of black electrical tape (or black paint) to indicate that it is "hot." The black side of the traveler cable is connected to the black side of the fixture. The traveler cable is run to the switch box where both wires are connected to the switch terminals. Again, make sure the white wire is marked so anyone working on the system in the future will know it is hot.

Partially Switched Circuits

A third possible way to wire a switched circuit is called a combination circuit. In a combination circuit, the switch falls in the middle of the run, but doesn't control everything beyond it. This is accomplished by using a length of three-conductor wire between the switch and the fixture it controls. In the three-conductor wire, the white wire is the neutral, the black is always hot, and the red wire is controlled by the switch. Be aware that adding three-conductor wire in a circuit can bring the number of connections in a box over the limit allowed by the code. If this is the case, install a bigger box. Three-conductor wire is also used when you are installing multiple switches to control a single circuit.

> **CAUTION!** Combination circuits are not allowed in kitchen wiring, as the code requires kitchen outlets to be on a dedicated circuit.

Wiring Simple Switches

Middle-of-the-Run Switch

In the switch box, attach the black wires of both the incoming and outgoing cables to the switch terminals. Twist the white wires together, finishing the connection with a wire nut. Twist the ground wires together, too, along with a jumper to attach to the switch and cap the ground connection with a wire nut as well. Add a second jumper to screw to the box if the box is metal.

Connect the black and white wires to the appropriate wires or terminals in the fixture box. Be sure to ground the fixture (and the fixture box, if it is metal).

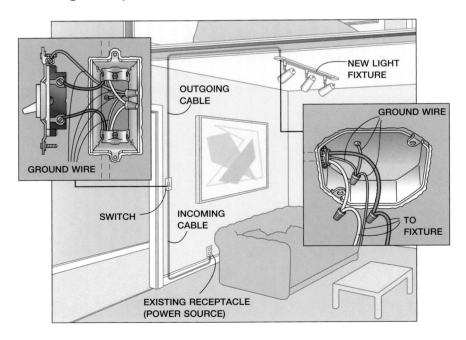

NEW LIGHT FIXTURE

OUTGOING CABLE

GROUND WIRE

GROUND WIRE

SWITCH

INCOMING CABLE

TO FIXTURE

EXISTING RECEPTACLE (POWER SOURCE)

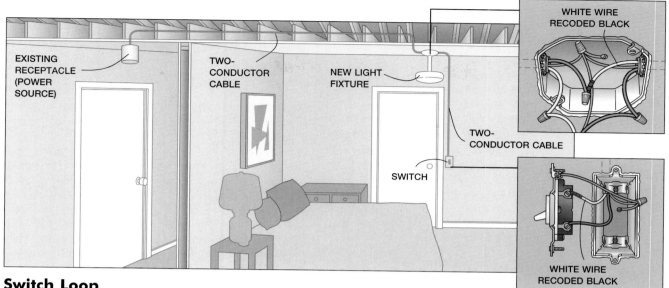

WHITE WIRE
RECODED BLACK

EXISTING
RECEPTACLE
(POWER
SOURCE)

TWO-
CONDUCTOR
CABLE

NEW LIGHT
FIXTURE

TWO-
CONDUCTOR CABLE

SWITCH

WHITE WIRE
RECODED BLACK

Switch Loop

In the fixture box, connect the incoming white wire to the white fixture wire or terminal. Mark the end of the white switch wire to show it is hot. Connect the marked wire to the black wire of the incoming cable.

Connect the black switch wire to the black fixture wire or terminal. Connect the ground wires (and add a jumper to the box if it is metal).

In the switch box, connect the switch wires to the two switch terminals. (Mark the white wire to indicate that it is hot.) Connect the ground wire to the switch (and the box if it is metal).

Combination Circuit

Run two-conductor cable from the power source to the switch box and from the new fixture to the unswitched receptacle. Run three-conductor cable from the switch box to the new fixture.

In the switch box, join the black wires together along with a jumper that runs to one side of the switch. Join the red wire to the other switch terminal. Connect the white wires and ground the switch and box as usual.

At the new fixture box, join the black wires together, as well as all of the white wires including the one from the fixture. Connect the black fixture wire to the red wire. Connect all the ground wires including the one from the fixture. Add a jumper to the box if necessary.

In the receptacle box, join the black wire to one side of the receptacle and the white to the other. Connect the ground to the ground screw (and to the box with a jumper).

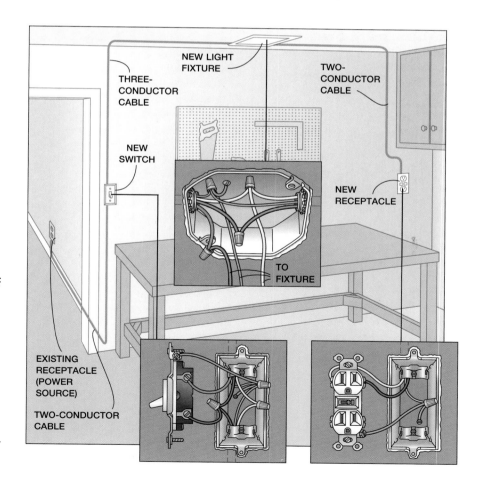

NEW LIGHT
FIXTURE

THREE-
CONDUCTOR
CABLE

TWO-
CONDUCTOR
CABLE

NEW
SWITCH

NEW
RECEPTACLE

TO
FIXTURE

EXISTING
RECEPTACLE
(POWER
SOURCE)

TWO-CONDUCTOR
CABLE

Wiring Three- and Four-way Switches

A pair of three-way switches, controlling a light from two locations, is more than a simple convenience. Stairways should have a switch at the top and the bottom. Long hallways should have switches at either end, and any room with two entrances should have a switch at both. You may even want to consider installing a second (or third) switch for your outside lights in an upstairs bedroom for security purposes. Four-way switches are used to add an additional switch(es) to a three-way switch circuit. They are wired into the three-conductor wire that runs between the two three-way switches.

Planning for Multiple Switches

Generally, a circuit that incorporates three-way switches involves running a length of three-conductor cable between the switches. Two-conductor cable is all that is necessary to run power to the first switch and from the second switch to the light.

Connecting the Switches

Three-conductor cable contains a black, a white, and a red wire as well as a bare ground wire. Usually the red and black wires provide alternate paths for the hot side of the circuit while the white is neutral. Occasionally, however, the white is used as a hot wire, in which case you must mark it so it will not be mistaken for a neutral wire later. The diagrams that follow show how the various wires are connected to the switches depending on your wiring scheme. Note the extra wire in three-conductor cable may require you to install a larger box than you might otherwise expect to keep the number of connections inside the box within the code specifications. Also note that in all situations, the fixtures and boxes should be properly grounded.

Basic Three-way Switch Installations

From Light to Switch to Switch

For the installation shown here, two-conductor cable brings power to the fixture box and runs from the fixture box to the first switch box. The only neutral wire is the white wire in the incoming cable—all the other white wires should be marked as hot.

In the fixture box, connect the incoming white wire to the fixture's white wire. Connect the incoming black wire to the outgoing white (marked) wire and the fixture's black wire to the outgoing black wire.

At the first switch box, connect the incoming white (marked) wire to the black wire in the outgoing, three-conductor cable. Connect the incoming black wire to the common terminal on the switch. Finally, connect the red and white (marked) wires from the three-conductor cable to the traveler terminals on the switch.

In the second switch box, connect the red and white (marked) wires to the traveler terminals on the switch and the black wire to the common terminal.

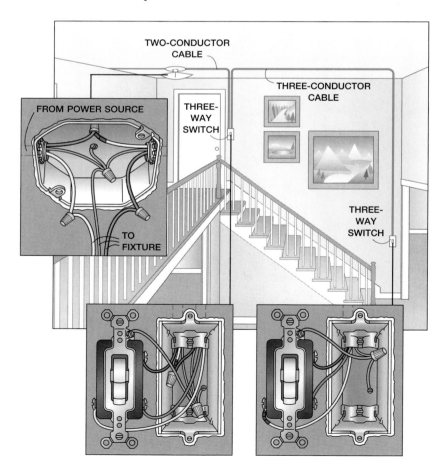

From Switch to Switch to Light

In the installation shown at right, two-conductor cable brings power to the first three-way switch box. From there, three-conductor cable runs to the second switch box, and two-conductor cable completes the trip to the fixture box. All of the white wires are neutral.

In the first switch box, connect the incoming white wire to the white wire in the three-conductor cable. Connect the incoming black wire to the common terminal on the three-way switch, and connect the black and red wires from the three-conductor cable to the traveler terminals on the switch.

In the second switch box, connect the black and red wires from the three-conductor wire to the traveler terminals on the second three-way switch. Connect the two white wires together and connect the outgoing black wire to the common terminal on the switch.

In the fixture box, connect the incoming black and white wires to the black and white wires or terminals on the fixture.

From Switch to Light to Switch

In the final situation, right, the light fixture is wired in between the two three-way switches. A two-conductor cable brings power to the first switch. Then a three-conductor wire runs from the first switch box to the fixture box, and from there to the second switch box. The white wire from the power source through the first switch to the light fixture is neutral. Beyond the light fixture, the white wire is hot and should be marked as a reminder.

In the first switch box, connect the incoming white wire to the white wire in the three-conductor cable. Connect the incoming black wire to the common terminal on the switch. Connect the black and red wires from the three-conductor cable to the traveler terminals on the switch.

In the fixture box, connect the incoming white wire to the white wire or terminal on the fixture. Connect the incoming black wire to the outgoing white (marked) wire, and connect the two red wires together. Finally, connect the outgoing black wire to the black wire or terminal on the fixture.

At the second three-way switch box, connect the red and white (marked) wires to the traveler terminals on the switch; connect the black wire to the common terminal.

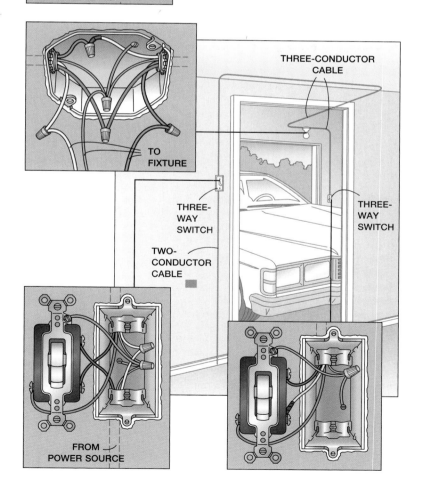

Adding a Four-way Switch

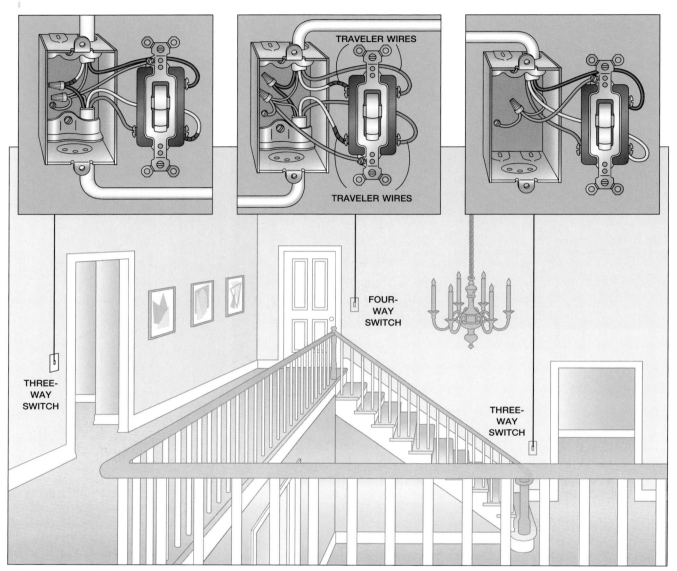

TRAVELER WIRES

TRAVELER WIRES

FOUR-WAY SWITCH

THREE-WAY SWITCH

THREE-WAY SWITCH

A four-way switch's purpose is not to cut off the flow of electricity but rather to redirect it. They can be added to any of the three-way switch circuits on the previous pages—the wiring is quite simple. They are installed in between the three-way switches. The two traveler wires that run between the three-way switches are cut and the resulting ends are attached to the four terminals on the four-way switch as shown. The terminal configuration on all four-way switches is not the same. If your switch doesn't function correctly, remove two of the wires on one side of the switch and reverse them.

Three-way Switches in Older Homes

Changes in the electric code mean that some of the three-way switches in older houses may be wired differently than those shown in this book. Working with these older switches can be frustrating and even dangerous. If you are updating an old system, it is better to run new cable and install new three-way switches rather than try to cobble onto the existing wiring.

he NEC requires that all electrical boxes and fixtures be properly grounded. The grounding system provides an alternate path for electricity to travel should something go awry. If you are working with cable that contains a ground wire, any of the diagrams here will result in adequate grounding. Use whichever works best in a given situation.

Metal Box with One Cable

Some switches don't have a ground terminal—the metal mounting plate serves to ground the switch, provided it is mounted to a metal box.

For switches with a ground terminal, make a pigtail connection attaching two jumper wires to the ground. Attach one of the jumpers to the box with a ground screw and fasten the other to the ground terminal on the switch.

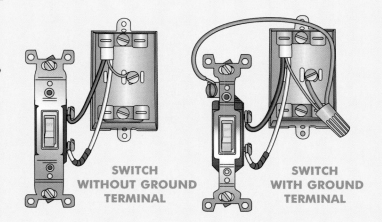

SWITCH
WITHOUT GROUND
TERMINAL

SWITCH
WITH GROUND
TERMINAL

Metal Box with Two Cables

For a switch without a ground terminal, make a pigtail connection with the two ground wires and a jumper wire. Attach the jumper to the box with a ground screw.

For a switch with a ground terminal, add a second jumper to the pigtail and attach it to the terminal on the switch.

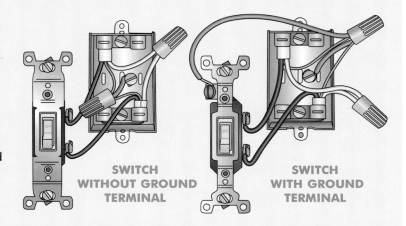

SWITCH
WITHOUT GROUND
TERMINAL

SWITCH
WITH GROUND
TERMINAL

Plastic Boxes

When working with plastic boxes, the box itself is insulated, and can't substitute for a ground terminal on the switch. Code does make provisions for switches without ground screws, but it's safer and easier to use one with a ground screw. Connect the ground wire directly to the ground screw if there is only one cable. If there is more than one cable in the box, make a pigtail connection with the ground wires, adding a jumper wire to connect to the ground terminal.

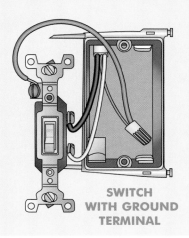

SWITCH
WITH GROUND
TERMINAL

Installing a Time-Clock Switch

1 Label the wires.

A time-clock switch can only be used in middle-of-the-run wiring, as the timer must have a source of constant power to drive it. Mark the incoming black wire so you know which of the black wires in the box is hot *(right)*.

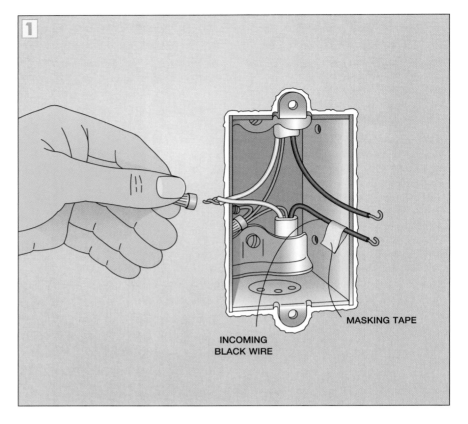

MASKING TAPE

INCOMING
BLACK WIRE

2 Install the switch.

Connect the incoming hot (marked) wire to the black wire attached to the switch.

Connect the outgoing black wire to the red wire from the switch.

Connect all of the white wires together *(right)*.

Most timer switches are not grounded so you won't have to worry about attaching a ground wire to the switch itself. Connect both of the ground wires. If you are working with a metal box, add a jumper wire to the ground pigtail and screw it to the box. No jumper is needed for a plastic box.

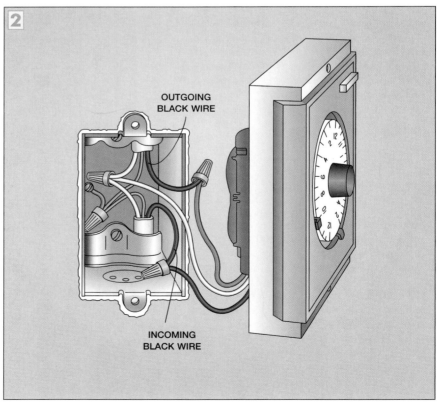

OUTGOING
BLACK WIRE

INCOMING
BLACK WIRE

Connecting the Switch

This type of switch, like the timer switch on the opposite page, requires a constant source of electricity. Therefore it must be wired in a middle-of-the-run situation.

- Mark the incoming black wire so you can tell it is hot.

- One side of a pilot light switch has two brass terminals connected by a brass strip. Connect the outgoing black wire to either of these terminals.

- Fasten the incoming black (marked) wire to the brass terminal on the opposite side of the switch.

- Make a pigtail connection with the two white wires and a jumper wire. Fasten the jumper to the silver terminal on the switch.

- Some switches only have two brass terminals, one on either side. In this case, attach the black wires to the terminals in random order. Turn the power on and try the switch. If the pilot light remains on, even when the switch is off, turn off the power and switch the black wires.

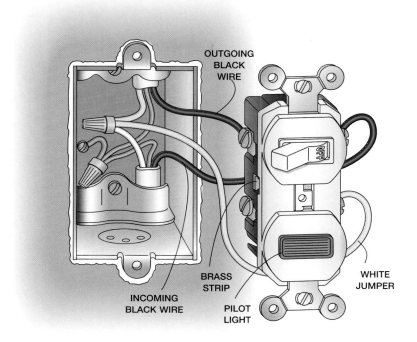

OUTGOING BLACK WIRE

BRASS STRIP

INCOMING BLACK WIRE

PILOT LIGHT

WHITE JUMPER

Choosing Receptacles

When it comes to basic receptacles, you don't have many choices. Unless you have to accommodate an appliance with a special plug (which probably means it needs more current than a standard receptacle can provide), your choice is essentially limited to the quality of the receptacle and what color it is. Lesser quality receptacles tend to wear faster, particularly if you swap plugs in and out of them frequently.

Double Duty

If you are pressed for space, you can install a light/receptacle combination, which can control a light and provide a place to plug in an appliance within the same box. Some light fixtures also include a receptacle that can be pressed into service.

Special Situations

Other receptacles are designed specifically for certain applications. Floor outlets, for example, are designed to be recessed into the floor so you can plug in a lamp or other appliance at the center of a large room, such as a great room. These receptacles include a cover to protect the receptacle when it is not in use. A locking receptacle prevents a plug from being pulled out accidentally. There are also several types of safety receptacles that close automatically when they are not in use, preventing toddlers from playing with them.

Older Houses

Receptacles in older houses can present a problem. Before the early 1960s, it was common practice to install ungrounded receptacles throughout a house. You'll recognize these outlets because they lack the third opening. When working on the electrical system in an older house, many local electrical codes require that you bring the old wiring up to date. This generally means replacing these old receptacles with grounded receptacles, except when there is not a separate ground wire. In this situation, you can gain some measure of added protection by installing a GFCI receptacle as described on page 146.

CAUTION! *Almost all electrical appliances available today make use of polarized plugs (which have one wide and one narrow prong) or they have a plug with an integral grounding prong. These are safety features meant to ensure the appliance is properly grounded. These new plugs won't fit in the older, two-slot receptacles. Avoid the temptation to cut the grounding prong off or file down the wider prong. It is far safer to replace the receptacle instead.*

Types of Receptacles and Their Plugs

120-Volt, 15-Amp, Ungrounded

This receptacle is typical of those found in homes built prior to the early 1960s. When wired correctly, the wide slot on the left is the neutral and the narrow slot is the hot. An appliance or lamp with a polarized plug will only fit into this receptacle one way, ensuring correct polarity within the appliance. In some older receptacles, the slots are both narrow and polarized plugs will not fit.

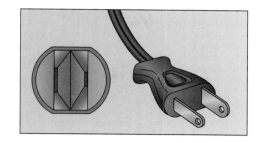

120/240-Volt, 30-Amp

This style of receptacle and its mating plug are commonly found in existing circuits designed especially for electric clothes dryers. They supply both 240 volts for the dryer's heating elements and 120 volts for accessories such as the dryer's timer and pilot light. The receptacle is grounded in its box with the ground wire. Some dryer receptacles and plugs (required in Canada) feature a fourth slot/prong for the ground (inset). New installations are required to have a fourth prong for the ground (inset).

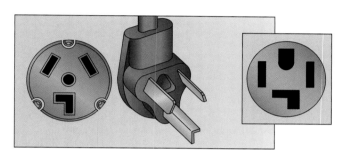

120-Volt, Grounded

These are the receptacles you are most likely to install. They have two slots (one wide and one narrow for polarity) and a U-shaped hole for the ground prong. On a 20-amp receptacle, one of the slots has a T-shape to accommodate appliances with 20-amp plugs. The Canadian version of a 20-amp receptacle is shown in the inset. Twenty-amp receptacles require heavier wire (usually 12-gauge) than needed for 15-amp receptacles.

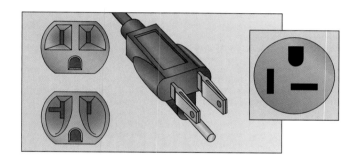

120/240-Volt, 50-Amp

This heavy-duty receptacle is generally used for an electric range. It supplies the electric heating elements with 240 volts and the oven light, timer, and other accessories with 120 volts. The newer version, required in all new installations, is shown in the inset drawing—it has a separate ground opening.

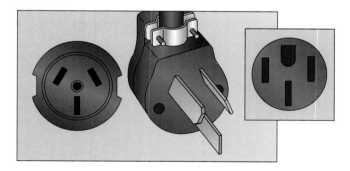

240-Volt, 30-Amp

Unlike the two other heavy-duty receptacles on this page, this receptacle supplies only 240 volts. It is used with appliances such as window air conditioners. Both slots are hot, while the U-shaped slot is for the ground. The Canadian version has a fourth slot for a neutral wire (inset).

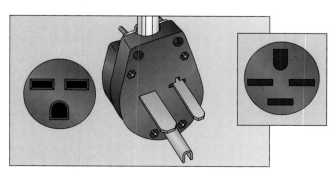

Wiring Receptacles

Wiring receptacles is fairly straightforward business. In almost all situations, you'll have two or three wires plus a bare ground wire coming into the box. These wires will be attached to terminals on the receptacle. Generally the black wire goes to the brass terminal, the white wire goes to the silver terminal, and the ground wire attaches to the green terminal. The only thing that might complicate matters is if you have to continue the cable beyond the receptacle, such as might be the case if you are adding a number of new receptacles to a single circuit in an addition.

Dealing with Continuing Wires

If you have two cable ends in a box, there are two ways to connect things so the outgoing cable has power, as does the receptacle. The first method is to connect the incoming wires to one set of brass and silver terminals on the receptacle and to connect the outgoing wires to the other set of terminals. The ground wires get twisted together along with two jumpers. One jumper is attached to the receptacle; the other is attached to the box (assuming the box is metal). The only problem with this approach is that it relies on a little strip of metal on the receptacle to maintain continuity between the two sets of wires. If the strip gives out, everything beyond that receptacle will be dead. A better way to deal with the situation is to twist the outgoing and incoming wires together along with a jumper wire that is attached to the receptacle. This way, if the receptacle goes bad, the rest of the devices downstream will remain unaffected.

Swapping GFCIs for Ungrounded Receptacles

Because there would be no way to ground the new receptacle, electrical codes forbid replacing a two-slot, ungrounded receptacle on an ungrounded system with a three-slot receptacle. If your system has black wires and white wires, but no bare copper ground wires, it's not grounded. (If you have a ground wire, you can just swap the old outlets for new ones, as described in Upgrading a Two-slot Receptacle on page 149.)

Fortunately, if your system is ungrounded, there's still a solution. Code allows you to substitute a three-hole GFCI receptacle for the old, two-slot unit. Although the GFCI itself wouldn't be grounded in this case, it will still protect you. If it detects more power in either the black or the white wire—as there might be in a defective lamp for example—the GFCI shuts down the power to the receptacle.

As an added bonus, a single GFCI receptacle protects all the other receptacles downstream from it, too. You can replace all the other downstream receptacles with regular, three-slot receptacles. They won't be truly grounded, so if you go this route, the code requires that these downstream receptacles be marked as being GFCI-protected. Most GFCI receptacles come with stickers for just this purpose.

There are two instances where this solution doesn't meet code. In the first case, it won't do the trick if you're installing a GFCI as the GFCI required in wet or damp locations. For this, you'll need to be able to attach a true ground wire. In the second case, the GFCI won't meet code in your shop, or anywhere else you're running equipment with a three-pronged plug. The third prong is a safety device. If a machine accidentally gets electrified, power runs through the third prong into the ground instead of through your body. When you're using a GFCI because the circuit is ungrounded, there's nowhere for that power to go. The GFCI will shut off power to the circuit, but it won't meet code requirements for heavy-duty equipment.

To put a GFCI in an ungrounded system, install it as explained on page 151. When the directions tell you to attach the ground wire, however, you won't have one. Simply leave the ground screw bare. (If the GFCI has a green wire instead of a screw, cap it with a wirecap and tape.)

Basic 120-Volt Receptacles

Middle-of-the-Run, Plastic-sheathed Cable

To wire a receptacle in the middle of a run:

- Connect the two black wires to the two brass terminals in any order.
- Connect the white wire to the silver terminals.
- In a metal box, attach a short jumper wire to the box with a green ground screw and another jumper to the ground terminal on the receptacle.
- Fasten the two jumpers to the two ground wires with a wire nut.

Middle-of-the-Run, Armored Cable

Attaching a receptacle to armored cable is identical to attaching it to plastic cable except the ground connections are different because the metal sheathing on the cable serves as the ground.

- Connect the black and white wires to the brass and silver terminals, respectively.
- Run a green jumper wire from the ground terminal on the receptacle to a green ground screw fastened to the box. The clamp holding the cable in place will ground the box to the metal sheathing.

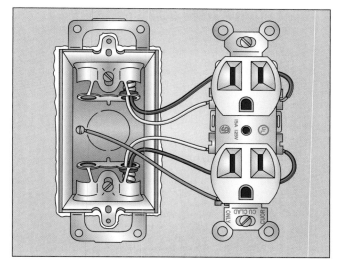

End-of-the-Run

Only one cable will enter an end-of-the-run box.

- Connect the black wire to the brass terminal; connect the white wire to the silver terminal.
- With a metal box and plastic-sheathed cable, attach ground jumpers to the box (with a green ground screw) and to the ground terminal on the receptacle. With a plastic box, there is no jumper to the box.
- Twist the ground wire and jumpers together and fasten them with a wire nut.
- With armored cable (which doesn't have a separate ground wire) run a jumper from the ground terminal on the receptacle to a screw in the back of the box.

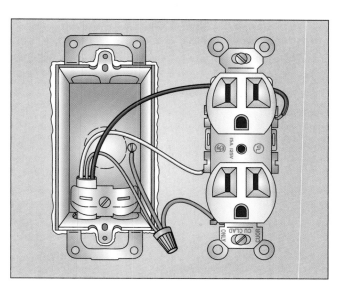

*I*f you are tying your new wiring into an existing receptacle box, make sure the old work is properly grounded. Check this easily with a circuit analyzer, as explained in Circuit Testing Techniques on page 94, or by visually inspecting the wiring and comparing it to the diagrams on this page.

In a metal box (upper right), proper grounding consists of two green jumper wires joined to the bare copper wires with a wire nut or crimped connector. One jumper should run to the ground terminal on the receptacle, and the other should run to a green ground screw in the back of the box. In a plastic box, the wiring is identical except there is no wire running to the box.

If you are adding on to a system that uses ungrounded receptacles (two-slot), you can check visually to see if they are attached to a grounded system (there will be a ground wire attached to the box) or with a voltage tester as described on the facing page. If you need to plug a three-pronged plug into a two-slot receptacle (it should be properly grounded, of course), you can install an adapter as shown (lower right). To ground the adapter properly, connect its ground terminal to the box via the cover screw.

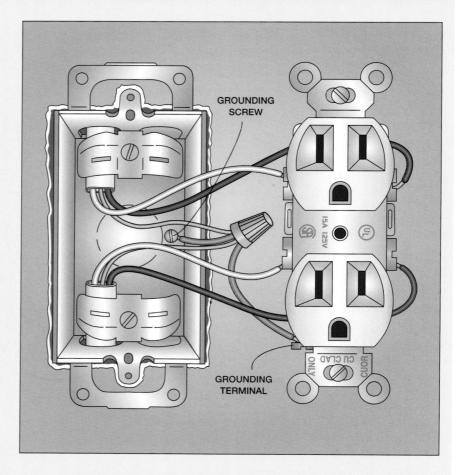

GROUNDING SCREW

15A 125V

GROUNDING TERMINAL

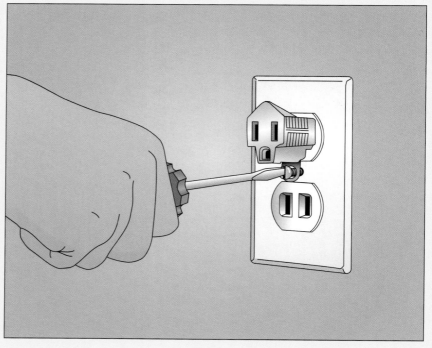

1 Test for a ground.

You can swap a three-slot, grounded receptacle for a two-slot, ungrounded receptacle as long as the outlet box itself is grounded. To check for a ground, break out your multitester or voltage checker.

Set the multitester on the 250 VAC (volts, alternating current) range. Place one probe on the screw attaching the cover plate (scrape off a little paint to expose bare metal). Put the second probe into one of the slots and then the other (right). Be careful—the receptacle is live. If the receptacle is grounded, the meter should register 120 volts (or close to it, depending on local variations) with the probe in one slot or the other.

If the meter shows 0 voltage at both slots, the box is not grounded. You'll have to run a new piece of three-conductor cable to it, or install a GFCI receptacle as described on page 146.

If the test shows the box is grounded, you can safely replace the old receptacle with a new, grounded unit.

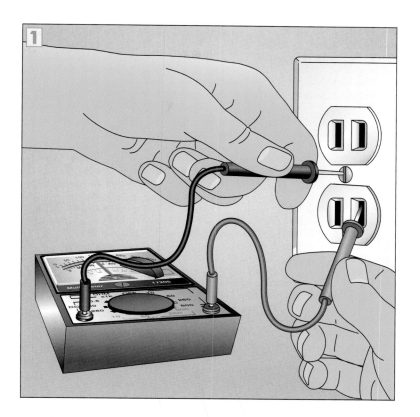

2 Connect the new receptacle.

Turn off the power and remove the old receptacle from the box.

Disconnect the ground wire from the box.

Connect it to a pair of jumper wires with a wire nut.

Connect one of the jumpers to the box and the other to the ground terminal on the new receptacle (right).

Connect the black wire to the brass terminal on the receptacle and the white wire to the silver terminal.

Fold the wires into the box, screw the receptacle in position, and replace the cover.

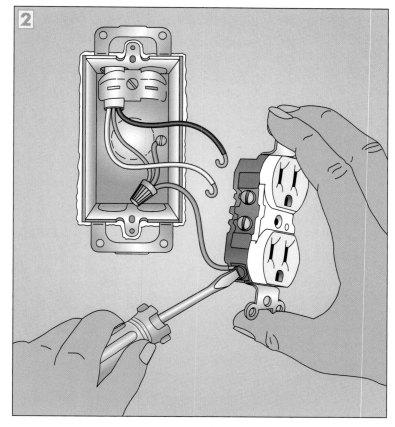

As useful as electricity is, it can also be deadly, even in very small doses. A current not much larger than 5 milliamps—$\frac{5}{1000}$ of an ampere, or about $\frac{1}{3000}$ of the current necessary to trip a 15-amp circuit breaker—can fatally disrupt the rhythm of your heart. So what are the circuit breakers or fuses in your house protecting? They are there to protect the wiring (and the house) from circuit overloads, not to protect people. People aren't supposed to come in contact with electricity. And if it stays in the wires, nobody will get hurt.

Deviant Currents

The problem is, you cannot count on electricity to stay where it is supposed to. Through wear, damage, or careless work, occasionally current in a hot wire will leak to a cover plate, box, or other conductor. These tiny leaks may well go unnoticed—until you touch a charged object when you happen to be a good conductor yourself, say, when you are barefoot outdoors on the damp ground. Then that tiny charge will race through your body on its way to the earth, at best giving you a little jolt—at worst, killing you. Such a shift in the current flow is called a ground fault.

An Electronic Sentinel

In the mid-1970s, electrical codes began to require the installation of a safety device called a ground-fault circuit interrupter (GFCI) in places where people might cause a ground fault. (See the box on the opposite page.) GFCIs compare the current in the hot side of the circuit to that in the neutral side. Normally the current flow is identical. However when a ground fault occurs, there will be a slight difference. When the GFCI detects a difference of 5 milliamps or more, it trips, shutting off current flow to the circuit within $\frac{1}{40}$ second.

Two Styles of Protection

GFCIs are available either as individual receptacles, or as circuit breakers that are installed in the service panel. A receptacle-style GFCI offers protection at the point where it is installed, as well as to any receptacles downstream from it. A GFCI circuit breaker offers protection to the entire circuit to which it is attached. (If you are replacing a breaker with a GFCI breaker, buy one of the same capacity.)

Both styles of GFCI will protect you from ground faults; however, tiny leaks can add up over a long run of cable (200 feet or more) and cause a GFCI breaker to trip erratically. In such a situation, it might be better to install individual GFCI receptacles at the points where they are truly necessary.

Maintenance

Unlike other receptacles and breakers, GFCI equipment needs a periodic check to make sure it is functioning properly. Both styles have a test button that simulates a ground fault, cutting the power. Push this test button monthly and replace any GFCI that does not immediately respond.

CAUTION! A GFCI offers no protection if you touch both the hot and neutral wires at the same time.

Hire an electrician to install any GFCI devices on a circuit having aluminum wires, even if they are copper-clad.

GFCI protection is required for new receptacles in bathrooms, garages, and crawlspaces.

You'll also need them outdoors, when the outlets are less than 6½ feet above ground level (8 feet, 2½ inches in Canada).

Code requires GFCIs within 6 feet of a kitchen sink or wet bar. Note: The Canadian code does not require GFCIs in kitchens; instead it calls for split receptacles that cannot be protected by a GFCI.

You'll need GFCIs anywhere within 20 feet of a swimming pool or similar installation, including underwater lighting. The Canadian code also requires GFCI protection in associated shower and locker rooms.

In addition, all receptacles downstream from a GFCI must be marked as GFCI protected. Stickers for this purpose are usually included with the devices.

Installing a GFCI Receptacle

1 Wire the device.

Determine which is the incoming cable as described in *Double-checking Receptacle Wiring*, page 95. Mark the cable, then turn off the power at the service panel.

Connect the incoming wires to the side of the GFCI marked "line," with the black wire to the brass terminal, and the white wire to the silver terminal. (*Note:* some GFCI units have wires to connect to, rather than terminals. In this situation, use wire nuts to connect like-colored wires.)

Connect the outgoing wires to the "load" side of the GFCI, again matching the color of each wire to its terminal (or wire). If there is no outgoing cable, and your GFCI has wire connections, cap the "load" wires with wire nuts.

In a plastic box, join the bare copper wires from the cables to the ground wire from the GFCI with a wire nut. If the box is metal, run a jumper wire from the ground connection to a ground screw in the box.

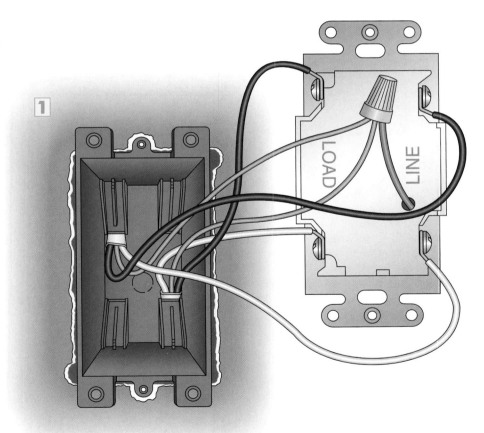

(continued on next page)

2 Mount the receptacle.

After making all the necessary connections, fold the wires into the box, being careful not to loosen any of the connections.

Push the receptacle into the box (*right*) and secure it with the mounting screws provided.

Screw the cover plate in place.

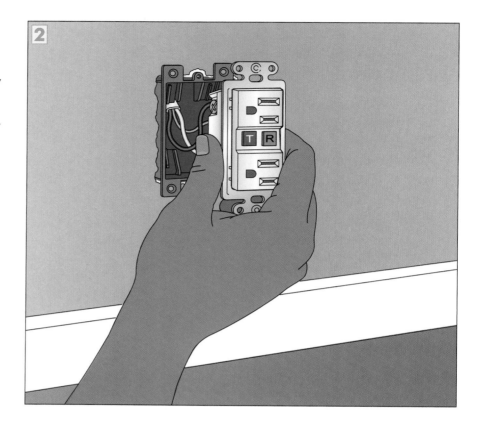

3 Test the device.

Turn the power back on at the service panel. Plug a radio into the first receptacle downstream from the GFCI and turn it on. Press the test button. You should hear a "snap" and the radio should turn off (*right*). If so, the GFCI is working properly.

Press reset and check the other receptacles downstream.

If you get other results, turn the power off again at the service panel. Double-check your wiring connections confirming that the incoming cable is connected to the "line" side of the unit and the outgoing cable to the "load" side. If the GFCI is wired properly, swap it for another unit and test again. If the problem persists, contact an electrician.

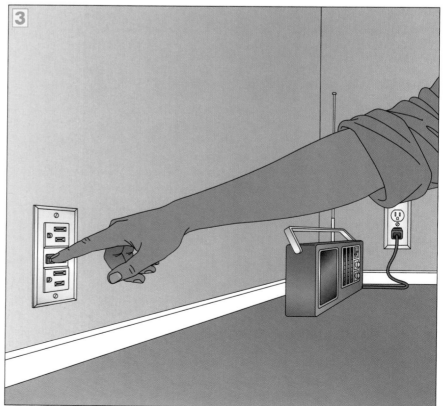

1 Mount a GFCI breaker.

Turn off the power to the panel by throwing the main breaker, or, on a split-bus panel, throwing the two high-voltage breakers. Remove the cover from the panel to expose the breakers.

Detach the black wire from the existing breaker and pull the device loose from the panel *(right)*. Most breakers clip in place down the center of the panel. To remove one, pivot it away from the center connection.

Turn the GFCI breaker off and clip it into the vacant place in the panel.

For a new circuit, choose an unoccupied slot and remove the knockout from the panel cover. Install the GFCI breaker and wire it as described below.

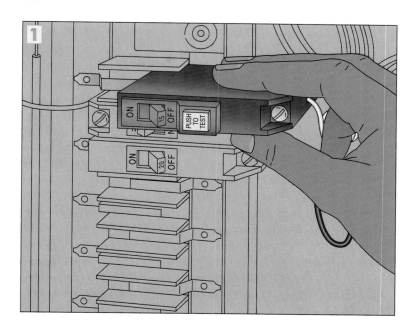

2 Wire the GFCI breaker.

Attach the black wire from the circuit you want to protect to the terminal on the breaker marked "load" or "load power."

Connect the white circuit wire to a terminal or wire marked "load neutral" on the GFCI.

Screw the GFCI wire marked "panel neutral" or "neutral bus" to any vacant terminal on the neutral bus bar.

In a new circuit, connect the ground wire to the panel grounding bar. (In some panels, this is the same as the neutral bus bar.)

Restore power to the panel and turn the GFCI breaker on. Push its test button. The breaker should trip. If it doesn't, try the remedies listed in Step 3 on the previous page. If the breaker trips, reset it as you would with an ordinary breaker.

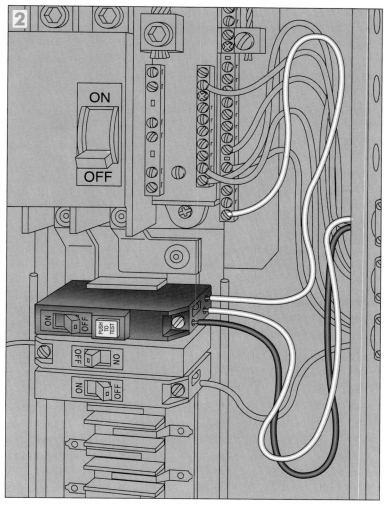

Adding a Receptacle to a 120-Volt Box

Many switch and receptacle boxes are designed so they can be screwed side by side with another box, allowing a second fixture to be installed. This process is known as ganging the boxes together. If you want to add another receptacle or two to a circuit, this is an easy way to proceed, as you don't have to run more cable, you only have to cut a bigger opening for the expanded box.

■ Once the ganged box is installed, attach the incoming black wire to one of the brass terminals on the first receptacle. Attach the incoming white wire to one of the silver terminals on the same receptacle.

■ Run a black jumper wire from the other brass terminal on the receptacle to one of the brass terminals on the second receptacle. Run a white jumper wire from silver terminal to silver terminal.

■ Run green jumper wires from the ground terminals on the receptacles to the ground wires of the cables. Also run a jumper to the box itself. Finish the ground connection with a wire nut.

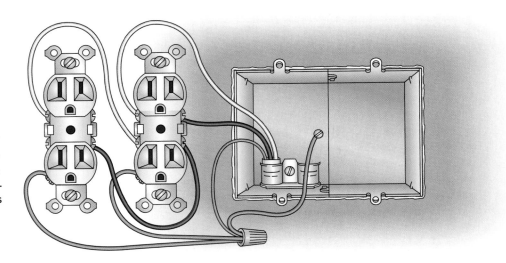

Splitting a 240-Volt Circuit

Because a 240-volt circuit has 120 volts in each of the hot wires, you can split it to deliver current to two 120-volt receptacles provided the circuit uses three-conductor wire. Install a ganged box to hold the receptacles, then follow the steps below.

■ Run the black wire from the 240-volt circuit to the brass terminal of one of the receptacles.

■ Run the red wire from the circuit to the brass terminal of the second receptacle.

■ Attach white jumper wires to the silver terminals on both receptacles. Connect these jumpers to the white wire from the 240-volt circuit. Finish the connection with a wire nut.

■ Ground the receptacles as described above.

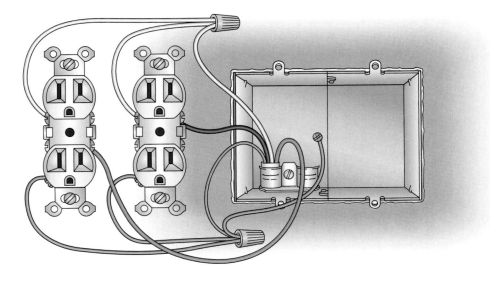

Switch Loop

This is the setup to use when it is easier to run the cable to the receptacle than to the switch.

- Run cable to the receptacle box. Then run a length of two-conductor cable to the switch box.

- In the receptacle box, connect the incoming black wire to the white wire of the outgoing cable. This makes the white wire hot, so mark it to signify the change.

- Attach the incoming white wire to one of the silver terminals on the receptacle. Attach the black wire from the outgoing cable to one of the receptacle's brass terminals.

- Twist the ground wires together along with two green jumper wires and cap them with a wire nut. Connect one jumper to the ground terminal on the receptacle, and the other to the box with a green ground screw. (If the box is plastic, skip the jumper to the box.)

- In the switch box, connect the black wire to one side of the switch and the white wire to the other side. The white wire is hot in this situation, so mark it with a black mark.

- Ground the switch with a jumper connected to the ground wire. Also ground the box if it is metal.

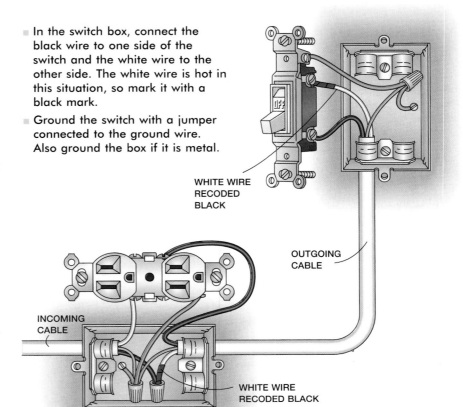

WHITE WIRE
RECODED
BLACK

OUTGOING
CABLE

INCOMING
CABLE

WHITE WIRE
RECODED BLACK

Middle-of-the-Run Switch

When it is easier to run the cable to the switch first, use this scheme.

- Run cable to the switch box and then to the receptacle box.

- At the switch, twist the ground wires together, adding two jumper wires to the connection. Cap the joint with a wire nut. Connect one jumper to the ground terminal on the switch and the other to a green ground screw in the box. (If the box is plastic, omit this jumper.)

- Connect the white wires together. Connect the black wires to the terminals on either side of the switch.

- At the receptacle, ground both the fixture and the box. Then connect the black wire to the brass terminal and the white to the silver terminal.

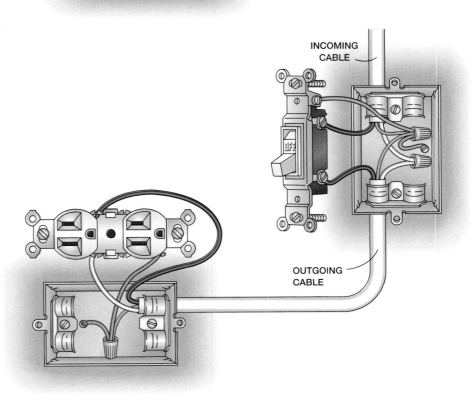

INCOMING
CABLE

OUTGOING
CABLE

Middle-of-the-Run Installation

For this type of fixture, the ideal situation is when the cable reaches the fixture before running to the switch. This way you can wire it so the receptacle remains hot and the switch controls only the light. The wiring is similar to the switch loop shown on page 155.

- Run cable to the fixture and then on to the switch.
- Connect the ground wires with a wire nut, adding jumper wires to the fixture and the box as shown.
- Connect the incoming black wire to the black wire from the receptacles and to the white wire in the cable that runs to the switch. Mark this white wire to indicate it is hot.
- Connect the incoming white wire to the two white wires from the fixture.
- Connect the black wire from the switch to the black wire from the light.
- In the switch box, connect the white and black wires to the two switch terminals. Ground the switch and box as usual.

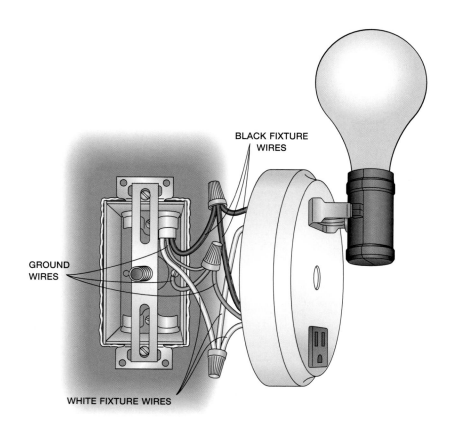

INCOMING CABLE

GROUND WIRES

CABLE TO SWITCH

WHITE WIRE RECODED BLACK

BLACK FIXTURE WIRES

GROUND WIRES

WHITE FIXTURE WIRES

End-of-the-Run Installation

When the fixture is located downstream from the switch, the switch will control both the receptacle and the light.

- Run cable to the switch, then on to the fixture.
- In the switch box, join the two white wires with a wire nut. Also join the ground wires, adding jumper wires to ground the switch and the box.
- Connect the black wires to the two switch terminals.
- In the fixture box, join the incoming black wire to the two black wires from the fixture. Also join the white wires together.
- Ground the fixture and the box as usual.

CAUTION! If this type of fixture is used in a bathroom, the electric code requires that the incoming cable be protected by a GFCI.

Split Circuit Receptacles

Removing the Hot Side Bridge

Usually an individual duplex receptacle is served by a single circuit. However, there are occasions when you might want to have each individual receptacle served by a separate circuit. One case is when you want one of the receptacles to be operated with a switch and the other to remain hot. To achieve this, you'll have to modify the receptacle by removing the metal bridge that connects the brass terminals on the fixture. To remove the bridge, grasp it with long-nosed pliers and bend it back and forth until it snaps off.

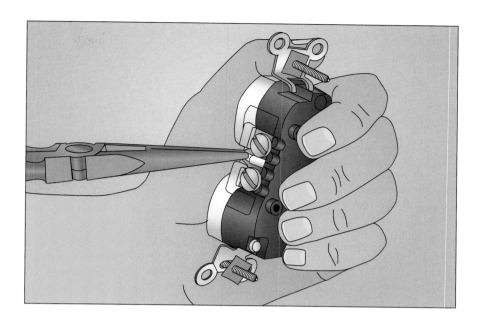

Adding a Switch Loop to a Split Receptacle

- Run cable to the receptacle box and then on to the switch box.
- Connect the ground wires as usual, adding jumper wires for the box and the receptacle.
- Connect the incoming white wire to a silver terminal on the receptacle.
- Connect the incoming black wire to a black jumper wire and the white wire leading to the switch. Mark this white wire to indicate it is now hot. Connect the jumper wire to the brass terminal on the receptacle that corresponds to the half of the receptacle you wish to remain hot all the time.
- In the switch box, connect the white and black wires to the two switch terminals. Mark the white wire to indicate it is hot. Ground the switch and box as usual.

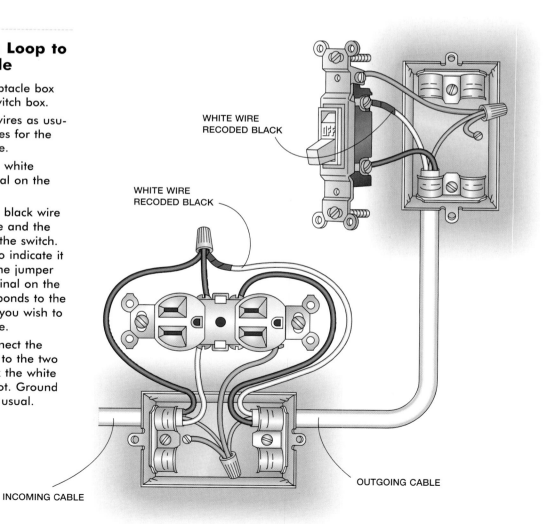

WHITE WIRE RECODED BLACK

WHITE WIRE RECODED BLACK

INCOMING CABLE

OUTGOING CABLE

Adding a Middle-of-the-Run Switch to a Split Receptacle

- Run two-wire cable to the switch box. Then run three-wire cable from the switch box to the receptacle box.

- At the switch connect the incoming black wire to the outgoing black wire and a black jumper wire. Connect the jumper wire to one of the terminals on the switch. Connect the red wire to the second switch terminal.

- Connect the two white wires together. Connect the ground wires and ground the switch and box as usual.

- In the receptacle box, connect the white wire to the silver terminal and the black and red wires to the brass terminals. Ground the receptacle and the box in the usual way.

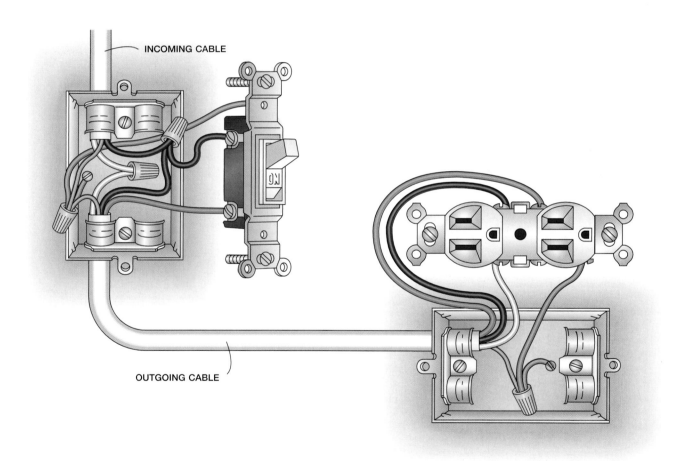

INCOMING CABLE

OUTGOING CABLE

Surface Wiring

A Short Cut

In houses where routing wire through the walls and ceilings proves to be more of a job than you are willing to tackle, surface wiring can be a practical alternative. Surface wiring, also called raceway, consists of a system of metal channels and outlet boxes that contain the wiring as it runs from place to place. With thoughtful installation along a room's trim, and a matching paint job, raceway can virtually disappear "into the woodwork."

Components

Raceway is available in metal or plastic. Fittings, such as boxes and elbows, consist of two parts—a back plate that screws to the wall and a cover, which snaps in place over the plate, containing the connections within. The back plates have a series of tongues, which mate with the channel that carries the wire from place to place. The channel is available in three widths. Which one to use depends on the number and gauge of the conductors within.

Wiring

Metal raceway systems can accommodate regular cable, but it is easier to install individual wires (labeled TW on their insulation). Only the hot and neutral wires are needed—the raceway serves as the ground. Plastic raceway systems require running a separate ground wire along with the hot and the neutral wires.

Getting Started

Start planning a raceway circuit as you would a regular electric circuit—sketch the locations of fixtures on a floor plan. Then transfer the drawing to the corresponding walls and ceiling. This will help you visualize actual layout of all the pieces. Measure the various distances and develop a shopping list of the pieces you will need.

Installation proceeds as follows: Start with the first fixture, then a piece of channel for the outgoing wires, then the next fixture, and so on. To protect the wires from abrasion by the sharp edges of the channels, file the burrs from any edges you cut. As a further precaution, insert a bushing into the ends of each cut section.

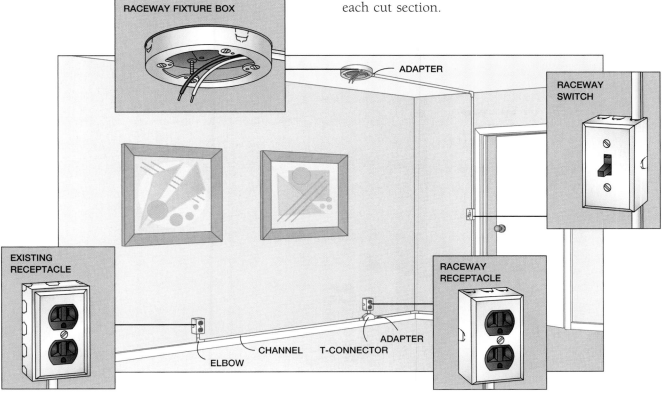

RACEWAY FIXTURE BOX

ADAPTER

RACEWAY SWITCH

EXISTING RECEPTACLE

RACEWAY RECEPTACLE

ELBOW

CHANNEL

T-CONNECTOR

ADAPTER

Finding a Source of Power

Tapping an existing box is often the easiest way to provide power for your new raceway circuit. If one is not available, run a new cable using conventional techniques until it is as close as possible to your raceway system. With either approach, at this point you'll have to install a two-part adapter box to make the transition from conventional wiring to raceway.

- Turn off the current and remove the old fixture from its box without disconnecting the wiring.
- Slip the adapter's tongued plate over the receptacle.
- Remove the twist-out on the frame where the channel will connect.
- Slide the channel onto the corresponding tongue; then screw the extension frame to the tongued plate. Thread hot and neutral wires through the channel into the box. Connect the black to the brass terminal on the fixture and

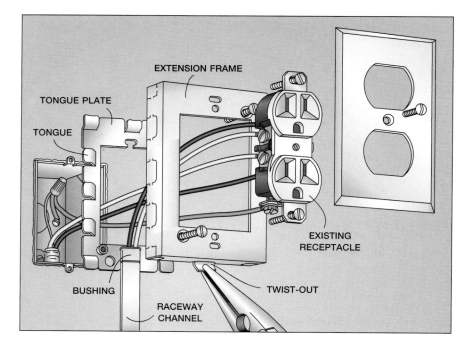

white to the silver terminal—the exact wiring depends on what kind of circuit you are building.

- Screw the receptacle in place, then attach the cover.

A Raceway Receptacle or Switch

- Slip one tongue on the box's base plate into the incoming channel, then fasten the plate to the wall. Fish the wires through the channel. If the wiring continues beyond this point, add another length of channel.
- Connect the black and white wires to the appropriate terminals on the fixture. Add a jumper wire from the fixture's ground terminal and the ground screw on the base plate.
- Remove the appropriate twist-out from the box cover, and screw the cover to the base plate.
- Screw the fixture to the cover, then add a cover plate (not shown).

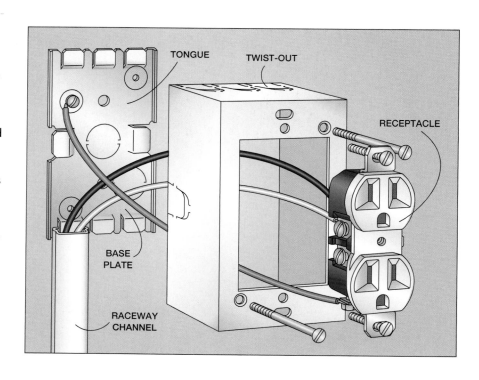

Raceway Channel Fittings

- Support raceway channel every two feet or so by screwing snap-in clips to the wall. If you need to join lengths of channel, use an extension connector.

- Slide the connector onto the first length of channel and screw it to the wall. Then slip the next length of raceway onto the connector. Hide the junction with a snap-on cover.

- To turn a corner, use a two-part elbow. Fasten the base plate to the free end of the channel, then screw it to the wall.

- Add the next section of channel, then snap the cover in place.

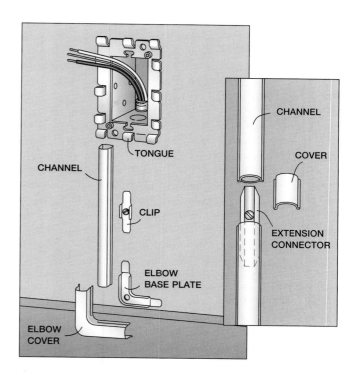

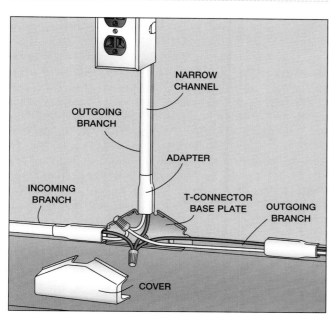

T-Connector Junction Box

This fitting allows you to create a branch in your wiring. The adapters shown here make the transition from the junction box to the narrowest pieces of channel. They are not necessary when using the two wider sizes.

- Slip the narrow end of an adapter onto the channel, then attach the connector base plate to the adapter. Screw the base to the wall.

- Join the incoming wires to those in the outgoing branches.

- Slide an adapter onto the connector to continue the raceway. Snap the cover in place to finish the job.

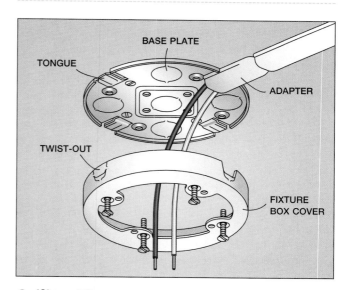

Ceiling Fixture

- Attach the base plate to the end of the channel. An adapter may be necessary if you are using the smallest channel. Screw the base plate securely to the ceiling.

- Remove a twist-out from the box cover to accommodate the channel adapter, then screw the cover to the base plate.

- Attach the fixture to the wires as necessary—black to black, white to white, and ground to ground.

Installing Fixtures

Once the switches and receptacles are in place, it's time for the real glory work—hooking up the actual lighting fixtures. Usually these are very straightforward to install. Before you begin, though, make sure the box is the right size and is mounted securely. This is particularly important when dealing with a heavy unit such as a ceiling fan.

Even though installing the fixtures is one of the last stages of the project, you should get the fixtures first. Hold the fixture in place, and check to make sure it won't interfere with doors, windows, curtains and the like, before you mount the box for it. This way you can design your wiring system around their requirements rather than having to modify things after the fact to make them work.

Lighting Fixtures

Choosing the right lighting fixture can mean the difference between a room that is truly inviting and one that is merely adequate. This is the kind of design issue that is covered in detail in the front part of this book. But in brief, you need to answer a number of questions when you are choosing what kind of fixture to install. These include:

Is the lighting meant to provide atmosphere?

Or is it more to provide task lighting—illuminating a certain area, such as above a counter or desk?

How will the fixture be installed—mounted on the ceiling or on the wall?

How will the fixture be controlled?

What type of light do you prefer? Incandescent bulbs provide a softer, more natural light. Fluorescent bulbs cost more than incandescents, but they last a lot longer. Halogen bulbs have crisp, white light and produce light more efficiently than incandescents. When you are choosing a fixture, ask what type of light bulb it uses.

Installing New Fixtures

If your project involves running new wire and boxes for the new fixtures, be sure to install boxes that the fixtures will fit and make sure the boxes are mounted securely enough to support the weight of the new fixture. The code requires that some fixtures, such as chandeliers and ceiling fans, be mounted to boxes that are specifically designed to take the added strain. If you are replacing an older unit, check the existing box to see if the new equipment will fit and to see if the box is attached securely enough to stand up to the stress. Also check to make sure the new fixture won't draw more current than the circuit can handle.

Connecting a Simple Fixture

The most basic of all lighting fixtures is a single bulb socket set in a porcelain or plastic base *(below)*. These fixtures are inexpensive and are often used in garages, basements, and attics. To install:

- Connect the black wire to the brass terminal, the white wire to the silver terminal, and the ground to a green grounding screw in the box—this type of fixture rarely has a ground terminal of its own.
- Attach the fixture to the box with machine screws. Don't overtighten the screws or you may crack the base.

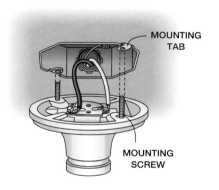

Attaching a Fixture with an Adapter

Light fixtures are often fastened to boxes via the mounting tabs at the box corners. The fixtures often make use of a dome-shaped piece of metal called a canopy, which serves as a cover for the box. Sometimes the holes in the canopy don't match those on the box. Fortunately, there is a fix for this problem available in the form of a slotted crossbar.

- Screw the crossbar to the mounting tabs. Or, if the box has a mounting stud, slip the crossbar on the stud and secure it with a lock nut *(below, left)*.
- Screw the canopy to the threaded holes in the crossbar *(below, right)*. Clip the screws short if necessary so they don't drive into the back of the box.

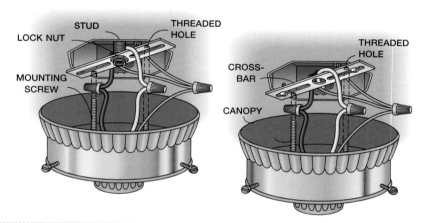

Securing Center-mounted Fixtures

If the box has a built-in stud, extend it with a smaller diameter nipple attached to the stud with a reducing nut *(right)*. If there isn't a stud in the box, install a crossbar with a threaded collar in the center. Screw a nipple into the crossbar and secure it with a lock nut *(lower right)*.

- To hang chandeliers or other large fixtures whose wires pass up through the canopy, attach a nipple to the stud with a C-shaped adapter called a hickey *(upper right)*. Lock both the nipple and the hickey in place with lock nuts. Slip the wires through the stud and into the box.
- With the nipple in place, connect the fixture's black, white, and ground wires to corresponding wires in the incoming cable.
- Fold the wires gently into the box.
- Fasten the fixture to the nipple with a cap nut, drawing the canopy tight to the ceiling or wall.

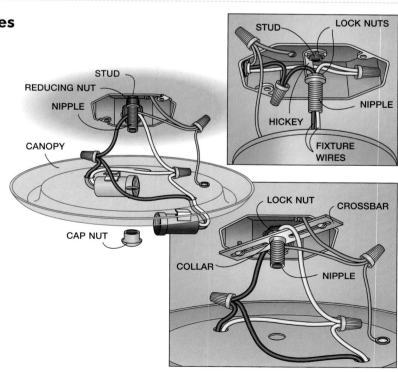

Fluorescent Lighting

Fluorescent lighting has a number of advantages and may be an appropriate choice in many areas. While the bulbs and fixtures are more expensive to purchase than incandescent light bulbs, they also use less electricity and last longer, so in the long run, the added expense is worthwhile. The light they cast is even, and, with the right choice of bulbs, can approach that of natural sunlight.

The heart of every fluorescent light is an electrical device called a ballast. It provides a surge of voltage to start the tube; then it limits the current while the tube is lit. Ballasts last approximately 10 years. When they fail, it may be cheaper to replace the entire fixture than trying to replace just the ballast.

Types of Fixtures

Fluorescent fixtures come in a wide variety of shapes and sizes. These can be broken down into three basic types:

First are rapid-start fixtures, which light after a second or two of delay. These tend to be inexpensive units and are often employed in home workshops, garages, and laundry rooms. They don't work especially well in cold areas, and may flicker more than more costly units. Flipping them on and off frequently in a short amount of time can cause the ballast to malfunction.

Instant-start fixtures come on as soon as the switch is thrown. This requires a high voltage surge of current, which causes the units to wear out somewhat faster than the rapid-start designs.

Compact fluorescents are the latest addition to the family. These self-contained fixtures have the ballast built into the base of the tube. They are quite small compared to standard fluorescents, which means they can be installed in more places. They also have a standard, threaded base, which means you can screw them into a regular light socket—no extra wiring is involved.

The Changing Fluorescent Scene

Federal environmental regulations call for changes in the fluorescent fixtures we use. Suppliers have been phasing out the old-style tubes designated T-12 and replacing them with the new T-8 types. Unfortunately, these new tubes won't work with the magnetic ballasts found in older fixtures. Either replace the fixture entirely or just replace the ballast. To replace it, turn the power off, remove the ballast and note how its wires are connected. Then, have your electrical supplier match the old ballast to a new, electronic one. Install the new one with the same connections the old one used.

Troubleshooting Fluorescents

Problem	Solution
Tube will not light.	Replace the fuse or reset circuit breaker.
	Replace tube.
	Rapid-start: Rotate tube on holder.
	Instant-start: Make sure pins are fully seated in sockets.
	Check to be sure the tube wattage equals that shown on the ballast.
Ends of tube light glow, but center doesn't light.	Check the attachment of the fixture's ground wire to the house's ground wire.
Tube flickers, blinks, or spirals.	This is normal with a new tube. Should improve with use.
	Replace tube.
	Rapid-start: Rotate tube on holder.
	Instant-start: Make sure pins are fully seated in sockets.
Fixture hums or buzzes.	Tighten the ballast connections.
Blackening at the ends of the tube.	These indicate the tube is wearing out and should be replaced.

Mounting a One-Tube Ceiling Fixture

- Position the fixture with the knock-out hole for the wires centered on the ceiling box. Mark the ceiling through the fixture-mounting holes. Set the fixture aside and drill a hole through the ceiling for a toggle bolt. The exact size hole depends on the toggle. Ask at the store.

- Push toggle bolts through the mounting holes in the fixture and thread the toggles onto their ends.

- Thread a hickey onto the stud in the box and a nipple onto the

hickey. If there is no stud, install a crossbar and thread the nipple onto that. The nipple will protect the wires from the sharp edges of the fixture's box.

- Have a helper support the fixture (or hang it from the box with a length of wire coat hanger) as you feed the wires from the ballast up through the nipple into the ceiling box. Connect the wires black to black, white to white, and ground to ground—make sure there is also a jumper ground wire running to the box.

- Push the fixture up against the ceiling, folding the wires into the box as you go. Push the toggles into the holes you drilled in the ceiling and guide the nipple through the knockout hole. Tighten the toggle bolts to hold the fixture in place.

- Install the cover panel and fluorescent tube to finish the job.

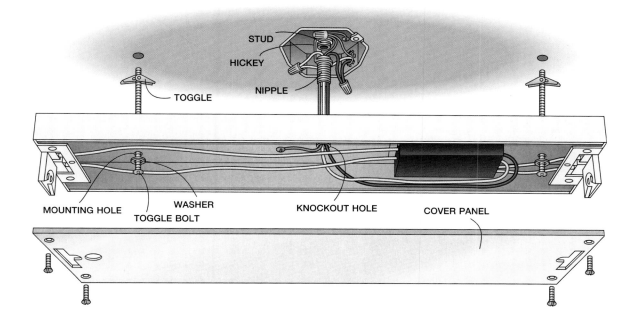

Hanging a Circular Fixture

- Thread a reducing nut onto the stud, and screw a nipple onto the nut.

- Connect the fixture wires to the house wires—black to black, white to white, and ground to ground. (Don't forget to run a jumper wire to the box, if it is metal.)

- Raise the fixture up to the ceiling, folding the wires into place in the box. Maneuver the fixture until the nipple pops through the center hole. Thread on a cap nut to secure the fixture against the ceiling.

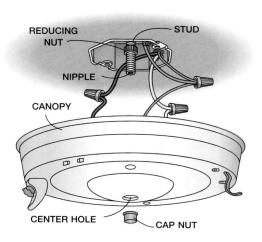

Track and Recessed Lighting

For spot lighting from above, it is hard to find a better system than a series of recessed (canister) or track lights. Track lighting offers more flexibility than canister lights, but canisters are less obtrusive and are harder to focus on something you want to highlight..

Selecting the Fixtures

Both systems are available in kit form or as individual units. Track comes in 2-, 4-, and 8-foot lengths that can be snapped together to form straight runs, right angles, Ts, and Xs. Installation depends on the manufacturer—most systems are not compatible with those from another manufacturer. The light units slide on the track and can be positioned anywhere along its length.

The working parts of recessed fixtures are usually available separately from the trim. Some types are designed specifically to install before the drywall goes up; others can be retrofit into a finished ceiling. One critical factor to consider is whether your ceiling is insulated. If so, you'll want to find IC (insulation covered) fixtures that are rated for use under insulation. Covering a non-IC fixture with insulation can result in a fire.

Wiring Requirements

In most situations, a 15-amp circuit is adequate for track or recessed lighting. The only time you might run into trouble is if you try to add too many individual lights to a circuit that is already close to the maximum. If you are in doubt about a circuit's ability to handle new connections, calculate the load on the circuit as described in *Calculating the Load on a Circuit* on page 84. Track lights can be connected to a regular ceiling box at any point along their length using a special connector called a canopy.

Recessed fixtures have their own junction boxes built in. If you are installing several units, make sure that all but one are rated for "through wiring" so the cable can continue from one fixture to the next. The last fixture needs only to accommodate a single cable and doesn't need to be rated for through wiring.

The following instructions follow the general procedure for installing track and recessed fixtures. Due to variations from manufacturer to manufacturer, the fixtures you purchase may not match those shown here exactly. Read the instructions that come with your fixtures carefully before you begin.

Wiring Track Lighting

1 Remove knockouts.

Hold a length of track in position so it crosses the ceiling box. Mark the large circular knockout in the track that is closest to the center of the junction box *(right)*.

Lay the track upside down across two pieces of scrap wood. Punch out the marked knockout and the small circular knockout next to it with a hammer and a nail set.

In the same manner, punch out a keyhole-shaped knockout at the far end of the track.

Install any required end caps at this point.

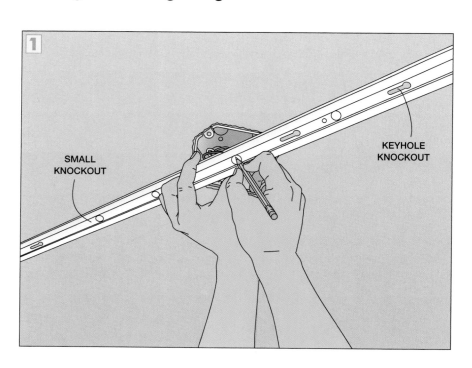

SMALL KNOCKOUT

KEYHOLE KNOCKOUT

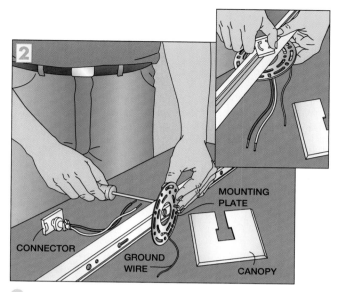

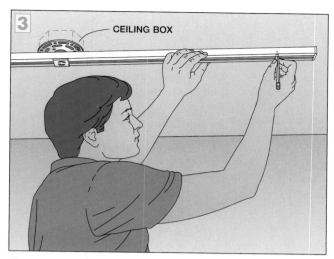

2 Attach the mounting plate.

Hold the mounting plate on the ceiling side of the track with the ground wire on top. Position the center hole over the large knockout opening and align one of the threaded holes over the smaller knockout opening. Join the pieces loosely with the screw provided, leaving a ⅛-inch space between the track and the plate for the canopy (above).

Thread the connector wires up through the center hole, and lock the connector itself to the track by turning it clockwise.

3 Mark the ceiling.

Fasten the mounting plate to the ceiling box temporarily using the screws provided with the ceiling box.

Pivot the track to align where you want it—usually parallel to a wall. Mark the ceiling at the midpoint of each keyhole slot (above).

Unfasten the mounting plate from the box and drill ⅝-inch holes in the ceiling for the toggle bolts at each mark.

Slip the bolts through the holes and add the toggles on their ends.

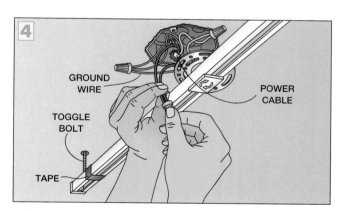

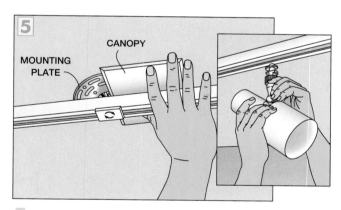

4 Wire the track.

Poke the toggles up into the ceiling, leaving the track suspended below. Tape the bolt heads to hold them in position.

Fasten the track wiring to the household wiring as usual—black to black and white to white (above).

Connect the ground wire from the mounting plate to the household ground and to the box if the box is metal.

5 Add the canopy.

Fold all the wiring up into the ceiling box. Then tighten the mounting screws, securing the plate to the ceiling box.

Slide the canopy in between the mounting plate and the track, covering the ceiling box (above). Tighten the mounting screw in the track to lock the canopy in place.

Take the tape off the bolts and tighten them, fastening the track securely to the ceiling.

Extend the track as desired, fastening each additional piece to the ceiling with more toggle bolts.

Slide the light fixtures onto the track, positioning them as desired.

1 Prepare the mounting frame.

Remove the frame's mounting bars and place the frame on a piece of cardboard. Outline the frame and the circular opening on the cardboard. Cut along the lines to make a template.

With tin snips, cut out the removable section of frame opposite the wiring box *(right)*.

Lift the spring clip on top of the wiring box and remove one of its two detachable doors. Unscrew the cable clamps from inside the box and cut away the center parts, modifying them for use with plastic-sheathed cable as directed by the manufacturer.

Reinstall the clamps and remove one of the knockouts from above each clamp.

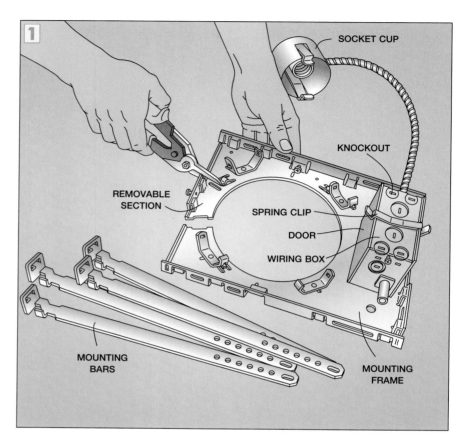

2 Open the ceiling.

With a stud finder, locate and mark the ceiling joists. Using the cardboard template, mark the locations of the fixtures on the ceiling, staying at least 2 inches away from the joists *(right)*.

Drill a small hole in the center of each circular area. Bend a length of coat hanger into an L shape. (The leg of the L should be slightly longer than the radius of the circular mark.) Insert the hanger into the hole and spin it around to check for obstructions. If the wire touches anything, you'll need to relocate the fixture. If it doesn't, cut a hole in the ceiling along the layout line with a drywall saw.

If you have to run a cable through any of the joists on its way from fixture to fixture, cut an access hole at each joist and drill a ¾-inch hole through its center.

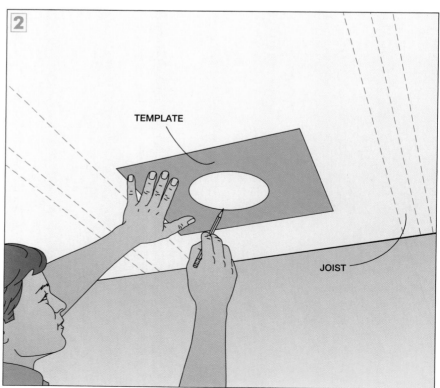

3 Run the wiring connections.

Run a two-conductor cable from a power source to the first fixture opening. Run more cable from the first opening to the next and so on, until there is cable running to each opening.

At the first opening, balance a mounting frame on top of your ladder while you connect the household wires to the fixture wires. The red wire nuts in the drawing show the connections you'll need to make (right).

Reattach the box door.

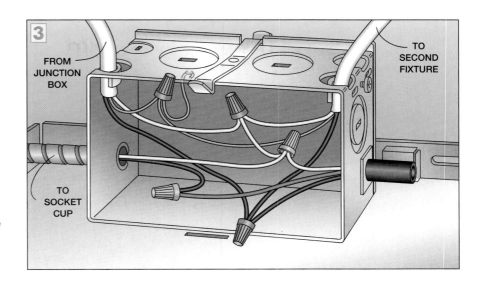

4 Install the mounting frame.

Push the socket cup through the ceiling opening and set it on top of the ceiling beside the hole.

Hook the frame up into the ceiling (right). Rest it on the drywall with the round opening aligned with the opening in the ceiling.

Slide the long ends of the four nail clips provided with the fixture into the brackets on the frame. Align the short ends of the clips with the center of the drywall and tap them in with a hammer.

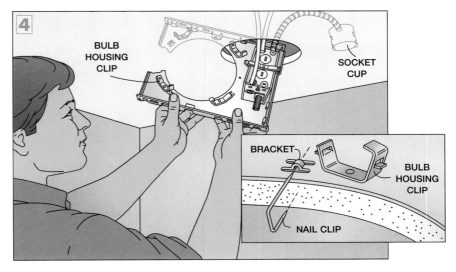

5 Install the bulb housing.

Reach into the ceiling and bring the socket cup back down into the room. Rotate the bulb housing clips inward.

Insert the socket cup into the top of the bulb housing so that the tabs in the cup snap into the slots in the housing.

Push the assembly into the opening until the flange rests tightly against the ceiling, completing the installation (right).

Repeat the process at each fixture.

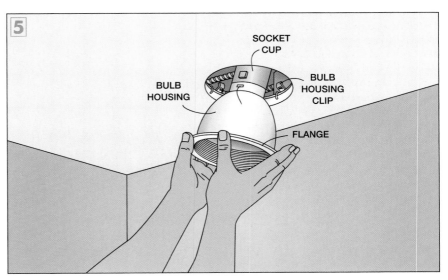

Ceiling Fans

Ceiling fans can make a huge difference in your house's comfort without costing much money to operate. During the summer you can run them on high, creating a cooling breeze, while during the winter, you can run them in reverse to push the warm air down.

Proper Support

Because ceiling fans weigh between 30 and 50 pounds and because they move and potentially could vibrate loose, it is critical that they are mounted securely in place. The mounting box should be a metal or plastic box designed specifically for fans—and it should be attached rigidly to the house framing.

Placement Considerations

For safety, a fan's blades should be no lower than 7 feet above the floor and no closer than 24 inches from the nearest obstruction. Where vertical clearance is tight, look for a model that can be mounted against the ceiling. In places where you have a little more room, you'll get better air circulation if the fan hangs down away from the ceiling slightly on the end of a rod called a downpipe. A downpipe is essential if you are hanging a fan from a sloping ceiling. Fans should not be placed in damp locations, such as on open porches, unless they are rated for such use.

Installation

Fans are sold in kits, which include all the necessary parts and hardware with the exception of an appropriate ceiling box. Such boxes are usually available from any electrical supplier. Before starting, turn off the power to the ceiling box at the service panel. The following instructions will work with most fans, but review the instructions that come with the fan you buy to check for any discrepancies. If the fan wobbles after installation, you may be able to fix the problem by swapping two of the blades to help even out the weight. Many fans also come with a balance kit that will solve the problem.

Installing a Ceiling Fan

The Anatomy of the Ceiling Fan

Ceiling fans are mounted to electrical boxes that are fastened securely to the frame of a house. Many codes require using specially designed boxes that are labeled "OK for Ceiling Fan Support." The fan hangs from a plate attached to the box. Some fans include a hook that allows you to hang the motor near the box while you are making the wiring connections.

Often, a downpipe is installed to lower the fan away from the ceiling, improving air circulation. For most fans you can purchase a light kit, which attaches to the switch housing. The lights are wired separately from the fan motor, allowing the lights to function even if the fan is not running.

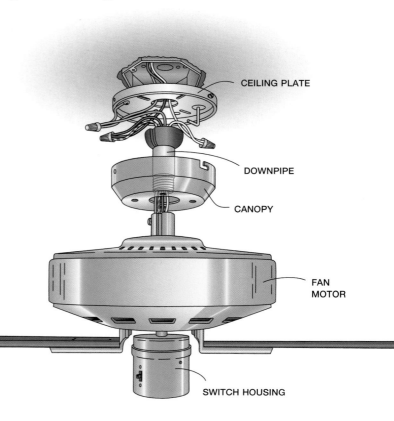

CEILING PLATE

DOWNPIPE

CANOPY

FAN MOTOR

SWITCH HOUSING

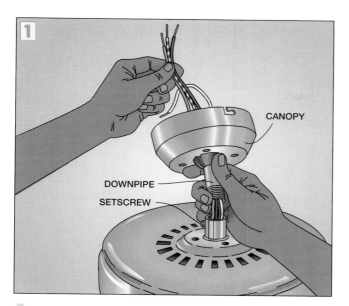

1 Assemble the fan.

Insert the downpipe in the canopy and feed the wires up through the pipe *(above)*.

Screw the downpipe into the top of the motor housing and tighten the setscrew to lock it in place.

To omit the downpipe, feed the wires through the canopy and screw it to the motor housing with the screws provided.

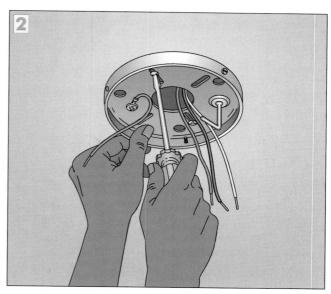

2 Attach the ceiling plate.

Feed the wires from the junction box down through the hole in the center of the ceiling plate.

Position the plate on the box and fasten it in place with the screws that come with the box *(above)*.

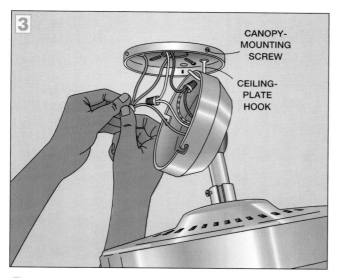

3 Connect the wires.

Support the fan by hanging it from a hook in the ceiling plate.

Connect the black and black-and-white fan motor wires to the black household wire. (Different manufacturers may color code their wires differently; check the instructions to see which wires get connected where.)

Join the white wires, then connect the three ground wires as shown *(above)*.

Hook the canopy onto the mounting screws on the plate and tighten them to secure the fan to the plate.

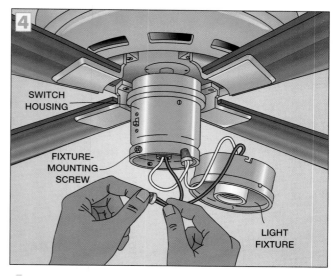

4 Attach a light kit.

Remove the cover from the bottom of the switch housing.

Connect the wires from the light kit to those in the switch housing—black to black and white to white *(above)*.

Attach the kit to the switch housing with the screws provided.

Outdoor Lighting

MAKING THE YARD SAFE

In recent years, the variety of outdoor lighting products readily available to homeowners has really taken off. Instead of the standard floodlights at the corners and a lamppost beside the driveway, you can create an artfully lit landscape that combines security and safety, utility and atmosphere, all without breaking the bank.

Once you have a good idea of what you want to achieve, this chapter will provide the technical details of how to accomplish your plan. You'll find that doing exterior wiring is not that much different from interior wiring. The only real trick is to put things together so they won't succumb to the ravages of the great outdoors. For this, there are a number of special fittings designed to keep nature at bay.

Outdoor Wiring Basics

*B*ecause of its exposure to the harsh conditions out-side, exterior wiring requires special materials and installation techniques. The basic idea behind exterior wiring, however, is identical to that of interior wiring—one wire carries the current to the various fixtures, another wire carries it back, while a third wire provides an alternative path to ground should something go amiss.

When you embark on an outdoor wiring project, start with a diagram of your house and yard. The drawing need not be to scale (although a scale drawing can be beneficial). This will help you work out the optimal positioning of the fixtures as well as serve as the start of a shopping list. Note as many details as possible on the drawing, such as the distance from fixture to fixture and the need for special boxes.

Finding a Source of Power

As with any new circuitry, you'll need to find a place to tie the new wiring into the existing system. If you already have some outside wiring, such as a doorway light or an exterior receptacle, you may be able to tap it for power. Or you may find it easier to drill through a wall to get at the indoor wiring. If you are extending an existing circuit, make sure it has enough unused capacity to supply all the new fixtures. If not, you may need to run an entirely new line from the service panel.

No matter what the source of power, all exterior wiring must be protected by a GFCI device—either a receptacle or a circuit breaker (see page 150). *Note:* A single GFCI receptacle will protect all the devices downstream from the original installation.

Protecting the Wires

Exterior wiring must be protected from physical damage and from the destructive effects of the elements, particularly sunlight. The most common way to protect exterior wires is to run them inside pipe, called conduit. Conduit is available in three materials, any of which is acceptable, depending on your local electrical code. The three include: polyvinyl chloride (PVC) plastic, thin-wall metal, and rigid or heavy-wall metal.

Of the three types of conduit, PVC and thin-wall metal are the easiest to work with; however, they must be buried at least 12 inches underground. Rigid conduit is more difficult to bend into shape, but it is often more convenient because it only has to be buried 6 inches. For most circuits, ½-inch conduit is adequate.

Wiring Choices

There are two main types of wires used for outdoor circuits. The first consists of individual TW wires, which must be run through conduit. The second option (if your local code permits it) is UF cable. This is a plastic sheathed cable similar to that which is run inside, but the plastic sheathing is much tougher. UF cable is rated for direct burial (no conduit) but it must be buried at least 12 inches deep. Above ground, it should be run in conduit for protection.

CAUTION! *Before excavating, find out what else is buried in your lawn. Most states have an excavation hotline that you must call at least 48 hours before you dig. This service will get in contact with all the local utility companies and let them know you will be digging. The utility companies, in turn, will come and locate all of their underground lines that cross your property. If you neglect to call and then cut a utility line, the repair can be quite expensive. Also, do not run electric lines through a septic drain field or under areas where water pools—there is too much risk of corrosion and premature line failure.*

A Low-voltage Alternative

In recent years, a number of manufacturers have begun to offer low-voltage lighting fixtures for outdoor lighting. Installing low-voltage lighting is much less involved than installing regular voltage fixtures—the wires don't need to be buried deeply, nor do they need to be run in conduit.

Low-voltage systems consist of a series of low-voltage lighting fixtures, which are connected to a transformer that you plug into a regular 120-volt circuit. If your only need for outdoor electricity is to provide a little light along a path, for example, a low-voltage system is a very viable choice. The only drawback seems to be that the lights tend to dim in circuits that include 100 feet of cable or more. This is usually easily remedied by adding a second circuit with an additional transformer.

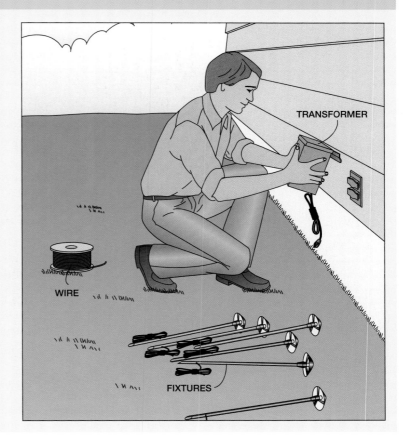

TRANSFORMER

WIRE

FIXTURES

Outdoor Wiring Components

Your local home center will have a wide variety of outdoor electric fixtures and their accompanying supplies. These items are designed to protect the wires and connections within from rain, snow, and physical damage. In contrast with indoor fittings, which are generally buried in the walls, outdoor equipment is much more robust. Boxes are made of heavy, rustproof metal castings. Instead of knockouts, they have threaded openings that accept conduit, or which can be sealed with threaded plugs designed for the purpose. Special cover plates protect the receptacles and switches and are sealed with rubber gaskets to keep moisture away from the terminals and twisted connections.

Even these special boxes aren't adequate if a box must be installed where it might be submerged by a heavy rain or runoff from melting snow. If you have to install a box in such a location, special, watertight hardware is available.

A Typical Outdoor Wiring Scheme

Several outdoor circuits provide outdoor lighting and convenience for the house shown here. A receptacle near the front porch provides a source of power for the lamppost by the walk and the low garden lights across the front. The floodlight over the garage door draws power from the garage circuit. Out back, a wall-mounted fixture is the source of power for a series of low lights and two receptacles near the back of the property.

Note: The cable feeding the fixtures in the backyard branches in several places. These branches occur in boxes that are buried. Such boxes must be clearly identified and accessible for excavation. A separate circuit serves the shed. Even though the receptacle is inside, a GFCI device still must protect it.

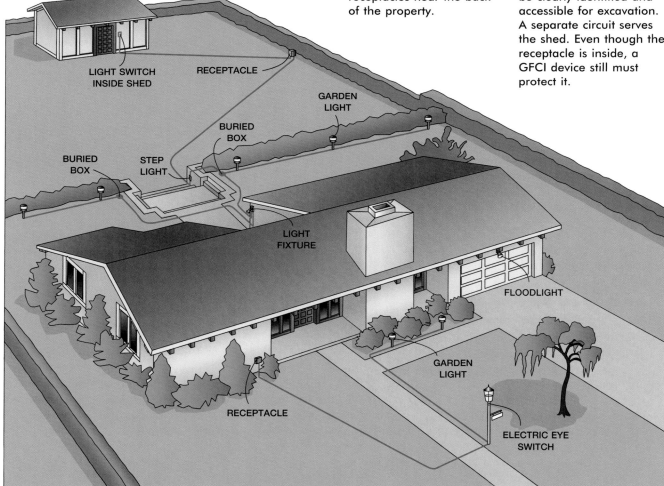

LIGHT SWITCH INSIDE SHED

RECEPTACLE

GARDEN LIGHT

BURIED BOX

BURIED BOX

STEP LIGHT

LIGHT FIXTURE

FLOODLIGHT

GARDEN LIGHT

RECEPTACLE

ELECTRIC EYE SWITCH

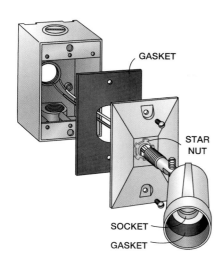

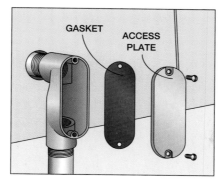

The LB Fitting

This fitting protects wires that emerge from a house and then turn down toward the ground—the basic configuration of a cable used for an outdoor circuit. The letters indicate that the fitting is used to turn a corner—"L"—and that it has an opening in the back—"B." The back opening makes turning the corner much easier. *Note:* There is not enough room inside the fitting for a junction between two cables. It is only to be used to help continuous wires turn the corner.

A Weather-resistant Light Fixture

As with other outdoor fixtures, this light holder is mounted to an outdoor box with a gasket between the cover and box to seal out moisture. Other configurations are available, such as a holder designed for two bulbs. When you purchase the bulbs for such a fixture, be sure to get those rated for outdoor use. These are made from glass specially formulated not to shatter when cooled suddenly by rain or snow.

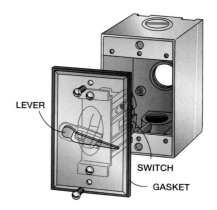

An Outdoor Switch

To control exterior lights from an outdoor location, a regular switch is used inside an outdoor box with a special cover. A lever on the cover extends inside the box to flip the switch. The switch itself is attached to the cover rather than to the box.

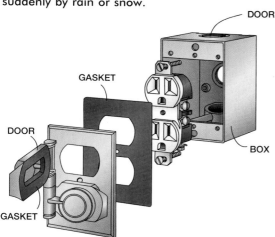

A Basic Receptacle

Most outdoor installations make use of standard fixtures such as duplex receptacles. The difference is in the box. In this fixture, two gasketed doors seal off the receptacle when it is not in use. The gasket forms a seal between the cover plate and the box. This type of cover is not to be used for equipment that stays plugged in for long periods of time. For receptacles that you want to leave appliances plugged into, you'll need a continuous-use GFCI receptacle.

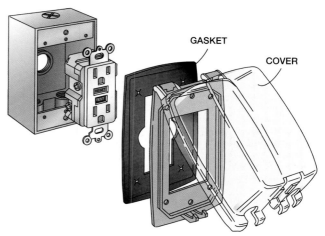

A Continuous-use GFCI Receptacle

The clear cover on this fixture is made from a tough, impact-resistant plastic. It is designed to protect the receptacle from weather even when cords are left plugged into the receptacle. The cover is shown here with a GFCI receptacle, but is also available configured for a regular receptacle. Note that all outdoor fixtures should have GFCI protection. A single GFCI receptacle can protect an entire outdoor circuit if it is the first fixture the circuit serves.

Creating a Path for an Outdoor Circuit

The easiest place to tap to power an outdoor circuit is an existing outdoor fixture—either a light or a receptacle. This way you won't have to drill a hole through one of you home's walls. However, drilling isn't an insurmountable task. If you have to go this route, the best place to drill is through a basement or an attic wall.

In the basement, try to locate your hole so it exits the house below the ground floor but above ground level. You'll probably find it easiest to drill through the rim joist that sits on top of the foundation. If this is unacceptable, you can drill through the foundation wall itself. If the wall is concrete block, try to drill through one of the voids in a block in the second row down from the top. (The top row is usually filled solid with concrete.) If you have to drill through a solid concrete wall, rent a heavy-duty hammer drill with the appropriate bit. In a house without a basement or crawlspace, try drilling down from the attic into the soffit.

If you must, you can drill a hole right through the wall near an existing receptacle. Open up an access area in the inside wall surface. Carefully move the insulation aside; then drill a small hole through the sheathing and siding from inside. Enlarge the hole from the outside. When you are finished running the conduit and cables, be sure to seal the exit hole carefully to keep insects and other critters from finding their way inside.

A Minimal Circuit

The simplest outside circuit consists of a single fixture, either a receptacle, or a light, in a box mounted to an exterior wall. With this type of circuit you can simply run the cable out through the hole you drilled in the wall directly into the box. Mount the box on the surface of the wall and seal around it with caulk. This may be all the circuit you need, or it can serve as a starting point for a more elaborate plan. It you extend the cable beyond this first box, you'll need to encase it in conduit along at least part of its route.

Working with Conduit

Of the three types of conduit, PVC is the easiest to use. It can be cut readily with a hacksaw, and the fittings go together quickly with a little solvent to make the joint. While PVC can be bent by applying heat, the usual process is to make straight runs with elbows in between to go around corners.

Both types of metal conduit are a little more difficult to work with, although they can be readily bent to shape with the aid of a special bending tool. You'll also need a hacksaw to cut the pieces to length and a file to deburr the rough edges. For heavy-wall conduit, you'll also need two pipe wrenches to twist the fittings together and a $1\frac{1}{8}$-inch open-end wrench to fit the threadless couplings on to the ends of trimmed tubing. The couplings and fittings for thin-wall conduit are all threadless and are secured with built-in setscrews.

Digging Trenches

Try to keep your trenches as straight as possible to make pulling the wires through the conduit easier. When you need to turn a corner, use a fitting with an access plate or a junction box to make the corner. This gives you access to the cable, making it much easier to feed through the conduit. You'll also find it easier to put the pieces together into larger assemblies alongside the trench before lowering them into place.

Tapping an Existing Fixture

1 Modify the box.

Turn off the power to the fixture at the service panel. Remove the cover plate from the box. Disconnect the wires from the fixture and set the fixture aside.

If you need additional space inside the box for the added wires, screw a box extender (*right*) in place to make the box bigger.

Screw a nipple (a short length of conduit) into one of the holes in the box (or extender). Screw an elbow or an LB fitting to the other end of the nipple.

Clamp the nipple to the wall with a conduit strap. Caulk the junction between the box and the wall to seal it.

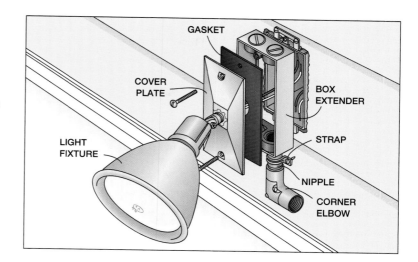

2 Run the conduit.

Run conduit from the elbow on the nipple down the side of the house toward the trench. Use elbows and other fittings as needed (*right*).

Bend a piece of conduit (see *Bending Conduit* on page 183) to make the transition from vertical to horizontal in the ditch. Join this bent piece to the other conduit with a threadless coupling.

Continue running the conduit to the other fixtures in your plan.

1 Drill the exit hole.

Outside, locate an exit point above the sill plate where your hole won't run into the end of a joist or a joint in the siding.

Drill a ¼-inch test hole through the siding and framing. Check inside to make sure the location is suitable. If so, enlarge the hole with a ⅞-inch spade bit.

In a concrete block wall, drill a ¼-inch test hole through both sides of a block in the second course of blocks. Enlarge the holes with a hammer and star drill, turning the drill ⅛ turn after each hammer blow.

Select a nipple long enough to reach inside the house. Thread it onto an LB fitting (for UF cable) *(right)* or into the back of an outlet box (for TW wire).

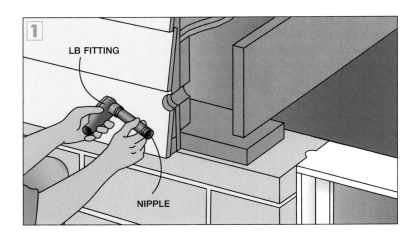

2 Install the fitting.

Temporarily insert the nipple into the hole *(right)* and cut a length of conduit to run from the fitting into the trench.

Withdraw the fitting from the hole and attach it to the conduit. Reinsert the nipple into the hole and seal around it with caulk.

Fasten the conduit to the house with straps. If you used an outlet box, it too should be fastened in place and caulked.

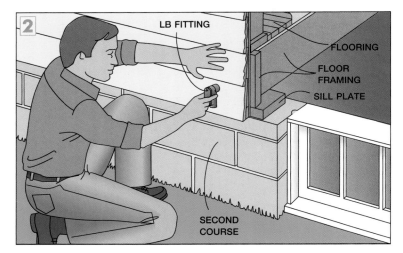

Dropping a Circuit through an Eave

Installing a Box on the Soffit

- Fasten together an outdoor box, a nipple, a corner elbow, and a section of conduit.

- Hold this assembly up against the soffit between two rafters. (Look for the nail heads to show you where the rafters are.) Mark the center of the cable hole in the back of the box and the location of the mounting tabs on the box's sides. Drill a ⅞-inch hole for the cable and pilot holes for the mounting screws.

- Fish a cable from an interior circuit out to the box and secure it with a two-part cable clamp.

- Screw the box to the soffit. Strap the nipple and the conduit in place *(right)*.

- You can make the conduit less conspicuous by running it right along a rain gutter.

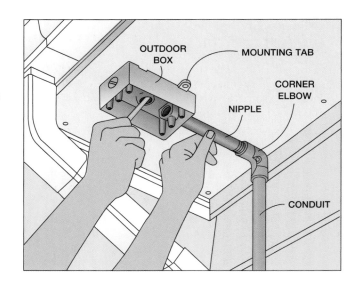

Connections for Heavy-wall Conduit

An Array of Fittings

These are the most common fittings used with heavy-wall conduit. Elbows are for turning corners. They have curved access plates for helping to pull wires through. The covers must be sealed with caulking cord to keep out the elements. Offsets help conduit jog neatly past small obstacles. Screw-on plastic bushings keep the insulation from chafing against the raw conduit ends. The C-body (C stands for continuous) provides access to the inside of a piece of conduit. It is helpful when pulling wire through a particularly long or twisting run of conduit. The T-body allows a circuit to branch.

If you bury a junction box, a T-body, a C-body, or an elbow, you must permanently mark the location with a fixture or a stake.

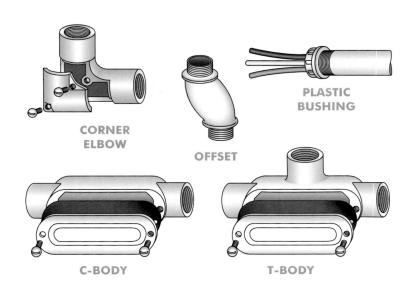

CORNER ELBOW

OFFSET

PLASTIC BUSHING

C-BODY

T-BODY

Couplings and Connectors

Couplings join lengths of conduit, while connectors attach conduit to other pieces of hardware. Threaded couplers join uncut lengths of conduit that still are threaded. Threadless couplers join pieces of conduit whose threaded ends have been cut away. After inserting the conduit into the fitting, tighten the nut until the conduit is secure. Threadless connectors join cut ends of conduit to a junction box.

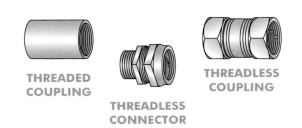

THREADED COUPLING

THREADLESS CONNECTOR

THREADLESS COUPLING

Bending Conduit

- Pencil a mark on the conduit where the bend is to begin.
- Slip the conduit into the bender until the mark aligns with the arrow on the tool.
- Step on the rocker tread and pull on the handle (*right*). To get proper leverage, you might need to brace the opposite end of the conduit against a wall. (Be careful not to damage the wall.)
- Some benders are equipped with 45- and 90-degree levels to help you bend the conduit to the desired angle. If yours isn't, go by the following gauge: For a 45-degree bend, pull the handle until it is vertical; for a 90-degree bend, continue pulling until the handle is halfway to the ground.
- Most benders leave you with a bend that is about 6 inches across (*inset*).

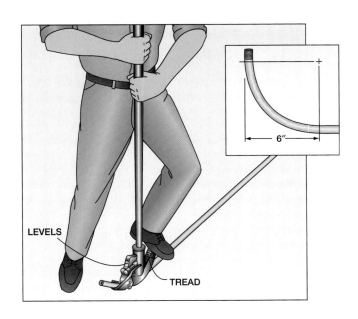

LEVELS

TREAD

6"

1 Make the opening.

For a cleaner look in a block wall, you can cut a hole and mount a regular box flush with the surface.

Center the box on a block and outline it with electrical tape. If the seams between the blocks have been stuccoed over, drill a test hole with a small masonry bit in an electric drill to find a hollow in the block. Insert a bent wire into the hole and twist it from side to side to locate the webs inside the block.

Drill a series of ½-inch holes inside the layout *(right)*. Finish the opening with a cold chisel, making the hole about ¼ inch wider and taller than the box.

Attach an extension to the drill bit and drill through the opposite side of the wall for the cable. Enlarge the hole with a star drill to accommodate the cable.

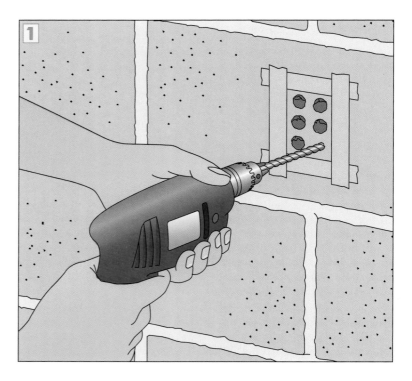

2 Mortar the box into place.

Insert screws loosely into the box's fixture mounting screw holes to keep them from being fouled with mortar.

Adjust the ears on the box so the edge of the box is about ⅟₁₆ inch in front of the wall surface *(right)*. This slight extension allows the gasket of the cover to form a tight seal.

Clamp the cable to the box.

Slip the box in place and press mortar into the gaps on all sides with a putty knife. To ensure a weatherproof joint, there should be no gaps in the mortar.

When the mortar dries, continue with the installation.

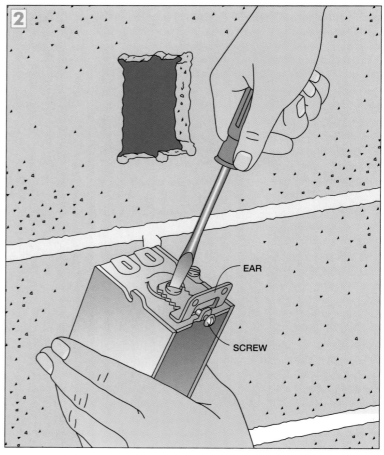

EAR

SCREW

Setting Up a Lamppost

1 Slot the post for conduit.

Scribe two parallel lines from the end of the post to a point slightly past the UF cable hole. Cut along the lines with a hacksaw *(right)*.

Bend the resulting strip of metal back and cut it off. Apply an exterior metal spray paint over the cut to protect the metal from rust.

HACKSAW

CABLE HOLE

SCRIBE LINES

2 Anchor the post.

Dig an 8-inch-diameter hole about 2 feet deep with a posthole digger.

Cut and bend a length of conduit so it will emerge from its trench in the middle of the posthole. It should extend above the surface almost to the lock ring on the post (or almost to the top of a fixed length post). Cap the top of the conduit with a plastic bushing to avoid damage to the wires.

Slide the post over the conduit. Tamp alternate layers of dirt and stones around the post with a scrap 2x4, checking with a level to make sure the post is standing straight up as you go *(right)*.

Fill only to the bottom of the conduit trench for now. You can fill in the rest of the hole and the trench after all the wiring is complete and tested.

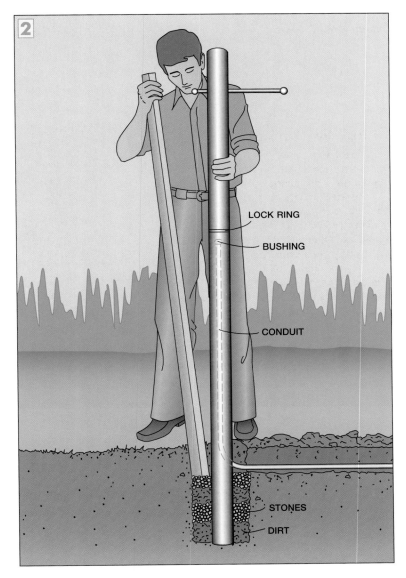

LOCK RING

BUSHING

CONDUIT

STONES

DIRT

Recessing a Light into a Brick Wall

Securing the Fixture

- Some fixtures are designed to fit in a brick wall. Decide where you want the fixture. Then chip away that brick and its surrounding mortar with a cold chisel. Hold the chisel at an angle so it's easier to control.

- Dig a trench for the necessary cable. Bore through the back of the wall and into the trench with a masonry bit. Enlarge the hole to ⅞ inch with a star drill.

- Assemble the fixture, threading a nipple into the back of the box that is long enough to extend

through the wall into the trench (below).

- Push the fixture into place, using pebbles to shim the fixture into the center of the opening. Pack mortar around the fixture and around the nipple where it protrudes from the back of the wall.

- When the mortar dries, thread an outdoor box onto the end of the nipple. Fish the fixture wires through the nipple and into the box. Run conduit and cable to the box and make the necessary connections.

COVER PLATE

NIPPLE

FIXTURE

Installing Light-sensitive Switches

A Variety of Sensors

For convenience and security, you might want to install a light-sensitive switch that will turn on your outdoor lights when it begins to get dark. These switches are built around a photocell that detects changes in the ambient light. Also part of the circuitry is a time-delay feature that prevents the switch from being fooled by car headlights or lightning.

There are a number of styles of light-sensitive switches available. Some lampposts have them built right in (*right*). Others are separate fixtures, which can control an entire circuit. These are mounted on their own outdoor box (*top, far right*). For added sensitivity, one style has an adjustable wand that can be pointed at the sky (*bottom, far right*).

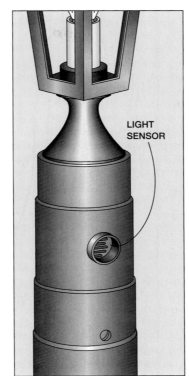

LIGHT SENSOR

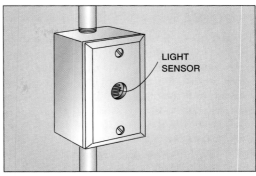

LIGHT SENSOR

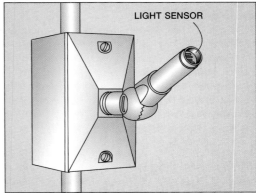

LIGHT SENSOR

Connecting a Light-sensitive Switch

- Join the white wire from the switch to the other white wires in the box with a wire nut.

- Join the black wire from the switch to the incoming black wire and the red wire from the switch to the outgoing black wire.

- Attach the ground wires to each other, along with a jumper wire to the box.

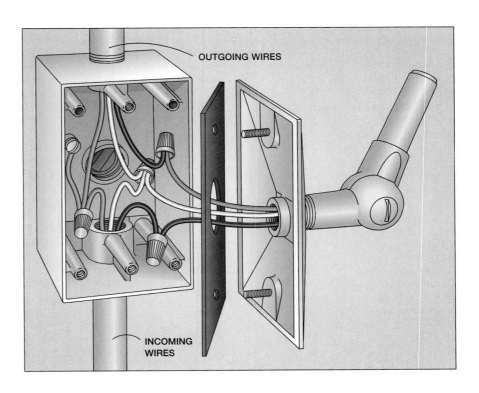

OUTGOING WIRES

INCOMING WIRES

1 Install the switch module.

Motion-sensitive switches, like those attached to some security lights, are also available separately so that you can connect them to an existing fixture. You'll need to install a double-width box to hold both the switch module and the light fixture.

Turn off the power at the service panel and remove the old fixture. Install a double-width box if necessary.

Join the switch module's white wire to the incoming white wire and the white wire from the fixture.

Connect the switch module's red wire to the fixture's black wire.

Connect the incoming black wire to the switch module's black wire *(right)*.

Run the remote sensor's wires in through the bottom of the box. Plug the remote sensor into the switch module.

Reinstall the fixture on the box.

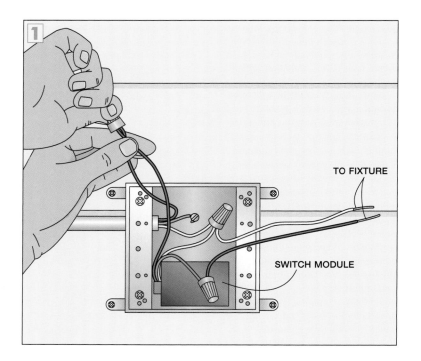

TO FIXTURE

SWITCH MODULE

2 Install the remote sensor.

Screw the motion sensor in position below the light fixture, about 5 feet above the ground *(right)*.

Allow the cord to the switch to droop below the sensor. This way any water running along the wires will drip off rather than run into the sensor.

Fasten the cord in place with staples.

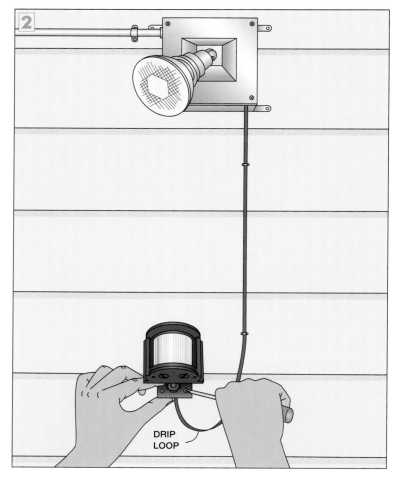

DRIP LOOP

Installing Outlying Receptacles

1 Attach an end-of-the-run box.

Dig a trench running to the various receptacle locations. Enlarge the end of the trench so it can accommodate a 4-inch-tall concrete block.

Cut and bend a length of conduit so it rises about 8 inches above the ground.

Fasten a box to the end of the conduit *(right)*.

2 Attach a middle-of-the-run box.

Enlarge the trench to accommodate a 4-inch-tall concrete block where you want the middle-of-the-run receptacles.

Cut and bend two lengths of conduit so they end 8 inches above the ground.

Use threadless connectors to fasten a box with two conduit openings in one end to the pieces of conduit *(above)*.

3 Make a sturdy base.

Place concrete blocks in the trench over the boxes. Fill in the voids in the block with gravel to anchor the boxes in place *(above)*.

Fish cable through the conduit and install the receptacles and cover plates. As with all outdoor fixtures, these receptacles should also be under GFCI protection.

Index

Acknowledgments

The editors gratefully acknowledge the following for their assistance with this book:

Bertie Bonner
Registered architect
Media, PA

Marty Peck
Lighting Designer
Milwaukee, WI

Paul Hafner
Philips Lighting Center Training Room
Somerset, NJ

T.J. Tindall
Lighting Designer/President
The Light Gallery
Princeton, NJ

Tom Callahan
President
Sawyers Electronic Control Systems
Frenchtown, NJ

JoAnne Lindsley, FIALD
Professor, NJIT/President,
Lindsley Consultants Incorporated
New York, NY

Ace Rosenstein
Director of Sales and Marketing
Seagull Lighting,
Riverside, NJ

Susan Reminger
Manager of Corporate Communications
OSRAM-SYLVANIA, Inc.
Danvers, MA

Photos courtesy of the following:

American Lighting Association
P.O. Box 420288, Dallas, TX 75342 ▪
www.americanlightingassoc.com ▪ Pages
9, 29, 34–36, 46–47, 55, 72, 74, 162.

Angelo Brothers Company
12401 McNulty Road, Philadelphia, PA
19154 ▪ www.angelobrothers.com ▪
Pages 23–25, 67.

Architectural Area Lighting
14249 Artesia Blvd., La Mirada, CA
90638 ▪ www.aal.net ▪ Page 37.

Baga s.r.l. c/o Axl, Inc.
301 North Harrison Street, #308,
Princeton, NJ 08540 ▪ www.axlinc.com
▪ Pages 23, 28, 51, *back cover.*

Bookworks, Inc.
P.O. Box 204, West Milton, OH 45383
▪ Page 128

Brass Light Gallery
131 S. 1st Street, Milwaukee, WI 53204
▪ www.brasslight.com ▪ Pages 51, 55,
59-61, 65, 70, *cover.*

Cooper Lighting
1121 Highway 74, South Peachtree City,
GA 30269 ▪ www.cooperlighting.com ▪
Pages 10–11, 26, 67.

Designer's Fountain
20101 South Santa Fe Ave., Rancho
Dominguez, CA 90221 ▪ Page 28.

Eurofase, Inc.
4590 Dufferin Street, Toronto, Ontario,
Canada ▪ www.eurofase.com ▪ Pages 23,
27, 37.

Frank Peluso Photography
15 Caspar Berger Road, Whitehouse
Station, NJ 08889 ▪ Pages 76, 100.

General Electric Company
1975 Noble Road, Nela Park, Cleveland,
OH 44112 ▪ www.ge.com ▪ Page 92.

Hadco
GT Genlyte Thomas Group, LLC, 100
Craftway, P.O. Box 128, Littlestown, PA
17340 ▪ www.hadcolighting.com ▪ Pages
36, 71–72.

Intermatic, Incorporated
Spring Grove, IL ▪ www.Intermatic.com
▪ Pages 34, 75.

KraftMaid Cabinetry
P.O. Box 1055, Middlefield, OH 44802 ▪
www.kraftmaid.com ▪ Pages 31, 48.

Leviton Manufacturing Co., Inc.
59–25 Little Neck Parkway, Little Neck,
NY 11362 ▪ www.leviton.com ▪ Pages
134–135.

Lightolier, a Genlyte Thomas Company
631 Airport Road, Fall River, MA 02720
▪ www.lightolier.com ▪ Pages 38–39.

LumiSource, Inc.
2950 Old Higgins Road, Elk Grove
Village, IL 60007 ▪ Page 29.

Lutron Electronics Co., Inc.
7200 Suter Road, Coopersburg, PA
18036 ▪ www.lutron.com ▪ Pages
38, 40, *back cover.*

Maxi Aids
42 Executive Blvd., Farmingdale, NY
11735 ▪ www.maxiaids.com ▪ Page 29.

National Kitchen and Bath Association
687 Willow Grove Street, Hackettstown,
NJ 07840 ▪ Pages 16, 30–31, 48, 50, 62.

Photographic Illustrators
467 Sagamore Street, Hamilton, MA
01936 ▪ Pages 18, 33, 54.

Philips Lighting Company
200 Franklin Square Drive, Somerset, NJ
08875 ▪ www.lighting.philips.com ▪
Pages 10, 17, 26, 28, 30–33, 43–44, 47,
52–54, 56–59, 61–62, 66, 69, 73, 75,
174, *back cover.*

Progress Lighting
101 Corporate Drive, Spartanburg, SC
29303 ▪ www.progresslighting.com ▪
Pages 6, 14.

Seagull Lighting
301 West Washington Street, Riverside,
NJ 08075 ▪ www.seagulllighting.com ▪
Pages 11, 17, 29, 36–37, 70, 73.

Thomas Lighting
950 Breckenridge Lane, Louisville, KY
40207 ▪ www.thomaslighting.com ▪
Pages 16, 20, 27, 34, 64.

W.A.C. Lighting Co.
615 South Street, Garden City, NY
11530 ▪ www.waclighting.com ▪ Pages
25, 28, 62.

Weather Shield Window & Doors
1 Weather Shield Plaza, Medford, WI
54457 ▪ www.weathershield.com ▪ Pages
49, 52, 56, 63.

Wood–Mode Fine Cabinetry
One Second Street, Kreamer, PA 17833
▪ www.wood-mode.com ▪ Page 49.